9/17/08

JAMES DAVID
JORDAN

Forsaken

A NOVEL

Nashville, Tennessee

978-0-8054-4749-1

Published by B&H Publishing Group,
Nashville, Tennessee

Dewey Decimal Classification: F
Subject Heading: TERRORISM—FICTION \
SUSPENSE FICTION \ EVANGELISTS—FICTION

1 2 3 4 5 6 7 8 • 11 10 09 08

TO MY SISTER, CARLA, WHO IS ALWAYS
THERE FOR EVERYONE.

ACKNOWLEDGMENTS

I GRATEFULLY ACKNOWLEDGE THE help and support of my wife, Sue, and my kids, Allie and Johnathan. Without them there would have been no book. I also acknowledge my agent, Tina Jacobson. Without her, there would have been a book, but it never would have been published. Finally, I acknowledge my editor, Karen Ball. Without her there would have been a book, and it would have been published, but it sure wouldn't have been as good. Oops, I almost forgot my old friend, Dale Willis. Without his advice the book would still have had guns, but not the right ones.

CHAPTER
ONE

EVEN IN HIGH SCHOOL I didn't mind sleeping on the ground. When your father is a retired Special Forces officer, you pick up things that most girls don't learn. As the years passed, I slept in lots of places a good girl shouldn't sleep. It's a part of my past I don't brag about, like ugly wallpaper that won't come unstuck. No matter how hard I scrape, it just hangs on in big, obscene blotches. I'm twenty-nine years old now, and I've done my best to paint over it. But it's still there under the surface, making everything rougher, less presentable than it should be, though I want more than anything to be smooth and fresh and clean.

Sometimes I wonder what will happen if the paint begins to fade. Will the wallpaper show? I thought so for a long time. But I have hope now that it won't. Simon Mason helped me find that hope. That's why it's important for me to tell our story. There must be others who need hope too. There must be others who are afraid that their ugly wallpaper might bleed through.

What does sleeping on the ground have to do with a world-famous preacher like Simon Mason? The story begins twelve years ago—eleven years before I met Simon. My dad and I packed our camping gear and went fishing. It was mid-May, and the trip was a present for my seventeenth birthday. Not exactly every high school girl's dream, but my dad wasn't like most dads. He taught me to camp and fish and, particularly, to shoot. He had trained me in self-defense since I was nine, the year Mom fell apart and left for good. With my long legs, long arms, and Dad's athletic genes, I could handle myself even back then. I suppose I wasn't like most other girls.

After what happened on that fishing trip, I know I wasn't.

Fishing with my dad didn't mean renting a cane pole and buying bait pellets out of a dispenser at some catfish tank near an RV park. It generally meant tramping miles across a field to a glassy pond on some war buddy's ranch, or winding through dense woods, pitching a tent, and fly fishing an icy stream far from the nearest telephone. The trips were rough, but they were the bright times of my life—and his too. They let him forget the things that haunted him and remember how to be happy.

This particular outing was to a ranch in the Texas Panhandle, owned by a former Defense Department bigwig. The ranch bordered one of the few sizeable lakes in a corner of Texas that is brown and rocky and dry. We loaded Dad's new Chevy pickup with cheese puffs and soft drinks—healthy eating wouldn't begin until the first fish hit the skillet—and left Dallas just before noon with the bass boat in tow. The drive was long, but we had leather interior, plenty of tunes, and time to talk. Dad and I could always talk.

The heat rose early that year, and the temperature hung in the nineties. Two hours after we left Dallas, the brand-new air conditioner in the brand-new truck rattled and clicked and dropped dead. We drove the rest of the way with the windows down while the high Texas sun tried to burn a hole through the roof.

Around 5:30 we stopped to use the bathroom at a rundown gas station somewhere southeast of Amarillo. The station was nothing but a twisted gray shack dropped in the middle of a hundred square miles of blistering hard pan. It hadn't rained for a month in that part of Texas, and the place was so baked that even the brittle weeds rolled over on their bellies, as if preparing a last-ditch effort to drag themselves to shade.

The restroom door was on the outside of the station, isolated from the rest of the building. There was no hope of cooling off until I finished my business and got around to the little store in the front, where a rusty air conditioner chugged in the window. When I walked into the bathroom, I had to cover my nose and mouth with my hand. A mound of rotting trash leaned like a grimy snow drift against a metal garbage can in the corner. Thick, black flies zipped and bounced from floor to wall and ceiling to floor, occasionally smacking my arms and legs as if I were a bumper in a buzzing pinball machine. It was the filthiest place I'd ever been.

Looking back, it was an apt spot to begin the filthiest night of my life.

I had just leaned over the rust-ringed sink to inspect my teeth in the sole remaining corner of a shattered mirror when someone pounded on the door.

"Just a minute!" I turned on the faucet. A soupy liquid dribbled out, followed by the steamy smell of rotten eggs. I turned off the faucet, pulled my sport bottle from the holster on my hip, and squirted water on my face and in my mouth. I wiped my face on the sleeve of my T-shirt.

My blue-jean cutoffs were short and tight, and I pried free a tube of lotion that was wedged into my front pocket. I raised one foot at a time to the edge of the toilet seat and did my best to brush the dust from my legs. Then I spread the lotion over them. The ride may have turned me into a dust ball, but I was determined at least to be a soft dust ball with a coconut scent.

Before leaving I took one last look in my little corner of mirror. The hair was auburn, the dust was beige. I gave the hair a shake, sending tiny flecks floating through a slash of light that cut the room diagonally from a hole in the roof. Someone pounded on the door again. I turned away from the mirror.

"Okay, okay, I'm coming!"

When I pulled open the door and stepped into the light, I shaded my eyes and blinked to clear away the spots. All that I could think about was the little air conditioner in the front window and how great it would feel when I got inside. That's probably why I was completely unprepared when a man's hand reached from beside the door and clamped hard onto my wrist.

CHAPTER
TWO

AFTER ABOUT A THOUSAND hours of self-defense classes, I expected my training would kick in when I needed it, and it did. I yanked my arm down, pulling the man with it. Pivoting on my left foot, I swung my fist in a roundhouse hammer chop. Just before it landed on his ear, his other hand shot up and caught my arm.

"Knock it off, Taylor," he whispered. It was Dad.

I pulled my arms free. "Are you trying to give me a heart attack?"

"Would you keep it down?"

I lowered my voice. "Okay, but why are we whispering?"

He looked over his shoulder, then back at me. "I think someone is about to rob the gas station."

"What gas station?"

He squinted at me. Without a word, he turned and pointed at the low row of faded red gas pumps next to which we'd parked just a few minutes earlier.

I got the point, but I do think that a lot of other people might have said something just as dumb under the circumstances. I shrugged. "Okay, *this* gas station. But why do you think someone's going to rob it?"

He put his finger to his mouth. "Shhh! I told you to keep it down." His hand trembled. He lowered it and shoved it into his pocket. The trembling didn't embarrass him, at least not around me. He may well have been afraid—he never pretended to be a superhero—but fear didn't make his hands shake. This was child's play compared to what he went through in the Special Forces. No, the trembling had been there for more than a decade, a function of too much stress and even more alcohol. When the drinking finally stopped, the trembling stuck around, sort of a perpetual tickler for the twelve-step program.

"It's just a hunch," he said. Two guys—a strange pair—a huge one dressed like a preppy and a little fire plug who looks like he got drunk in a tattoo parlor. Preppy was doing the talking. Tattoo Man just stood back and watched. He's got snake eyes, the little one. The owner's an older woman. She seemed scared to death."

"What did you do?"

"I walked out. What did you expect me to do, throw a pack of beef jerky at them?"

A drop of sweat worked its way down the back of my neck. I reached beneath my hair and swiped at it. "So what do you want to do now?"

"I'm going back in there to see what's going on. I want you to stay out of this except to back me up. It's probably just my imagination anyway. Here's what we'll do. You go to the truck and get the shotgun. I'll go into the station. You just come to the door nice and easy, carrying the shotgun. They sell ammo in there, so I suspect people bring their guns in all the time. You're just buying some shells. Keep your eyes on me, and don't come into the store. Just stand in the doorway."

"You want me to carry a shotgun into the gas station? You don't have to bring a gun with you to buy shells. The owner will think *I'm* robbing her."

"If your point is that the plan's not perfect, I'm sorry that I forgot to bring my instruction manual for busting up a robbery. Have you got a better idea?"

I brushed my hair behind my ears and stared across the road. No inspiration there. Nothing but brown flatness stretching to the horizon. I shrugged.

"Okay, then, would you please just do as I say?"

"Fine, but if something happens, do you really expect me to shoot somebody?"

"Absolutely not! If something happens I expect you to turn around and run for the truck. Let me handle it. The point to all of this is to *prevent* something from happening. You're posing with the gun, that's all."

"Speaking of guns, do they have any?"

"I don't know. Now, go get the shotgun."

I have to admit that I found the whole thing exciting. For some reason, probably the invincibility of youth, I didn't sense much danger. I suppose I just had so much confidence in Dad that I couldn't imagine anything happening that he couldn't handle. I walked quickly across the crusty parking area and past the gas pumps.

Reaching into the bed of the truck, I grabbed our old Browning Over/Under. Here's where I made my first mistake. In hindsight, though, I'm glad I didn't do everything perfectly. It provided the last big laugh that my father and I ever had together.

You see, being the daughter of a Special Forces guy is not the same as being a Special Forces guy. I proved the point by opening the breech of the shotgun and draping the barrel over my forearm as I walked toward the door of the station. It was a gun safety point that my dad had drilled into me since I was big enough to hold a weapon. A gun with an open breech can't fire. Unfortunately, the whole world can see that it's not loaded. Given more time to think, it might have occurred to me that that wasn't the effect we were looking for.

When I appeared in the door of the gas station, Dad was standing at the counter next to Preppy, near the store's old-fashioned cash register. The place smelled of chewing tobacco and live bait, the latter of which struck me as odd since there couldn't have been any public water within fifty miles.

The owner, swarthy and solid, could have passed for a farming grandmother in a prairie painting if she had more teeth. She stood silent, one hand in the pocket of her faded jeans, the other resting on the closed drawer of the register. Her eyes moved from Dad to Preppy to Tattoo Man. She seemed too occupied to pay much attention to me. Although sweat glistened on her upper lip, I didn't think she looked scared, just hot. Everything was hot.

After saying something I couldn't catch, Dad pointed toward some boxes of shells on the shelf behind the owner's head. When she turned to look, I saw Preppy glance at the cash register. It was puzzling that such a clean-cut guy could give off such a creepy vibe, but I could see exactly what Dad meant. Preppy was up to no good.

I cleared my throat.

The three heads near the counter turned toward me at once. When Dad saw the open gun draped over my arm, he rolled his eyes. I looked down at the yawning breech and felt the blood rush to my neck. I knew my face would soon be glowing like a Christmas light. I hate it when that happens.

To make things worse, it occurred to me that I hadn't brought any shells from the truck, so I had no way to load the gun even if I wanted to. When you think about it, though, that part was not really so dumb. Why should I have brought shells into the store? The point of our whole cover story was that we were *buying* shells. I always made good grades, but Dad used to say that I sometimes thought so logically that I missed the forest for the trees. This may have been one of those instances.

In light of my mistakes I needed to redeem myself. I flashed my biggest smile. "Well, if we're going to do much shooting on this trip, we're going to need more than just the two shells in my pocket, wouldn't you say, Dad?" I squeezed my fingers into the front pocket of my shorts and jangled some change. Unfortunately, it sounded like change, not shotgun shells, so to divert their attention I wiggled the part of me that was in the shorts. That drew a smile from Preppy and appeared to take his mind off ammunition.

Dad frowned when he heard the change jingling, but he seemed unwilling to give up hope based on such scant evidence. He raised an eyebrow so obviously that he might as well have painted *Got shells?* on his forehead.

I looked him in the eye. "Too bad we forgot to bring the shells from home."

He understood my code. He rolled his eyes again, apparently his expression du jour, and turned back to the owner. "Twelve-gauge, double-ought buck." He drummed his fingers on the counter and kept one eye on Preppy while the owner turned, pulled a box of shells from a shelf, and set them next to Dad's hand.

"All I've got is number-six shot," she said.

"That will do."

I sashayed past a sagging rack of candy bars and headed for the cash register. Dad inched his hand across the counter and slipped it into the box of ammo. That's when I remembered I was supposed to stay in the doorway. Oh well, he always told me that the best battle plans weren't worth the paper they were written on once the shooting started. I kept walking toward the counter.

Tattoo Man slid in so close behind me that I could feel his hot breath on my shoulder. With shelves of pork rinds and motor oil on either side of me, there was nothing to do but continue walking. "Hey, fellas," I said, in the sultriest drawl I could conjure. I nodded toward Preppy. "What's your name, big guy?"

"My, my, what have we here?" Preppy waggled the matchstick that he held in the corner of his mouth. His eyes moved up and down my body, and I felt as if I'd been slimed. I'd created the distraction I needed, though. Behind me, Tattoo Man's footsteps stopped.

"I'm Chad," Preppy said.

It figured. I kept walking, extending the space between Tattoo Man and me. When I reached the counter, I moved past Dad to within a couple of feet of Chad. He really was huge. I'm five-feet-nine, and he could have rested his chin on my head. His biceps heaved against the banded sleeves of his polo shirt. It was time to keep my mouth shut and let Dad take over, but I had already developed an intense dislike for this guy. It must have gotten the better of me.

I pointed over my shoulder at Tattoo Man. "So the gangs have reached the high schools out here too? I'll bet you guys' civics teacher is all aflutter about it."

The smile disappeared from Chad's face. Tattoo Man's shoes began scraping toward me again. Dad's scowl told me my remark might leave me open to second-guessing when this was over.

Chad recovered his veneer and pointed toward his friend. "I appreciate a clever comment as much as the next person, but if I were you I would be careful around my compatriot, Will. I'm a good natured fellow, but Will—he's got what one might call a dark side. I believe the public schools took their leave of him years ago."

Will's footsteps stopped a few feet behind me.

Dad moved in next to me. "You're too young to be losing your memory, Taylor. You gave me the shells, remember?" Before anyone could move, he pulled the gun from my arm, popped two shells into the breech, and snapped it shut. He stared over my shoulder at Will while he tilted his head toward the owner. "Can I get a couple of boxes of these?"

"Sure." She reached for another box. "Need a bag?"

Will stepped up beside me. He slid his hand into his pocket. I took a step back; Dad took a step forward. Chad moved past us and put his hand on Will's arm. "My friend, these folks seem to have some business to conduct, so we should be moving on."

I turned, and for the first time I saw Will's eyes, which moved from me to Dad and back to me. They weren't hard, but pale and empty—more like smudged camera lenses than eyes. As expressionless as if he were surveying nothing more than a broomstick or a rock.

From the time I got out of the truck, I had longed for something cold. I found it in those eyes, and it made me wish we were back in Dallas.

Chad nodded. "A pleasant day to everyone. I hope we have an opportunity to meet again." With one hand he pulled the matchstick from his mouth. With the other, he grabbed Will's arm and directed him out the door.

When they were gone, the owner pulled a handkerchief from her back pocket, wiped her face, and looked up at Dad. "Something told me those fellas were up to no good."

"I had the same feeling. That's why I came back." He turned toward me. "But my plan of attack didn't work quite the way I envisioned it. Taylor, you looked really scary standing in the doorway with an empty shotgun. I'll bet they were terrified you were going to hit them with it."

I stuck my hands in my back pockets. "I guess I didn't think that one through very well."

"It's okay. I should have been more specific when I told you to get the shotgun." He walked to the door and looked out. "Their car's gone. Let's give them a few minutes' head start in case they went the same way we're going. I don't want to run into them on the road. Then we'll take off. I'd like to get camp set up before dark. Will you be okay here, ma'am?"

"Oh, I'll be fine. My husband'll be back any minute. Besides, I've got a friend of my own right here." She pulled her hand out of her pocket and placed a .38-caliber revolver next to the register.

"I'm guessing that one's loaded." Dad smiled.

The woman chuckled. "This one's always loaded, Mister. So's the shotgun under the counter. We're a long ways from any help out here. I wouldn't be too hard on your girl, though. She handled herself just fine."

Dad looked at me and smiled. "I was proud of her. I thought you showed a lot of guts, Taylor. You made a few mistakes, but you kept your cool, which is three-quarters of any battle. I didn't like the smart-aleck remark you made, though. Remember, the first line of defense is to defuse, not escalate."

"This is Texas, not a war zone, Dad."

His face darkened. "Same rules apply."

The old woman opened the swinging gate of the counter and stepped toward me. She placed her arm around my shoulder. "Why, honey, most girls would have been bawlin' their eyes out before they got through that door. And here you were walkin' right up to that big, smart one as if you enjoyed it. I was mighty glad you were here. I may be a well-armed old lady, but I'm still an old lady."

We turned to leave.

"If you need to use the bathroom, it's right over there." She pointed to an open door near the corner, behind which appeared to be a reasonably clean, well-lit restroom.

I brushed at my arm, as if to wipe away the memory of the black flies. "I used the one outside."

"Oh, no, honey. That one's been busted for years. It's supposed to be locked, but kids keep breakin' in and dumpin' garbage in it."

"It was fine."

She touched the boxes of ammo on the counter. "Say, didn't you want to buy some shells?"

"We don't need any. We've got plenty in the truck." I smiled at Dad. "Besides, we're fishing."

She scratched her head.

Dad opened the breech of the shotgun and the two shells popped out into his hand. "I'm glad you said something, though, or I'd have walked out with these." He dropped them onto the counter.

"Well, good luck then." She picked the shells up and placed them into the open box.

As we drove away from the station, fried weeds and scattered gravel crunched beneath the tires. A reddish-brown cloud drifted up behind the truck and followed us listlessly down the road. My stomach grumbled. I assumed that I was still nervous from the excitement and that it would pass.

Over the years since that day, I've had the same feeling in my stomach many times in a tight spot. It's the adrenaline-juiced feeling that keeps a person alert and can keep a person alive. It comes in handy in my line of work. But I wish I had known back then what I know now. It might have helped prepare me for what would happen later that evening. I no longer want that nervous feeling to go away too quickly. Because the bad guys don't always quit when you think they should.

CHAPTER
THREE

WHEN DAD AND I left the gas station, we drove north-west for another hour, most of it on a straight, two-lane farm road. Judging by the different twists of barbed wire on each side, the road must have cut a border between two huge ranches. After finding the turnoff on our hand-drawn map, we squeezed the truck down the last five hundred yards of a tight path edged by boulders the size of rolled-up sleeping bags.

The campsite was a hard, flat clearing on a rise sur-rounded by buffalo grass, prickly pear, and a smattering of scraggly mesquites. The clearing ended at a ledge that fell off to the lake past larger boulders, some as big as a bedroom dresser. In the center of the camp was a precisely cut fire pit encircled by six hewn logs, creating the effect of a rugged dining room table and chairs. The owner must have hauled the logs in, because aside from the mesquites there wasn't a tree in sight. The pristine scene at the fire pit gave me the hunch that the owner frequently brought his wife camping.

The clearing was just large enough that we could have driven the truck and boat in a comfortable circle around it. The owner had assured us that we would have the place to ourselves, so we left the pickup on the side of the road where it opened to the campsite. We unloaded from there.

The few clouds in the sky were nothing but wispy streaks, and rain was no more possible than snow. For Dad that meant no tents, so unpacking and setting up camp took little time. The sun was low enough to sniff the horizon beyond the lake when I changed into jeans and boots; this was rattler country. We walked to the edge of the drop-off to scout.

The lake extended dark and quiet to the opposite bank, which presented a mirror image of our side. Stubby, red-brown bluffs with limestone caps rose from the water, and desert shrubs and mesquites appeared as olive blotches on the rocks. From the gray flatness beyond the bluffs, shadowy mesas rose against the orange sunset, like giant hunting dogs warming on a rug in front of a fireplace.

We made our way down a path that funneled us to the water. The lake was deep and fell off quickly. We discussed whether we should begin the next morning by fishing from the bank. Looking diagonally across the water, we could see the boat ramp where we would put in, maybe a mile from where we stood. As is the case with all lake fishing, understanding the structure beneath the surface would be the key to success. Dad's friend had drawn a map of some of his favorite spots, a tribute to the seriousness of their friendship.

We took turns dipping in the lake to wash off the dust. Then we worked our way back up the path and started dinner. Within a half hour, Dad had steaks sizzling over the fire. Although I was an accomplished campfire chef, he insisted on doing the cooking since this trip was my birthday present.

By the time we finished eating, the sun had been down for more than an hour. The air was dry as lint, and the heat had backed away to the point where it was not uncomfortable to sit where the fire's warmth touched our feet and ankles. We left our dishes on the ground and lay back side by side, our heads propped on our rolled-up sleeping bags.

"We don't see enough stars in Dallas," Dad said.

I was so full and relaxed that moving my mouth seemed an effort. I didn't respond.

"There are two kinds of people in the world, kiddo. The kind who love stars and the kind who love lights. I always preferred the stars." Dad had a knack for boiling things down to essentials.

For a few moments I pondered his unspoken judgment on those poor souls who preferred the lights. I was about to comment on how shallow they must be, when he turned his head toward me.

"You like the lights, don't you, Taylor?"

Like heck I did. "How can you say that? Look at all the times we've gone camping together! I could live out here in the middle of nowhere, no problem."

"The middle of nowhere?"

Okay, it was poor phrasing, but he was parsing my words. "I meant out in the country. I'm just like you, Dad. I like the stars." And I did. At that moment I wanted more than anything to be just like him.

He stared up into the sky again. "No, you're not like me, and I don't want you to be."

I turned toward him and leaned on my elbow. "Of course, why would I want to be like a decorated war hero? That would be a real embarrassment."

"I've done things that I had to do—things that no human being should do to another. I would never wish that on my kid."

"You did your duty. You never have to be ashamed of that."

"I'm not ashamed. I'm proud that I did what a lot of people couldn't do. I'm proud that when the moment came, the moment when you're afraid and you want more than anything to run away, I stayed and fought. That's the moment that every man, I think, wonders about—wonders if he has what it takes to stay."

"You're very brave."

"I'm not sure I know what brave is. I just did the things that had to be done. But I'm a human being. I still did those things to other human beings. I killed them when I had to, and sometimes I wonder if I killed when I *didn't* really have to. I made choices when there was no time to think and no alternative but to choose. There's a responsibility that goes with that. No speeches, no parades, no medals can gloss that over or make it go away. It's a responsibility a person has to live with forever."

I put my hand on his shoulder. He covered my hand with his, and I could feel the tremors. I remembered the dark days, the drinking days. The mornings I found him on the floor and was afraid he would die and leave me alone. If he wanted to talk about responsibility, I had been too young to see that, too young for *that* responsibility—the responsibility of getting my own father into bed and making excuses for him with neighbors. Too young to have no mother and to be so afraid of being alone. What about *that* responsibility?

I shook my head. It was over now. We were whole again. But tears welled up just the same. I'd always been too quick to cry. I fought to hold the tears back, because I didn't want to cry here. Not now.

He squeezed my hand. "I shouldn't be talking about me." I swear, sometimes he could read my mind. "There were things that you missed out on, with your mother gone. Things she could have given you that I couldn't. I know that, and I'm sorry for it. When your mother was young, before her problems started, she had a type of strength— a faith—that I didn't have. She didn't cause her problems the way I caused mine. They were thrust on her when she was too young to deal with it. She tried. She fought if for a long time, as long as she could. In many ways she was stronger than I was. You have her strength, Taylor, but I hope I haven't cheated you of that faith she had in the beginning. It was a good thing. I've been thinking about that lately, and I'm going to work on it. I promise."

I didn't like to talk about Mom, especially not when I was about to cry. So I chewed my lip and pictured the happy times, with all of us together. That helped. Soon I regained control.

Dad sat up and patted me on the knee. "Well, I don't know why I'm being like this. It's almost your birthday. Look at the sky. The stars are out and we've got the world on a string, don't we, kiddo?" He pushed himself onto his feet and told me to relax while he cleaned up.

Before long, he had gathered the utensils for washing and headed down the embankment to the lake. I rested my head on my sleeping bag and studied the sky. Out here, the universe was brilliant, and it was all ours. Dad was right: We had the world on a string. I thought of a song. It was one of his songs, not mine. The tune stuck in my mind, and I started to hum. Then I started to sing softly, *"Don't you love her madly? Wanna be her daddy? Don't you love her as she's walkin' out the—"*

"Well, if it isn't Xena, the warrior princess! And she sings such an appropriate song."

I jumped to my feet and spun just in time to see Chad and Will from the gas station crunching through the brush next to our truck. Will carried a shotgun.

The breech was not open.

CHAPTER
FOUR

"WHERE'S YOUR SHOTGUN, BEAUTIFUL?" Chad walked toward the fire. "If I recall our earlier encounter, you were all about shotguns. Will brought his. We thought we could compare."

I looked toward the lake. Dad was nowhere in sight. Something in my stomach turned hot and began to tumble. I took a deep breath. "Hey, what are y'all doing out here?" I flashed a big smile and forced myself to think. I glanced at the ground near Dad's sleeping bag to see if he'd brought his pistol from the truck. If it was there, I couldn't make it out in the dark. The shotgun, which had not proved terribly useful so far that day, was still in the bed of the truck.

"We followed you, of course. Heaven knows, one has to make a special effort to get to know people out here in the sticks. In any event, I've not been able to get my mind off you since our last encounter."

I looked at Will. He'd only been there for a minute and a half, but he already seemed to be losing his focus. A field rat or something skittered through the nearby brush. He followed it with his eyes. He didn't seem to think any more than he talked.

"Why don't you just sit down by the fire and make yourself comfortable?" Chad nodded toward the sleeping bags. "Where's Daddy? Out shooting dinner?" He chewed on a reed as he talked. I remembered the match that he had waggled in his mouth back at the gas station and wondered if he had some sort of oral security thing going on, like a dog that's afraid to approach a human without picking up its favorite toy.

Chad looked toward the lake. "Here he is!" He waved. "Hey, Pops, we're back!"

My father's shadowy figure rose from behind a boulder at the edge of the campsite. In his right hand was a skillet. In the skillet were our steak knives, forks, and metal plates. Though the light was dim, I could see the muscles in his arms and chest, flexed tight against his olive T-shirt. "What do you fellas want here?" His voice was as hard as the rocks around him, and I wished more than anything that we were home.

Will's eyes focused on the knives in the skillet. He pointed the shotgun at Dad.

"Well, that's not a very hospitable greeting, Mr. . . ."

Chad cocked his head. "I don't believe I caught your name back at the gas station, sir."

"Roger Pasbury." He turned to Will. "If you're not looking to shoot someone, you ought to point that thing somewhere else, son."

Will smiled. "You're the one holding the knives, mister. And I'm not your son." His eyes brightened. It was the first time I had seen any life in those eyes. His smile frightened me more than anything because it was the smile of someone doing something he enjoyed.

Dad looked down at the utensils in his hands. "Oh, come on. These are what we ate dinner with. What do you think? I hid steak knives down by the lake in case someone showed up with a shotgun?"

Chad lifted his hand, palm out. It was a huge hand, the size of an oven mitt. "Wait a minute, gentlemen. There's no need to get testy. We're just looking for some good conversation in inviting surroundings."

He looked at me with the same all-over look he'd given me in the gas station. I shivered and rubbed my bare arms. He cocked his head. "School's out for the day, and we're just looking to blow off some steam." Another smile. "That's all right with you, isn't it, beautiful? That *is* what you said back there at the gas station, isn't it? Something about school?"

"My daughter's name is Taylor." The muscles in Dad's neck worked as he spoke. He glanced around the campsite, and I knew he was mentally mapping the objects, the terrain. He was preparing. I tried to swallow, but my throat may as well have been coated with chalk.

"She sometimes speaks before she thinks," Dad continued. "We all do. I'm sure she didn't mean anything by it."

"Well, Taylor, as I told you back at the gas station, my name is Chad and this is Will. Will loves his shotgun as much as you love yours. You two should hit it off just fine."

Will dipped the barrel of the gun, as if he were tipping his cap, but his blank expression didn't change.

"If you want some food, we can get you something," Dad said. "We just finished eating, but we've got some burgers in the cooler we could cook up for you."

"My, you're suddenly very welcoming. Now that's more like it. Why don't we all sit down around the fire and get acquainted."

Will took a step toward the fire pit.

Chad raised a hand. "Not you, Will. I think you'd better stand off a bit and keep an eye on things. I think you'll be happy enough with your role as the evening's events unfold."

I narrowed my eyes. "What role is that?"

"I was wondering if you were ever going to speak for yourself, or if you were going to allow Daddy to do all of your talking for you. You certainly didn't have any trouble expressing yourself at the gas station."

"Listen, you—"

"Taylor, shut up," Dad said.

Chad ran his hand through his hair and smiled. "You're really going to have to learn some manners,

Taylor. Perhaps we can explore that theme further when we get down to business. First, let's sit."

The three of us sat on the logs by the fire—Dad in the middle, flanked by Chad on his left and me on his right. Will stood a couple of steps behind me.

"So you were planning on doing some fishing tomorrow?" Chad said.

"Yes, we were."

I watched Dad's eyes. He continued to scout our surroundings. After a few seconds he focused on the fire—a particular point at the nearest edge of the fire—but I couldn't make out what had caught his eye.

"Large mouth?"

"Walleye. I understand this is one of the few walleye lakes in Texas."

Chad turned to me. "And you like to fish, too, beautiful?" His voice no longer sneered. It was detached, as though he had already recategorized us from humans to mere objects and was just going through the motions of completing the conversation he'd started.

"I like to fish," I said.

He picked up a stick and absently poked at the fire. "Plastic worms? Crank bait? What do you use here?"

"We've gotten some instructions from the locals." Dad's face brightened, perhaps hopeful that there might still be a safe resolution if he could engage Chad. "We're supposed to bounce around on the bottom using a leader and a spinner baited with night crawlers. Never tried it before. Do you fish?"

"No, I don't." Chad tossed the stick into the fire and stood up. "That's enough small talk. I think it's time to get down to business."

Dad looked over his shoulder at Will, then squinted up at Chad, who towered over him. "But we just started talking."

Chad folded his massive arms in front of his chest. "I said, I've had enough."

"Please don't do this, son." The light from the fire flickered across Dad's face, highlighting the lines in his forehead and making him look older than I'd ever seen him. But his eyes were fixed and hard, and the line of his jaw stretched tight as he spoke.

Looking back now, I realize that at that moment he, too, had moved into another world—a world of absolute concentration. He'd been there before and knew that total concentration was the minimum requirement. It was a world he had wished to avoid for the rest of his life and hoped I would never have to see. A world of brutality and survival.

I admired him so much for his calm in that moment, and I loved him. Dear, God, how I loved my dad.

Chad clucked his tongue. "You don't seem to understand, Mr. Pasbury. We have to do this. It's what we do, isn't it, Will? You see, sir, we came for your daughter. And we intend to take her."

Will laughed. It was a high-pitched, inhuman sound, more of a squeal. I trembled but didn't take my eyes off Dad.

"What do you mean you want to take her? Take her where?"

Chad chuckled. "More accurately, we simply want to use her for a while. Right, Will?"

Will stepped forward so he was standing to my right. He lifted the shotgun with one hand, resting the barrel on his shoulder.

Dad had been waiting for an opening. Will's nonchalance created one. From the corner of my eye I saw Dad pull one foot beneath him, so he was almost crouching rather than sitting on the log. He looked up at Chad. "I told you Taylor sometimes talks without thinking. If it's an apology you want, I'm sure she's thought better of her rudeness. Haven't you, Taylor?" He looked me in the eye.

"It's true, I've got a big mouth. Always been a problem. I didn't mean anything, though. I just joke around too much. If I offended you, I'm sorry." I turned my head to meet Chad's eyes.

"No offense taken, truly. Nevertheless, you could use some work on your manners. Perhaps I can teach you a few things, and Will can reinforce your learning a bit when I'm done."

Dad pointed over his shoulder. "I've got money in the truck. More than a thousand dollars. Just let me go get my wallet, and I'll give you all the cash we have. We'll forget this and you can move on."

The idea gave me hope. If Dad could get to the truck, he might be able to grab the pistol he kept in the cab.

Next to me, Will chuckled.

"Why, Mr. Pasbury," Chad said. "We didn't come all the way out here for your money. Although I appreciate that you pointed out where we can find it. We want your daughter. What we intend to do is show her a good time. We're not going to hurt her. In fact, by the time we're finished, she might just find that she's had the time of her life."

Dad looked him in the eye. "And you think I'll just sit by and watch?" He lowered his hand to his side, closing it around something on the ground, but I couldn't make out what it was.

"You certainly can watch if you'd like. That's an interesting thought. Not what I'd have expected of you. In any event, when we're done we will move on. We have no intention of hurting anyone as long as you behave yourself."

"You need to think about this." Dad held Chad's gaze. "Let's say you did this thing. And let's say you killed us both. You'd get caught eventually. The owner of the gas station saw you with us. It won't take the police long to figure it out. You can't wipe out all of your tracks, yours and your car's. You'll be throwing away your whole lives for one night."

"Mr. Pasbury, you assume way too much. First of all, we don't need to kill anyone. We're not from around here and no one knows us, certainly not your little woman at the gas station. Second, the car is stolen. We'll be driving something else a few hours from now. Third, you seem to jump to the erroneous conclusion that this is our first time. Actually, I like to think of us as professionals."

Dad turned his hand slightly and I saw what he had picked up. The plastic lighter-fluid bottle he used to start the fire. I wondered what Will would do if I turned and threw up on his shoes?

"Taylor, run!" Dad reached into the fire and grabbed a log. As the flames seared the skin from his hand, he screamed an animal scream—a sound I still hear in the night—and lunged at Chad. He squirted the lighter fluid onto Chad's face and slammed the burning log into the side of his head.

Chad howled. His cheek exploded in flames. He fell onto his side, thrashing at his head and hair as the flames melted his ear like candle wax. One arm lay twisted beneath him, snapped in the fall. He howled again.

Dad dropped the log and wheeled toward Will. "Run, Taylor!" He lowered his head and charged directly toward Will, who stood transfixed at my side. Then Will's eyes brightened. He dropped the shotgun from his shoulder to his hip and leveled it at Dad, who was too far away to reach him in time.

I have relived the next moment a thousand times over the years. I see myself diving at Will's legs, knocking him off balance. I see the shotgun's barrel lurch upward and hear its report slam the air above our heads. I see Dad lunge at Will and tackle him, and I know Will is no match for Dad in close quarters.

That's how I see it in my mind.

But I did not dive at Will's legs. I turned and ran toward the truck. I heard the shotgun blast, and I heard Dad moan. When I reached the truck, I dove into the front seat, where I finally took a breath.

I reached under the dash for the metal holster that hung there, and fumbled to find the release. Finally, my fingers hit the latch. Dad's 9MM, semi-automatic dropped into my hand. I opened the door and rolled out onto the ground behind the truck. The shotgun blasted again, and I hoped that Dad had somehow wrestled it from Will.

I rose and peered over the bed of the truck. Dad writhed in the dirt at Will's feet, his pant leg and shirt dark with blood. Will was facing my direction, but his attention was on the ground, not me. He grinned down at Dad as he reached into his pocket, found two shells, and loaded them. He lowered the barrel toward Dad's head. I braced my hands on the truck's fender and leveled the pistol at Will's chest. The shot was neither long nor difficult. An odd sense of calm drifted over me in the moment before I fired, so that everything seemed to move in slow motion. The middle of Will's chest seemed as big as a barn, and I squeezed my trigger before he squeezed his.

He fell across Dad's legs.

By the time I reached Dad, Will's eyes were glassy. The entry hole near his shirt pocket told me that he would be dead in minutes. I kicked him off of Dad's legs and knelt to the ground. Dad's skin was gray and his breath came in gasps. His eyes were closed.

I held his face in my hands and pressed my cheek against his. "Why did you do it?" I sat on the ground and pulled his head onto my lap. "I'm sorry! I'm so sorry."

He opened his eyes and looked up at me. "I'm proud of you, sweetie. You did it just right." He moaned and blood ran from the corner of his mouth.

"I should have hit him. I could have saved you, but I ran."

"We'd both be lying here if you had." He lifted his leg, exposing a dark puddle in the dirt beneath him where the blood splashed in pulses. I slid his head from my lap, tore off my shirt and wrapped it around his leg. I pulled it tight, but the blood was everywhere and I couldn't see where or how to stop it.

I was scared he was going to die. And when I'm scared, I talk. So I talked while I worked on his leg the best that I could. "I wasn't afraid of them. It happened so fast, I just couldn't think. I made the wrong choice."

"You made the right choice. Leave the leg alone. It's too late." He touched his side, which was soaked in blood. "There's no patching me out here. Come closer."

I looked at his leg. The blood still spurted, and I knew he was right. I couldn't stop it. His lips were tinting blue. I moved over and pulled his head close to my chest. "Why did you do it, Dad? You could have lived. You can't leave me. I don't have anyone else."

"There are things more important than living. You're one of them." He gasped and pulled one arm to his side. I wanted so badly to stop the pain, but I didn't know how.

"You're strong—stronger than you think. I've always known that." He coughed and blood came from his mouth again. His voice faded to a whisper. "You've made me happy. I'm happy now. You're alive, and that's what matters. I love you." He tilted his head up, and I pressed my cheek against his.

His head sagged. When I looked in his eyes, they were fixed at the stars.

I don't know how long I sat with my father's cheek pressed against mine, my tears smudging the dirt on his face. I do know that I moved only when I heard a groan behind me. I looked over my shoulder. Chad was dragging himself slowly away from me with his one good arm, trying to reach the brush at the edge of the campsite. I started to jump up, but I could see there was no rush.

I unrolled one of the sleeping bags, folded the end of it over, and placed it beneath Dad's head. Then I stood, picked up the pistol, and walked over to Chad. He was so weak I could have stopped his progress by placing my foot in front of him. But I didn't even have to do that. He curled himself into a ball and covered his head with his arm.

"We weren't going to kill you!" His voice was so high-pitched that it nearly squeaked. His legs worked back and forth in the dirt, and I had the strange thought of a child making a snow angel. "For the love of God, have mercy! Please don't kill me!"

I watched him for a moment, then looked out across the lake. For the first time that evening I noticed crickets chirping. In the distance a red light blinked on and off—a radio or television tower, I supposed. The night had swallowed the mesas that jutted so insistently into the horizon at sunset. Now it seemed everything twinkled, everything was a star or was brightened by starlight. I sucked in a long breath and let it out, and noticed that the air had turned crisp.

It seemed forever since I had felt cool.

When I turned back to Chad, he had quieted down, but one leg continued to work back and forth in the dirt. Although his arm still covered his head, there was an open spot near the crook of his elbow where I could see his hair just above his good ear. I leaned over and pointed the pistol just there.

Then I squeezed the trigger.

CHAPTER
FIVE

ELEVEN YEARS AFTER DAD was murdered, Simon Mason hired me. At first blush, it would be difficult to imagine an employer and employee less suited to one another. In little more than a decade, the plain-spoken son of a Dallas electrician had risen to become the world's most recognized Christian evangelist.

Even though we both lived in Dallas and he had an incredibly high profile, I hardly gave a thought to the man until the moment he called me on the telephone. What slight thought I *had* given him tended toward a caricature of television evangelists.

In other words, I assumed he was a greasy-suited charlatan.

That view had been reinforced only weeks before I met him when *The Times* ran a Sunday feature labeling him "The Best-Known Christian on the Planet." In response to that bit of hyperbole, Simon placed a well-publicized call to the Vatican, where his call was promptly accepted. He reportedly assured the Pope that those words had been the paper's, not his. He reportedly handled the situation with such sincerity that the Holy Father issued a press release to the effect that they both played on the same team—though presumably Simon dressed in the Protestant locker room—and His Holiness appreciated Simon's work in advancing the ball for Christ.

While Simon was molding himself into a first-round pick in the worldwide evangelical draft, I had done less to recommend myself to the squad. At first, things went well enough. I blew the doors off my entrance exams and attended Texas A&M on a full-ride scholarship. I graduated in three years with a major in sociology and a minor in business administration. My interest had always been criminal justice, though, and immediately after graduation I trained as a security specialist with the Dallas police SWAT unit.

After a year, on an impulse, I applied to the Secret Service. To my surprise I got hired, primarily, I'm sure, because of the well-publicized story of how I had dispatched two serial rapists at a Texas Panhandle campsite. Newspapers throughout the country had treated me as a tragic heroine, while the local authorities felt so sorry for me that they displayed a pointed lack of curiosity about the close-range shot to Chad's head. The Secret Service apparently determined that a female with that sort of calm under fire was just what they were looking for in a political climate that prized diversity.

I served four years in Washington and received two decorations for my work. One, in particular, recognized the "extraordinary commitment" that I demonstrated to a certain Arab dignitary from a tiny Middle Eastern emirate that was a particularly helpful ally to the United States. While working on the president's advance security team for an international conference on democracy, I foiled an assassination attempt on the sheik with what I will politely call my backside. The region's top surgeons labored for the better part of thirty minutes to remove three pieces of shrapnel from my left buttock.

The next morning most of the major American papers ran front-page photos of the dignitary standing next to my hospital bed, smiling broadly while handing me a medal signifying his nation's second-highest honor. The headlines can be summed up by the *Tribune's:* "Secret Service Hero Works Tail Off for Democracy."

That's where my government career peaked.

To say that I was drummed out of the Service would be an exaggeration, but I definitely didn't receive a farewell dinner and wristwatch. During the conversation in which my supervisor nudged me toward retirement, he said that I had developed quite a reputation, which was true. The combination of the Panhandle killings and the Dubai incident had made me into probably the best-known Secret Service agent since Kennedy's assassination.

Unfortunately, my Service account had some debits as well as credits. I was widely viewed as an agent inclined to shoot first and ask questions later. While I had never hurt anyone, I had shot out two tires and a security camera—all intentionally. (I won the Service's marksmanship contest three years straight.) In a service that doesn't do much shooting, that placed me in rarefied air.

More to the point, though, my supervisor noted that rumors about after-hours drinking and carousing had not enhanced my career standing. After all, propriety was one of the minimum requirements of the Service. He suggested that perhaps I should get some professional help, which angered me so much that I stalked out and headed for the nearest bar. There, as I vaguely recall, I picked up another in a long series of nameless, faceless, and generally shiftless guys in my continuing quest for the answer to the question: Are there any good men left out there?

With the promise of referrals from a Service eager to see its most publicized female agent leave quietly, I resigned and moved back to Dallas. Within weeks I opened Pasbury Security, whose strategic plan included the slogan, "Dallas businesses' choice for tough security assignments." The phrase didn't exactly roll trippingly off the tongue, but it must have worked. By the time Simon hired me, my company was already the best-known private security firm in the Southwest. And I was in a considerably stronger financial position than most twenty-nine-year-olds.

While my professional life was checkered, my personal life was blighted. I didn't drink every day, or even every week. But when I did drink, I drank too much. When I drank too much, I had a destructive tendency to become sexually aggressive. That led to a depressing pattern of poor choices in men—the sort of choices that one would expect from a half-sauced woman on the prowl. I spent far too many nights sleeping in strange apartments, with one hand on a loser's bare chest and the other hand wrapped around the neck of a bottle. To characterize me as a young woman tumbling toward the cliff's edge would be accurate, except that a fair segment of the population would not even consider me that young anymore.

I realize many people would be appalled that I can describe so flippantly a life drifting toward disaster. Many others, however, will understand perfectly. They are the ones who understand what it is like to work later than everyone else in the office because they have nothing to return home to but an empty apartment; the ones who dread weekends because they can only wander the malls alone so many times before the store clerks begin to pity them; the ones who lie in bed at night and cry because they don't understand why they can't be charming enough, or pretty enough—or good enough—to not be alone anymore. Those people will understand. Humor helps. Flippancy helps.

Crying changes nothing.

In any event, fate did not appear to be dragging Planet Pasbury and Planet Mason on a collision course.

In fact, we were orbiting in different solar systems, which is why he was the last person I expected to be on the other end of the line one Saturday morning in March when my cell phone beeped and woke me. I was sprawled on the couch of my office, a rambling loft in a rejuvenated warehouse near downtown Dallas. Wherever I had been the night before—and that recollection did not immediately come to me as I shook off sleep—I had found it more convenient to crash at the office than to make my way farther north to my apartment.

The phone beeped again. I rolled onto my back, freeing my left hand from between my hip and my leather Euro sofa. I must have slept on the hand for quite a while, because it felt like a giant sponge dangling from my wrist. I couldn't flex the fingers quickly enough to make them useful, so I dragged myself into a sitting position and slapped my bare feet onto the hardwood floor. The room smelled of bourbon—stale, open-all-night bourbon, but still good stuff. I scratched one foot with the other and kicked over the bottle on the floor next to the couch. Fortunately, it was nearly empty. Only a few drops slid out onto the floor before I righted the bottle and reached for the phone. "Hello."

"Taylor Pasbury?"

The floor was cold; my toes curled reflexively in an effort to generate warmth. I tucked one foot beneath me and tried to pull the hem of my black cocktail pants over the toes of my other foot with my sponge hand. "Speaking," I grunted. One of the advantages of being in the security business is that clients actually prefer a certain level of gruffness, particularly from a woman.

"I'm glad I caught you in your office. This is Simon Mason. Fred Skilling, at Skilling Oil, gave me your name."

"That was thoughtful of him." I tried to run my hand through my hair. The night on the couch had turned my usual gentle waves into a twisted mess that clumped in auburn hives about my neck and shoulders. I worked at the knots with my fingers.

"I'd like to talk to you about taking charge of my security. Is this a good time?"

I'm sure that most people go through their entire lives without receiving a phone call from someone famous. Because of my time in the Service, though, I had received many of them. I'm not bragging; it's just a fact. That is why it is odd that the name Simon Mason, which by then was already more recognized around the world than the Secretary of State's, did not register with me at all.

"Mr. Mason, I appreciate your call, and I hope that I can help you, but my office hours are Monday through Friday, eight-thirty to five-thirty. If you'll call back then, my assistant will set up a time for you to come in. She keeps my calendar. I couldn't even tell you right now where I'm going to be next week."

"I'm sorry to bother you on Saturday, Ms. Pasbury, but I've got a big Weekend of Glory celebration in Chicago tonight and tomorrow. I'm in Chicago right now. I was hoping you could come to at least one of the events and take a look at our set-up. We've had some threats. The FBI has convinced me we should take them seriously."

I sat up straight. "You mean, you're *that* Simon Mason?"

He chuckled. "Well, I'm not certain who *that* Simon Mason is. I'm the one who's a preacher. Have you heard of me?"

It had to be a prank. I tried to recall what male I had been with the night before. After a few muddled moments, I realized I had come back to the office alone, so I ran the male half (okay, quarter) of my telephone contact list through my mind to identify the most likely practical jokers. No one stood out. But my head hurt. I didn't feel like wasting any more time. "Mr. Mason, would you mind if I gave you a call right back? I've got something going on here . . . uh, I left some water running. If I could just get that taken care of. Uh, is there a number?"

Silence on the other end of the line.

"It's not just water, uh . . ." I spotted my space heater sitting on the floor next to the couch. "There's a space heater too . . . with the water, I mean. Dangerous combination. Is there a number?"

He cleared his throat. "Sure, I can give you the number here at the Palmer House. I really don't want to talk about this on my cell phone. Have you got a pencil?"

"I have one right here. Let her rip." I had neither a pencil nor any intention of playing along with this stupid game. I held the phone away from my mouth and yawned as he repeated the number slowly. "I'll call you in just a few minutes, Mr. Mason. Thank you."

"I'll only be here for another half hour. Can you call by then?"

"Oh, certainly." By this time I was studying a spot where the nail polish on my big toe was peeling. I had paid way too much for that pedicure to have the stuff coming off after two days. "I'll talk to you real soon, Mr. Mason. Good-bye." I clicked off the phone and was just setting it on the end table when it occurred to me to check his number in the incoming calls directory. I hit the menu button and clicked through to the folder. The number was in the 312 area code. Chicago.

I jumped up and brushed my hands over the wrinkles in my silk blouse, as if I thought Simon Mason was going to walk through the door of my office at any minute.

Realizing that panic was not a strategy, I took a deep breath and forced myself to think. I needed confirmation. I dialed information and asked for the number of the Palmer House in Chicago. It matched. Great, he really was Simon Mason. And now that he had had a few minutes to reflect on my running-water-and-space-heater story, he had without question concluded that I was a moron.

I had to find a way to make the story plausible. A space heater and running water—I had it! I dialed the Palmer House and asked for Simon's room.

"Hello?"

"Mr. Mason? It's Taylor Pasbury."

"Well, that didn't take long. I hope everything is okay."

It occurred to me that I was about to lie to the world's most famous preacher. It was a victimless lie, though, which helped. "I may as well come clean with you, Mr. Mason." I gave him an embarrassed laugh. "I was getting ready to take a bath when you called. That's why the water and the space heater were a problem." I silently applauded my clever escape.

"You have a bathtub in your office?"

This was a great example of how I sometimes completely overlook the obvious. Now that Simon Mason had voiced the question that would have been obvious to ninety-nine out of any randomly selected group of a hundred people, I—Old Number One Hundred—was stuck. I could cling to the implausible story that, yes, I did have a bathtub in my office. (After all, doesn't everyone?) But if we ended up working together, he was going to see my office eventually. I decided to throw myself on the mercy of a man of God, not so much from contrition as from a sense that the road of lies I would have to travel to get clear of this would be long and winding and far too exhausting.

"Okay, I'm going to give a confession. I'm not just a liar, I'm a serial liar. There is no water. There is no space heater. And there is no bathtub in my office. When you called, I didn't believe it was really you. I was sure it was someone playing a joke on me. So I gave you that excuse about running water and the rest. After I got off the phone, I figured out that it really was you. I think you can deduce where it all went from there." I held my breath.

He began to laugh—a clear-throated, energetic laugh—and I wondered if he might be younger than I imagined. "You know, I thought I was the only one who ever got caught in a dumb white lie."

I scratched my head. "Wait a minute. You're telling me that *you* lie?"

"I try not to make a habit of it. But, yes, I've told a lie or two. I'm not proud of it, but it's the truth." He paused. "It really is the truth. I wouldn't lie about lying." He laughed again.

Now, I was beginning to wonder about him.

"Listen, if perfection is one of your requirements for taking on a new client, we should cut this off right now."

"No, that's not a requirement. If it were, I would have a short client list, wouldn't I?"

"Yes, I think you would."

I walked over to my desk and picked up a pen and note pad. "So, Mr. Mason—I mean, *Reverend* Mason— what kind of threats have you received?"

"First of all, call me Simon. Okay if I call you Taylor?"

"Sure."

"Actually, I haven't personally received any threats. The FBI tells me that I've been the subject of terrorist chatter."

"You mean National Security Agency chatter?"

"I don't know. What is the National Security Agency?"

"It's an agency that monitors communications around the world for the U.S. government. Very secretive. These days they focus a lot of their attention on terrorist organizations."

"Well, apparently it didn't take a lot of sleuthing to uncover this threat. They tell me it's been posted on Web sites run by Islamic terror groups."

I scratched out notes as he spoke. "So you're being threatened by Muslim terrorists?"

"That's what I understand."

"What exactly is the nature of the threats?"

"It's not completely clear, but the educated guess is that they want to kill me."

"Of course. That's why they call them terrorists. But *why* do they want to kill you?"

"I don't know. The FBI supposes that it's simply that I'm a prominent Christian. You know, culture war. And haven't you heard? I'm as famous as the Pope."

"Yes, I read that. Congratulations."

"What a joke."

"Well, it's true, isn't it?"

"Of course it's not true. And it's not helpful to what I'm trying to do, that's for sure."

"What *are* you trying to do?" There was a pause. I leaned forward and quickly added, "I need to understand more about your business's—sorry, I'm not used to working for preachers—I mean your ministry's goals."

"My job, as I see it, is to lead people to the truth. The truth is Jesus, because he can save people's souls.

It's that simple, which is lucky because I'm not any great intellect. I'm a pretty simple guy."

I had to give him credit. He had a disarmingly genuine delivery of the *I'm-just-a-simple-preacher* thing. I was a long way from buying it, though.

"Anyway, I'm a much easier target than the Pope, there's no doubt about that. For most of my security I rely on the auditoriums where we hold our celebrations."

I shook my head. "You've got to be kidding me. You don't have a security team? You're an obvious target for any number of radical groups, not to mention hundreds of kooks."

"Look, I'm not some big shot in the way that you probably think. Fifteen years ago I was just a local sports-radio host. On weekends I traveled around preaching to groups that were sometimes smaller than twenty people. This fame thing came on quickly and snowballed to the point where it's ridiculous. If it weren't for the people it allows me to reach, I'd say no thanks."

I sat back down on the sofa and shifted the phone to my other ear. "That's good background. Let me get some more basics. Do you have a few minutes to answer some questions?"

"I have about fifteen minutes right now. I can make more time later."

"Okay. First, your family. Wife? Kids? Do they travel with you?"

"My wife died seventeen years ago. Ovarian cancer."

I wrote *wife dead* on the note pad. "I'm sorry. That must have been awful for you."

"It was. But God uses everything for his purposes, even tragedies."

"So you think God planned for your wife to die?" I might have phrased that better if I had given it some thought. I heard him take a deep breath before he spoke.

"No, God didn't give Marie cancer. Genetics did. God did have mercy on us, though. We had five years together before she died. And for three of those we had Kacey, also."

"Is that your son?"

"Daughter. She's twenty now. She goes to Southern Methodist University in Dallas."

"How old are you?"

"Forty-four."

"Does she travel with you?"

"Kacey?"

"Yes."

"Generally only in the summers, but she is here with me in Chicago. Travel doesn't work very well for her with school and all."

I wrote *daughter 20, no travel.* "Does she live at home?"

"She lives on campus during the school year and at home in the summer."

"There are no other children?"

"Just Kacey and me. That's our family."

"You say you're in Chicago for a meeting?" I set down my pad and pen and walked over to the small refrigerator behind my desk. I took out a bottle of water.

"Yes, at the Mid America Center. I'd like you to come up and take a look, if possible. I know this is short notice. Do you think you can make it?"

Was he kidding? This was the juiciest security assignment in America. "I think I can juggle some things and make it work. How about if I call you back in ten minutes or so after I check my schedule?" It's never good to seem too readily available.

"That's fine. Please don't be longer than that, though. I have to leave for the auditorium. We've got a rehearsal."

After I hung up, I danced around the couch and whooped. Simon Mason, the best-known Christian on the planet, was about to make me the best-known security consultant on the planet. How they would envy me back at the Secret Service. It was only 10:45 in the morning, but this day was starting out right. That called for a celebration. I set my bottle of water on the end table and picked up last night's bottle of bourbon. There was just enough left for a healthy slug.

CHAPTER
SIX

THE TAXI'S HEADLIGHTS SPARKLED off fat, wet snow-flakes that drifted down in lazy zigzags as the driver edged past a line of tour buses near the entrance to the Mid America Center in Chicago. Each bus had a sign of some sort in the window—*This Bus Headed for the Promised Land* or *Jesus Rocks at DuPage County Bible Church*. With a tweaking of the signs' language, I could as easily have been arriving at a Bulls game.

The air was just cold enough to allow the snow to gather in tiny drifts against the curbs. Winding lines of pedestrians flowed like narrow tributaries from the parking lots toward the arena, converging into broad streams at the crosswalks. Their momentum swept them along in clusters, families and friends huddled against the chill. As they moved, snowflakes swooped onto their jackets and hoods, sat up for an instant as if looking around, and then disappeared into wet splotches.

Blue jeans and sweaters appeared to be the favored dress for the evening. I brushed lint from my gray wool skirt, which had seemed a solid, businesslike choice when I was packing. Now it seemed I was going to look like an English nanny at a rock festival.

I twisted my fingers in my bangs, a habit I developed as a child when I triggered a crisis by losing my chewing gum in my hair. My mother, in the midst of one of her bad spells, pulled out her scissors and gave me something that I recall as essentially a crew cut. Whether it was actually as short as that, I couldn't swear, but she definitely intended it to punish. It served its purpose well. She sent me to school, where I sat alone and bawled while three-quarters of the kids in the second grade pointed at me and laughed. It really wasn't so bad, though; it's only stuck with me for about twenty years.

I'm often reminded that one thing hasn't changed since then: My sense of style is pathetic.

As if my fashion choice for the evening had not been bad enough, I left Dallas in such a rush that I forgot to check the forecast. Though I brought a raincoat, I packed nothing that would prepare me for a winter storm. I had no idea whether this was the beginning of a March blizzard or just seasonal flurries.

I leaned forward and tapped the driver. "Are we supposed to get much snow?"

He glanced over his shoulder. "It's just lake-effect stuff. It shouldn't amount to much. Tomorrow is supposed to be sunny and nearly fifty degrees." Several cars in front of us moved away from the curb, and we finally arrived at the drop-off point. I paid the driver and stepped onto a thin layer of slush that coated the edge of the walk.

At Simon's request, the FBI had briefed me by telephone on the threats, which were vague as to possible means but quite specific as to the target. Whoever these people were, they wanted Simon. I had no idea what to expect from his security operation or what exactly I was supposed to do that evening. I would have to play it by ear.

Simon had warned me that though tickets were free, they were still required. I followed his instructions and picked up my ticket from the will-call window near the entrance. Once inside the building I dragged my rolling suitcase down the concourse, clattering in and out of the streams of people. I'd never been to a religious event in a place like this. I was surprised that the vendor kiosks, with the notable exception of liquor stations, were open for business. The warm smell of popcorn drew me toward a skinny vendor in a White Sox cap. I checked my watch. I was already a half hour behind schedule. There was no time to eat. I tacked back out into traffic.

As I made my way through the concourse, I scanned the crowd. It was a much younger group than I had expected. I even passed a fair number of tattoos and body piercings. After I'd walked a quarter of the way around the building, I spotted the roped-off door that Simon had described to me over the phone. Above it was a red sign with white letters: *Private—No Admittance*. Two Chicago policemen sat on folding chairs just inside the ropes. As my suitcase and I rattled up to the rope, the taller of the two—a pale, skinny guy about my age—stood and held up his hand. "Sorry, this entrance is for the Mason team."

"I'm Taylor Pasbury. Reverend Mason invited me. He said he would leave my name with security."

"We don't have any names, ma'am," the shorter one said. "You'll have to turn around and head back that way." He pointed toward the concourse.

"Is there anyone you can check with? I'm a security consultant, here to work with Reverend Mason's security team."

The cops looked at each other and smiled. "Security, huh?" the short one said. "You look like you could be packing some heat. We may have to frisk you." He poked an elbow in his buddy's side.

"Hotter than either of you boys will ever get. Now, you've shown you're clever. Would you mind going in and checking with Mr. Mason? Your boss isn't going to like it if the *Tribune* reports that two Chicago cops were harassing one of Simon Mason's people—and a woman at that." Though I knew he'd only been joking, my Sig

Sauer .357 semi-automatic really was in my luggage. I was hoping they wouldn't check.

"Hey, we were just having some fun," the skinny one said. "No need to get worked up about it. I'll go check." He ducked inside the door.

That left the short one and me trying to look at anything but each other. He pulled a notepad out of his jacket pocket, flipped it open, and studied some handwriting on the first page.

"Are you a Simon Mason fan?" I preferred verbal awkwardness to silent awkwardness.

"I'm Catholic—" he scribbled something—"we don't go for this show biz stuff. I wouldn't be here at all, but my wife's been on me to work more overtime to pay off the Christmas bills."

The door opened and the skinny officer walked out. He unhooked the rope. "You can go in." He didn't even look at me, as if to drive home the point that he had already moved on to more important things.

"Oh, so they *were* expecting me. Thank you for your hospitality, gentlemen."

As I pulled my suitcase through the entrance, the short one muttered, "Mason will regret that hire."

On the other side of the door, a dimly lit hallway led to a flight of stairs that ended at another door. I picked up my suitcase and carried it down the steps. Several light bulbs were out, and I had the creepy sensation of descending into the belly of the building. When I reached the bottom, I opened the door and stepped into a huge, brightly lit staging area. I stopped until I could blink the sparklers from my eyes.

In front of me people scurried in all directions, some pulling handcarts loaded with everything from folding chairs to pianos. To my right a high school choir, the girls in plaid skirts and the boys in crisp slacks, stood in two rows in front of a concrete wall. They sang a vibrant gospel song, swaying and tapping their hands against their thighs. Their round, bald conductor rapped his wand against a book in his hand. The singing stopped abruptly, save for a few voices that straggled. The conductor barked out some commands. The rapping began again, this time rhythmically, and the choir sprang into motion, curving and dipping like a giant centipede before launching into another chorus.

To my left, a petite woman, her head wrapped in tight blonde curls, spoke into a headset. She pulled a phone from the pocket of her tan wool pants and tapped out something on its keyboard. When she finished, she slid the phone back into the pocket. I judged her to be a few years older than I was, but she had the sort of perky, turned-up nose that camouflages age, so I couldn't be sure. When I touched her on the shoulder, she jumped and spun around.

"Oh! You startled me." She pushed a curl off her forehead. It fell right back where it had started. "I guess I was concentrating so hard that I lost track of where I was."

"I'm looking for Simon Mason. Do you know where he is?"

"I'm his executive assistant. May I help you?"

"I'm Taylor Pasbury. I just got in from Dallas. Simon is expecting me."

She looked me up and down. *"You're* the security person?"

"That's me." I gave her what I thought was an engaging smile. She did not appear to be engaged.

"Right about now, he'll be practicing his Bible talk. He doesn't like to be disturbed when he's doing that."

I collapsed the telescoping handle of my suitcase. "How long does it usually take?"

"That's hard to say. Sometimes he goes through it once and he's fine. Sometimes he tweaks it right up until he goes on stage. He gets nervous before he speaks."

I laughed. "C'mon. Simon Mason gets nervous about speaking? I have a difficult time believing that."

She narrowed her eyebrows. "I've worked with him for five years. I think I know what I'm talking about."

"I'm sorry, I didn't mean to sound as if I were questioning you. It's just surprising that a man with his experience speaking all over the world would still get nervous about it. I recall, though, once hearing that Bob Hope always got nervous before going on. That was pretty amazing too."

"Well, I can tell you for sure that Simon is terrified right about now."

"If it bothers him so much, why does he do it?"

She crossed her arms in front of her. "He was *called* to do it. He has no choice."

"Of course." I looked away. I had no doubt that some people were called to God's work: Mother Teresa and Pope John Paul II, for example. I had lots of doubt, though, about whether a single televangelist anywhere fit with that company. I had a strong suspicion that they were called more by their wallets.

"Why are you in the security business?"

"My first choice was pool-sitting, but there wasn't enough money in it." I chuckled.

She just stared at me.

I cleared my throat. "Actually, I used to be a Secret Service agent. Opening a security business seemed the logical thing to do."

She looked me over again. "I suppose it would. You mean that you protected a president? Which one?"

"United States, for the most part. I helped with a few foreign ones when they came to visit."

She sighed. "I meant which United States president."

I began to hope really hard that she had no vote in the decision to hire me. Fortunately, before I could do any more damage, Simon Mason walked up. I recognized him immediately, although he was taller and more athletic than I recalled from television. He was almost completely bald except for a ring of tightly cropped sandy hair. His scalp glistened in the backstage lighting, and I realized he was sweating. I was surprised at his casual dress: a suede barn jacket over corduroy pants and a denim shirt.

"Taylor?" he said.

"That's me." I offered my hand.

He took it firmly and looked me in the eye. "Thank you for coming on such short notice. I think you can get a feel this evening for where we are from a security standpoint. Tomorrow morning we can get together for breakfast at the hotel and talk about what you think you can do for us. Did you check in before you came over?"

"I came straight from the airport. It's a pleasure to meet you, Reverend Mason."

"Simon. We're all on a first-name basis around here." He looked over my suit. "And we're casual too."

I must have blushed because he was quick to add, "You look very nice—professional. I should have warned you about the way we dress."

"It's okay. I've got years of experience at dressing inappropriately."

He laughed and his blue eyes brightened. "You should fit right in."

"Who's in charge of security?"

He looked at his assistant, whose expression made it clear she wasn't thrilled at our exchange. "We really haven't had to provide much in the way of our own security before now. Elise, here, is pretty much in charge of everything. You two have met, haven't you?"

"I hadn't caught your name." I held out my hand to her.

She didn't take it. "Elise Hovden." She took a step to her right, placing herself partially between Simon and me.

It didn't take a body language expert to conclude that she viewed Simon as something more than just her preacher. I wondered whether he viewed her as more than just his executive assistant. That determination was not on the critical path for the evening, though. I pointed toward the stage. "How do you screen the people who have access to this area back here?"

"Most are with our touring group or are volunteers from local churches," she said. "Some are provided by the arena or the Chicago police."

"I understand. But how do you *screen* them?"

She shifted her weight from one foot to the other. "We don't formally screen them. We haven't thought that was necessary to this point. We do keep our eyes open for anyone who looks suspicious. Obviously, it may be time to reevaluate that part of our program."

"How many are provided by the arena?"

"How many *what* are provided by the arena?"

"People. How many of these people milling around back here are provided by the arena?"

"I couldn't really say. Maybe thirty. Some of them aren't technically provided by the arena. They're with local providers of things like pianos, refreshments, that sort of thing."

I nodded toward a guy who was pulling a cart with speakers on it. "Has anyone checked any of this stuff?"

"The speakers?"

"Yes, and the pianos you just mentioned, the podiums, the backdrops."

"No, but the arena provided us a list of suggested vendors for many of the things. I hardly think the

Mid America Center is recommending terrorist organizations."

It was becoming obvious that prayer was likely to be our best defense for the evening. That was Simon's department. I would have to do what I could on the earthly side of things, and that wouldn't be much tonight. "At a minimum, can we get someone to check out anything that's being taken onto the stage and anything that's being left back here during the show?"

She folded her arms. "It's not a show. We call it a celebration, because we're celebrating God's Word. It begins in less than an hour. These people all have jobs to do to get Simon on stage on time. We can't divert them now."

"Okay, but do you mind if I snoop around before the show, um, celebration?"

She glared at me. I sensed we were not likely to become Bunco buddies.

"That would be fine," Simon said. "If anyone asks, just tell them they can check with Elise or me. In the meantime I'm going to have to excuse myself. I still have some rehearsing to do." He pulled a handkerchief from his pocket and wiped his forehead.

As he turned to walk away, a young woman walked up behind him. She was tall and lean, and her chestnut hair fell easily over her shoulders. She strongly resembled Simon, particularly in the energetic glow of her high cheekbones. "Dad, the limo is here." She pulled a hair clip out of the purse slung over her shoulder. In one motion she reached back and fastened her hair into a ponytail. "Cheryl and I are leaving for the airport."

"Okay, but I want you to meet someone first. Taylor Pasbury, this is my daughter, Kacey."

"Hi, Ms. Pasbury." She extended her hand and smiled. It was her dad's smile—an open smile that seemed to flip on a switch behind her hazel eyes. I had been prepared not to like her since she was almost certain to be a spoiled child-of-celebrity. I put that judgment on hold.

"Nice to meet you, Kacey. You can call me Taylor." I looked at Simon. "She's not riding to the airport alone, is she?"

He shook his head. "One of our graduate-student interns, Cheryl Granger, is riding with her. She'll make sure Kacey gets on her plane. My sister, Meg, is meeting her at the airport in Dallas."

I didn't like the arrangement, but I would have to address Kacey's security later. Right now I had my hands full with Simon and the "celebration."

"Are you the one who used to be a Secret Service agent?" Kacey said.

I smiled. "That's me."

"That is so cool. I wish we could talk sometime when you're not too busy. I'll bet you've got some great stories."

"I'd love to talk sometime."

Simon put his hand on her shoulder. "Kacey has always been a bit of a tomboy. She played basketball and soccer in high school."

She rolled her eyes. "Didn't the word *tomboy* go out about twenty years ago?"

"It's okay," I said. "I played sports in high school—basketball and softball. My dad used to call me a tomboy too. It bugged me to death."

Elise stepped toward Kacey and raised her hand. "I was a pom-pom girl in high school."

Kacey just looked at her. Simon lowered his eyes and studied the worn cover of the Bible he was holding. I wouldn't have wished that moment of silence on my worst enemy.

"Pom-pomming requires skills I've always admired," I said. *Sheesh! 'Skills I've always admired.' And was there even such a word as 'pom-pomming'?*

The base of Elise's neck reddened. "Well, I've got a lot of work to do." The color spread into her cheeks as she spoke. "If you'll excuse me." She walked over to Kacey, put her arm around her and squeezed. "Have fun back at school. Maybe you and I can have a girl talk when we get back to Dallas."

Kacey stood stiffly but smiled. "Sure thing. See you, Elise."

Elise straightened her headset and strode away.

"Let me walk you to the limo, Kace," Simon said. "Taylor, I'll see you after the show." I noted that he used Elise's forbidden word to refer to the event.

Being dropped into someone else's mess is a difficult thing, and the security situation for this event was definitely a mess. It occurred to me that no one had even officially told me I was hired. Nevertheless, I decided to do what I could before Simon took the stage.

If I had known what the next twenty-four hours would be like, I probably would never have stayed. Or maybe I would have been more determined to stay. I suppose it doesn't matter, because I did stay. One thing was clear: Simon Mason needed me.

What I didn't know yet was that I needed him even more.

CHAPTER

SEVEN

SINCE ALL OF THE action would be on the stage, I started there and worked from the bottom up. Although the stage was huge, the underbelly was not complex. A stage for a rock concert needs all kinds of hidden bells and whistles. But Simon was not going to rise through a trap door in a cloud of orange smoke. Beneath this stage was nothing but a labyrinth of metal supports. It only took ten minutes to check out the whole thing.

The stage itself was more of a challenge for the simple reason that there were so many things on it: two pianos; an electronic keyboard; a drum set; speakers and amplifiers; two sets of bleachers on which the choirs would stand; a glass pulpit; and twenty or so microphones, some standing, some dangling. The worst part, though, was the landscaping. There must have been a hundred potted trees and plants, and an artificial river wound across the stage. The place looked like Costa Rica.

The musical instruments and bleachers were easy to check. It was the speakers and plants that gave me heartburn. Since I couldn't dump all of the potting soil out on the stage or tear apart a gazillion dollars worth of speakers, I tried to get comfortable with the people who brought them. One of them happened to be pulling two eight-foot palms onto the stage on a cart as I inspected the back of a giant amplifier. He was young and red and doughy—an Irish potato with acne scars. Dried mud flaked off his tennis shoes as he walked. A rusty trowel jutted from his back pocket.

I tapped him on the shoulder. "You work for the Mid America Center?"

"No. O'Reilly's Interior Landscape." His breath smelled of onions and cigarettes. I turned my head away. He didn't seem to notice.

I had to force myself to look back at him. "Did O'Reilly's provide all of the plants?"

Fortunately for my nostrils, he was not about to stop for me. He dragged the cart across the stage, and I trotted after him. A trail of dirt clumps marked the cart's path like a brown vapor trail. "Far as I know." He stopped, pulled on a pair of leather garden gloves, and wrestled one of the palms onto the stage.

"Is your boss Mr. O'Reilly?"

"Mrs. O'Reilly. Dad's been gone for ten years."

"I'm sorry." I had no idea whether I should be sorry, because I had no idea why Mr. O'Reilly was gone, but I supposed it didn't matter for my purposes. "So Mrs. O'Reilly is your mother?"

"Yes."

"Is she here?"

He chuckled. "The nursing home doesn't let her deliver plants."

"I'm sorry."

He looked up at me and raised an eyebrow, as if to ask whether "I'm sorry" was going to be my response to everything he said. He pulled the trowel out of his pocket, bent over, and dug into the potted palm. "It's okay," he said over his shoulder. "She's still sharp as a tack. Just can't get around anymore." The conversation smelled better with his face over the planter.

"So are you in charge?"

He laughed. "Believe me, she's in charge. I'm responsible for important deliveries, that's all. I'm a CPA with an accounting firm in the Loop. I just do this to help Mom out. She doesn't trust the regular guys with this kind of thing. Simon Mason is big, you know. Are you a reporter or something?"

"I'm with the Mason staff. Where did all of these plants come from?"

"Our greenhouse in Elmwood Park. I've got the delivery ticket if you want to see it. Are we in some sort of trouble?"

"Not at all. Were you with the plants in the truck from the greenhouse?"

"I drove the truck. Look, I don't mean to be rude, but I've got to get finished here. This thing is starting in thirty minutes. There must be ten thousand people out there already." He pointed at the giant video screen that blocked the stage from the auditorium seats. For the first time, I noticed the low rumble of the entering crowd.

"How many more plants are you bringing out here?"

"These two are the last ones. Are you security?"

I threw up my hands. "You got me."

He looked me over. "Wow, security in our building doesn't look like you."

"Thanks." I thought about saying the polite thing: *You're not so bad yourself.* His breath and oily hair simply made it impossible. "How long has O'Reilly's been in business?"

"Forty years, last November." He rolled the other palm off the cart and stood it up.

"Good enough. Thank you for answering my questions."

"You're welcome." He slid a hand through his hair and then wiped it on the pocket of his khakis, leaving a greasy splotch. "What are you doing after the show?"

"Sorry, I've got a boyfriend." That was entirely untrue. "By the way, they tell me it's not a show. It's a celebration. They're very particular about that."

He shrugged and turned his back, then stuck a finger into the soil around one of the pots. He grabbed a plastic watering can from the cart, leaned over, and poured water around the base of the palm. As far as he was concerned, I was no longer there. I tapped my foot on the floor and watched him work. This guy was gross, but I would have liked to think that I could hold his attention for more than thirty seconds. I know exactly how ridiculous that sounds, but it's the way I think sometimes.

I turned to leave, then stopped and turned back. "One more thing: Do you know who's in charge of the sound system?"

"No idea." He didn't even look up. I was yesterday's news.

I walked to the back of the stage and examined a six-foot speaker. *Windy City Speaker Hut* appeared in white stenciled letters across the back. I trotted down the steps to the floor behind the stage and looked around. Though people were milling everywhere, they all appeared to be part of the show. I pulled out my phone, dialed information, and within a few seconds was listening to an after-hours recording for Windy City Speaker Hut. I punched zero for the operator but got another recording.

Only twenty minutes until the first performers were to take the stage. I bounded back up the stairs and moved from speaker to amplifier to speaker. Some of them had removable backs that I pulled away to check inside. Most were screwed shut. I shook the smaller ones to see if anything rattled. This was getting me nowhere. I headed backstage to look for Simon.

The area behind the stage was like a train station during rush hour. Any terrorist worth a nickel could have walked in with a grenade and wiped out half of the traveling cast. I finally found Simon walking up the steps from the lower concourse. Behind him Elise hurried to keep up, a laptop clutched tightly under her arm. I waited for them at the top of the stairs.

Simon carried a tattered leather Bible in one hand. He offered a tight-lipped smile and wiped his forehead with his sleeve. "Hi, Taylor." His eyes moved, from me, to the stage, then back to me. Elise had been right. He was nervous.

I gathered that this would be a poor time to talk about security details. Besides, there was little that could be done at this point. I motioned toward the stage. "I checked some things out. Maybe we can talk after the show."

Elise's face darkened.

"I mean, the celebration."

Simon moved over to the curtain that served as a stage door and pulled it aside. The youth choir that I had seen earlier was hustling onto the bleachers near the back of the stage. To the side of the bleachers, a rock band scrambled into position and screeched out a few tuning notes. The drummer climbed onto a glass-encased stand that held bright-orange drums of various sizes. Elevated and isolated, covered with tattoos and wearing a stocking cap, he reminded me of a clown perched on a trap door in a carnival dunking booth.

"Don't see any terrorists with machine guns," Simon said with a weak laugh. He stepped aside and held the curtain open for me. "Want to take a closer look?"

From where we were, just at the edge of the giant

screen, we could see both the stage and a part of the auditorium. People moved up and down the aisles. The floor seemed to vibrate with the buzz of thousands of conversations.

"Machine guns aren't what worry me at an event like this," I said. "Bombs loaded with nails and ball bearings are what keep me awake."

He cleared his throat. "Right."

The bass player thumped out the first chords of a gospel tune. The singers swayed on the bleachers. A few of them put their hands to their mouths for a last, throat-clearing cough. In front of them the giant screen scrolled up toward the ceiling. A wave of applause began in the front row of the auditorium and washed toward the back as the rising screen revealed the stage.

I frowned. "Hey, where did those two plants beside the podium come from?"

Simon looked around the curtain again. "What plants?"

"The bushy things on each side of the podium—those weren't there twenty minutes ago."

"I don't know what was there or not there. I've been practicing my Bible talk."

"It's a pulpit, not a podium," Elise said, nudging me aside. "Let me see." She peered through the gap in the curtain. "It doesn't look unusual to me. I don't remember for sure, but it seems that we always have plants beside the pulpit, don't we Simon?"

He extended his hands, palms up. "Honestly, I have no idea."

I looked again. "I know those were not there before."

"Someone must have brought them out after you left. What's so unusual about that?" Elise said.

"I was talking to the son of the landscape company's owner. He told me the two palm trees that he was taking off the cart were the last of the plants for the stage. Those two by the podium—the pulpit—were not there."

"What if they weren't?" Simon was frowning now. "Do you really think someone can hide a bomb in a potted plant?"

"You better believe someone can hide a bomb in a potted plant! Granted, the odds are overwhelmingly against it; but the odds are overwhelmingly against just about any threat. The point is that you are the focus of attention of some very dangerous people. If they did put a bomb in one of those plants, it would almost certainly kill you. Those plants weren't there when I checked the stage earlier, and according to the landscaping company they're not supposed to be there now. I'm telling you that it would be prudent to check them out."

Elise tapped her fingers on the laptop she was holding under her arm. "Well, what do you want us to do, call off the show because there are two potted plants that are unaccounted for?"

I raised an eyebrow. "The *show?*"

"The celebration." She scowled at me.

"No, we don't need to call off the celebration. We simply need to check out those two plants."

Simon sighed. "How are we going to do that in front

of fifteen thousand people? You know, Taylor, I'm not the president of the United States and it's not practical to do some of the things you may be accustomed to doing for security. Besides, if we check out the plants and they do contain bombs, won't whoever planted them just set them off?"

"It's possible. More likely there would be a timing device. Whoever planted them would probably stick out like a sore thumb in this crowd. Besides, the printed programs give a great timetable for what's going to happen and when it's going to happen. You're scheduled to be on the stage three-quarters of the time. A timer wouldn't have to be precise and would still work just fine."

He put a hand on his hip. "Fine, but that brings us back to the question: What now?"

"Can I see that?" I reached for the program Elise carried in her hand.

She pulled it away. "Why?"

I looked at my watch. "There's very little time. Would you please just give me the program?"

She glanced at Simon. He nodded. She handed me the program.

"The song leader's going to pray right at the beginning, isn't he?"

"That's right," Simon said.

"We can dim the lights. No one will think anything about it. I'll get the plants off during the prayer. Most of the people won't notice. If a bomb blows up, at least you're back here and not out on the stage. Elise, who's running the lighting?"

"Wait a minute," Simon said. "This seems like a huge overreaction to me. We can't cart potted plants around during a prayer. What will people think?"

I threw up my arms. "If you're dead, it won't matter what people think!"

He took a quick look around us to see if anyone had heard. "Okay, calm down. We get the point."

I lowered my voice. "I'm sorry if I sound impatient, but dangerous people have threatened your life and you are acting as if you don't take that seriously. Apparently you don't know what people like this are capable of, but I do. We are not overreacting. We are using common sense. Your life has changed. You'd better get used to it if you want to stay alive."

Elise chewed her lip. I wondered whether she had the authority to fire me before I'd been hired? I was just about to tell both of them that this was a bad fit and I should just hop a plane back to Dallas when she turned to Simon. "She's right. Your life is in danger, and we've got to get serious about protecting you."

I did a double take. "Excuse me?"

She turned back to me. "Whatever it takes to protect Simon, we'll do. The arena runs the lights, but the operators are way up in the third deck. We've got walkie-talkies to communicate with them."

There was no time to stand around with my mouth hanging open. "Get them on one of those things and tell them there's been a change and you want them to dim the lights real low during the opening prayer. I've got to find two strong guys and a cart." I took off down the stairs.

The plan was simple, and it could have gone off smoothly. I did find a cart, and I did find two strong guys, and the lights did go down during the prayer. On the other hand, we happened to choose Chicago's squeakiest cart, so everyone in the auditorium was already peeking toward the stage and wondering what was going on before we even got the cart to the pulpit. To top it off, the two big strong guys were actually much bigger than they were strong. They dropped one of the plants when they were loading it onto the cart. The pot shattered on the stage, spilling potting soil everywhere. At least that saved me the effort of digging through the dirt.

The song leader, whom I later learned was named Donny, was a young guy with leather pants, two arms covered in tattoos, and hair past his shoulders. He could have been a biker, but he was a real pro. He didn't miss a beat with his prayer while we were practically making mud pies on the stage. Fifteen thousand heads, though, were praying with one eye open. After the prayer there was nothing to do but send a maintenance guy out to sweep up the mess while the band played a few bars of a song that Elise identified as "Cleansing My Soul." Simon glared straight ahead the entire time. I almost hoped that I'd find a bomb in the stupid plant.

When the second pot finally made it off the stage, I dove into it with my hands. There was nothing there but potting soil. Elise didn't speak. Simon and ten members of the cast looked at me as if I had just arrived from Mars.

I was off to a great start.

I was feeling a bit put upon at the end of the show as Simon finally walked off the stage with the band playing a cool, bluesy version of "Amazing Grace." The whole situation seemed to have been set up to make me look bad. After all, at the last minute I had walked into a dreadfully planned—strike that—totally *unplanned* security situation. Yet everyone seemed to expect me to make lemonade out of a rotting lemon, with no inconvenience to anyone but me. To top it off, no one had even told me yet that I was hired. There was nothing fair about it; but let's face it, there's nothing fair about life. I braced myself for Simon's reaction to the plant fiasco.

To my surprise, there was little reaction at all. In fact, Simon barely acknowledged my presence as he came off the stage. He was busy shaking hands and talking to well-wishers and hangers-on. Finally, I tapped him on the shoulder. "Do you want to meet at the hotel restaurant for breakfast so we can talk about some things?"

"Actually, I'd rather talk now. We've got to discuss what went on tonight."

"What do you mean, 'what went on tonight'?"

"Frankly, I'm not sure this is a good fit."

"Fine. You invited me here; I didn't volunteer." I turned to walk away.

He touched my arm. "Hang on, Taylor. I said I'm not sure. Don't you think we should talk about this before either of us makes any decisions? How would you feel if you walked off and then I got whacked tonight? That's what they call it, isn't it? 'Whacked'?" He smiled, and

I noticed again how much he and his daughter looked alike, particularly when they smiled.

"That's what they call it on television. We used to call it 'popped.' It wouldn't make much difference to you, though. Either way you're stiff." It was my turn to smile.

"That's comforting, thanks. Listen, now that the show's over, the events manager for the arena is taking us out for dinner. Can you come along? We should be able to talk."

"I thought you didn't call it a show?"

"*Elise* doesn't call it a show. Everyone else does. It drives her crazy. Somehow I doubt if God gets very worked up over what we call it."

I looked at my watch. "When are you leaving?"

"Right now. We don't have to hang around here for anything. How about it?"

"I'm here because you asked me to be here. If you want me to go, I'll go. Elise put my suitcase somewhere. I need to take it with me."

Simon turned and waved at Elise. "Where is Taylor's suitcase?"

"It's in your dressing room. We can get it on the way to the car."

Simon touched my elbow. "You can follow me." He headed toward the back of the auditorium.

When we stopped by his dressing room, I excused myself to use the restroom and took my suitcase with me. I opened the suitcase and pulled my pistol out of its travel box, then got a loaded clip from my ammo box. Once I'd loaded the pistol, I transferred it to a purse I'd packed and slung the purse over my shoulder. When we left the dressing room, we wound through some tunnels to an underground driveway where a black Lincoln Town Car waited for us.

I stopped at the curb. "Who provided the car?"

"The same limo service that picked us up at the airport," Elise said. "We're meeting the arena person at the restaurant."

"Did anyone check them out?"

"No, but they were recommended by the Mid America Center. Seems pretty safe to me."

"That's a good start, but someone needs to check out the drivers and check the cars from now on. It's easy to do and eliminates a big risk factor."

Simon and Elise looked at each other. Neither responded. Why on earth was I bothering? We got in the car.

Elise leaned toward the driver. "We're going to Pascali's Taste of Italy, on the Loop. Do you know where it is?"

He nodded. "Sure." With that, we sped out of the tunnel.

The snow had stopped, and the streets were mostly clear. The only lights in the car were the instrument lights and a pin light over the driver's ID. I could see the back of the driver's head, but not much else. His hair was curly and black. I looked at his ID and sucked in a breath.

His name was Hakim Ahmad Malouf.

CHAPTER

EIGHT

"SO, HAKIM, HAVE YOU been in the United States long?"

Simon glanced at me, then at the driver's ID. When he looked back at me, I could see Hakim had his attention.

"Since I was twelve years old. I listened to your show on the radio while I waited in the car, Reverend Mason. Praise God for you, sir."

Simon raised an eyebrow. I leaned forward. "You sound a bit more open-minded than some of the Muslims we read about in the papers these days."

"I'm no Muslim, ma'am. I'm Baptist. My family is from Lebanon." He looked at me in the rearview mirror.

"There are many Christians in Lebanon. Always have been. During the civil war, when Syria got involved, many left. Things turned very bad. There are fewer Christians now, but they are still an important force in the country."

"I'm sorry. I just thought with your name and all . . ."

"Do you know any men named Peter or Paul?"

"Sure."

"Are they all Catholic?"

Simon laughed. "Fair point."

"Do you want me to tell you a fact you'll not believe?"

I moved my head to the side so I could see more of Hakim's face in the mirror. "What's that?"

"About seventy percent of Arabs in America are Christians."

"No way," Simon said. "Where did you get that information?"

Hakim smiled into the mirror. "I read it in one of the papers. People leave them in the car all the time. It's one of the great things about driving for a limo service. I never have to buy a paper. It's true, though. Only about twenty-five percent of Arabs in this country are Muslim."

Simon patted him on the shoulder. "I'm going to check you on that one. It sure doesn't sound right to me."

Hakim shrugged. "Reverend Mason, when are you going to Lebanon to preach to the Muslims?"

Simon laughed. "Now there's an invitation that I don't recall getting in the mail."

"I'm not sure the Middle East is ready for Christian revival meetings," Elise said.

Hakim took one hand off the wheel and turned his palm up. "Neither was Rome two thousand years ago, wouldn't you agree?"

Elise narrowed her eyebrows. "It would be suicide for a prominent Christian preacher like Simon to go to the Middle East and try to convert Muslims."

Hakim adjusted his mirror so he could see her face. "Suicide? Perhaps. I suppose one could say that Jesus' apostles committed suicide by spreading the Word in the Roman Empire. They were martyred you know, all except John. And they knew it was coming. Does that make it suicide? There is no place on earth where the people need Jesus more than in the Middle East. If Jesus gets a chance to compete for the people's hearts, he will win."

"Competing for hearts—I like that. I never thought of it that way," Simon said.

"Jesus is love. And given a choice, in the long run people will always choose love," Hakim said. "He conquered the Roman Empire without firing a shot because thousands were willing to be martyred to spread the gospel. That's a lot different than the way Islam spread."

"You know a lot more history than any cab driver I've ever met," I said.

He wagged a finger. "It's not a cab; it's a town car. Anyway, I only drive at night. I'm a seminary student at Lakeshore Bible Institute during the day."

"Now it's starting to make sense. So tell us how Islam spread."

"The prophet Muhammad was a warrior and a politician. The history of those who came immediately after him—his apostles, so to speak—was one of assassination and war and bloodshed, not peaceful martyrdom like Christ's apostles. Islam spread through military conquest and political domination—a starkly different beginning from Christianity." He pulled the limo to the curb in front of Pascali's. "Here we are."

Simon reached in his pocket and pulled out a money clip. He peeled off two bills and reached over the seat toward Hakim.

"No, no. The tip will be on the bill the limo service sends you for all of the rides during your visit."

"This is something extra. We appreciated the lesson. I'd like to continue this discussion when we finish dinner."

"Sorry, Reverend Mason. I won't be here. They're sending another car to pick you up. I've got to study for a test in the morning." He smiled. "It's eleven-thirty. Do you think I'm starting to study too soon?"

Simon and I laughed. Elise didn't seem to get it.

"That brings back some college memories," I said.

Simon leaned one arm across the back of the seat in front of him. "Do you have something with a phone number on it?"

Hakim grabbed a pen from the drink holder next to him. "I'll write it on the back of a receipt." He ripped a receipt off a pad, scribbled on the back, and handed it to Simon.

Simon put the receipt in the inside pocket of his jacket. "I get to Chicago fairly frequently. Okay if I call you sometime? Maybe we can get a cup of coffee."

Hakim turned around. "Are you kidding me? You're Simon Mason. If you call, I'll be available. Wait until my professors hear about this. Maybe you could come speak at school sometime. Do you think that would be possible?"

"I'm sure we could work it out. Elise, do you think we could schedule something?"

Elise sighed, pulled out her phone, and started punching buttons. She shoved the phone back in her purse. "I made a note in my calendar to call."

I reached for the door handle, then stopped. "By the way, do you know the driver who is coming to get us?"

"No, ma'am. But you can call the printed number on the receipt and ask. The dispatcher should know." He jumped out of the driver's side and came around to open our door.

As we got out of the car, I said, "Thank you, we'll do that."

When Hakim drove off, Simon looked at Elise. "Well, that was the strangest limo ride we've ever had. Wouldn't you say?"

"You're not really going to call him, are you?"

He studied Elise. "Sure I am. He was a good kid— had some interesting ideas too. Why wouldn't I?"

She shook her head. "You've got to start understanding that you're a celebrity. Everyone wants a piece of you."

He angled a look my way. "The minute I start thinking I'm a celebrity, shoot me, okay?"

I was afraid I would have to stand in line.

CHAPTER
NINE

DESPITE SIMON'S VIEWS ON his own celebrity, from the moment we entered the restaurant it was apparent how the staff saw him. They greeted us at the door and funneled us between two rows of red-clothed tables toward a wall of rich mahogany paneling adorned with autographed photos of famous people. A warm cloud of smells—garlic, oregano, and freshly baked bread—drifted through the restaurant. My nose reminded me that I hadn't eaten a thing since I grabbed a hot dog early that afternoon in the Dallas/Fort Worth airport.

Near the back, the maitre d' led us down a narrow hallway that ended in a private room. Three of the room's walls were brick. The fourth wall was a built-in oak wine rack. In the center of the room was a rectangular cutting-board table. Hanging above the table were two cast-iron chandeliers.

Simon and I sat at one end of the table. When Elise pulled out a chair next to Simon, he glanced at her. "Elise, would you mind entertaining everyone down at the other end? I want to talk over some security issues with Taylor."

She gripped the back of the chair with both hands. "Don't you think I should be part of the discussion?"

He smiled. "Now don't get worked up. We're not going to make any decisions without you. If all three of us are down here with our heads together, everyone else will feel left out. Do you mind?"

She looked at me, then back at Simon. "Of course not." Just then the other group of Simon's traveling crew walked into the room. Elise moved to the opposite end of the table and sat down.

Donny, the song leader, slapped me on the back as he walked past. "Hey, if it isn't the potted plant lady! Did you wash the dirt from under your nails before you came to the table?"

I held up a thumb. "It's green. Next time I thought we could go with a backyard garden theme."

"Great idea. Each of us can dress like a different vegetable." Everyone laughed except Elise, who was holding her knife up to the light and polishing it with her napkin.

After we all settled in, the events coordinator from the Mid America Center ordered a bottle of Chianti.

I felt the muscles in my neck relax. One bottle seemed light for a group of nine, but it was a start. It had been a stressful evening.

A white-coated waiter with a thick mustache and a towel draped over his arm selected the bottle from the rack behind Donny's head and moved from chair to chair, offering to fill glasses. As I stretched out my hand to steady my wine glass for the waiter, Simon turned his glass upside down. Everyone from the ministry followed suit. I swallowed hard. "Waiting for something with a bit more bounce?" I smiled hopefully.

"I don't drink. You go ahead if you'd like, though."

The waiter appeared next to me and extended the bottle toward my glass. His hand seemed to move in slow motion as I balanced risk and reward in my mind. Just as he tipped the bottle, I caught his hand. "No thanks. Just water."

Simon smiled. Good thing he didn't know me better, or he would have recognized the longing look that I gave to the bottle as it passed. I turned my glass over.

Donny said a prayer for the food and then loudly entertained the other end of the table with a high-pitched recap of his role in improvising music during the potted plant debacle. He smiled my way a number of times, presumably to assure me that he was not being critical.

Simon picked up his butter knife and twirled it between his fingers. "I understand you stepped into a difficult situation tonight. I think my problem was that we hadn't had any time to talk things over. I didn't know what to expect. If we could sit down and go through a sort of cost-benefit analysis on some of the security steps you would like for us to take—Elise is big on cost-benefit analysis—we can probably get to a point we both can live with. Are you willing to give that a try?"

I was pleasantly surprised. "Sure. I understand that you don't have an unlimited budget for this. Nobody does, except the president."

"Actually, I'm not as worried about the dollar cost as I am about the effect on my ability to reach people. I'm no PR genius, but I understand that much of my appeal is that ordinary people view me as one of them. Anything that would make me appear aloof or as if I were acting like a big shot . . . well, that's what I couldn't afford. Here's an example. We tell the car services never to send those big, long limousines to pick us up. We ride in regular town cars, even if it means taking two or three cars instead of one. Riding around looking like rock stars is not our thing."

"That makes perfect sense. I can work within your requirements. I'm all about compromise."

The waiter walked into the room and placed salads on the table. I must have glanced lovingly at my upside-down wine glass because Simon said, "You really wanted a glass of wine, didn't you?"

I considered how I had lied to him about the bath-tub during our first telephone conversation. I resolved not to lie to him again—at least not unnecessarily. "Yes, I would have liked a glass. Or two."

"You could have had it. I wouldn't have minded."

He looked at his watch, which must have been as old as he was, judging by the wear on its leather strap. "I've always told Kacey that most of the bad things in life happen after midnight and involve alcohol or drugs. It's five minutes after twelve."

I gave him a weak smile. "That late? Boy, time has really gotten away from me tonight."

"I don't have any problem with people who like to have a glass of wine now and then, so you don't need to worry. Even the apostle Paul said we should take a bit of wine for the stomach's sake."

"He really said that?" I rapped my fingers on the edge of the table. "Now, there's a portion of the Bible that's grossly underreported."

He laughed as he opened his menu. "We had them bring the same salad for everyone because we're usually starving by the time we get to dinner after a show. You can order your entrée off the menu."

After a few moments he closed the menu and set it on the table. "I don't drink because there are always those in the press out to snap a picture that will prove that people like me are nothing but fakes. Though it's still difficult for me to believe, millions of people look up to me. One photo with a goofy look on my face and a wine glass in my hand could do a lot of damage. I'm determined not to let that happen."

The waiter came around to take our orders. As I watched Simon pick up his menu and point to something, I couldn't help feeling a bit sorry for him. Because of my stint in the Secret Service, I knew the fishbowl in which politicians swim. Until that moment, though, I never considered that people like Simon were in the same sort of situation.

Actually worse, if they took their responsibility seriously.

The public expected politicians to have vices. They did not cut preachers the same slack. One public slipup would not only irreparably injure his career but could damage the whole point of it. People looked to him for guidance on how to live their lives. That was quite a burden to carry around every day. I thanked my lucky stars I was far too socially irresponsible to have any influence over anyone.

We spent the rest of the dinner chatting about a variety of things, including the next weekend's International Celebration of Hope in Dallas. It would be his largest event ever and would be telecast around the world. Because the event had been planned for months, I would not be able to have much impact on security. There were a few areas, though, where I could provide security upgrades, even on such short notice. We discussed my ideas as we ate.

From time to time Elise eyed us from the other end of the table. She frowned through the entire dinner, as if she had been permanently exiled. Her frown particularly deepened whenever Simon said something that made me laugh, which was frequently. He was a witty guy.

One thing seemed obvious: Elise was likely to create obstacles to my efforts to do my job. Nevertheless, she had made it clear at the auditorium that she would do what was best for Simon, no matter what her personal interest—at least, it seemed that way. That impressed me. I was curious to learn more about her. And about her relationship with Simon.

Of course, that was the last thing that should have been occupying my mind. I was about to learn that, where Simon Mason was involved, there was no time to sweat the small stuff.

CHAPTER
TEN

AFTER DINNER WE MADE our way toward the front of the restaurant. Simon walked in front of me and pulled my suitcase as our group moved single file down the narrow hallway and then wound through several tightly packed tables. Before we reached the front, I turned to him. "Can I take a look at the receipt Hakim gave you?"

He reached in his coat pocket and handed it to me. "Why do you want that?"

"I'm going to call and check on the new driver."

He stopped. "Now, this is an example of what I was talking about, Taylor. I don't really think it's necessary to check out the driver of a reputable limousine service that was recommended by the auditorium. That seems like overkill to me."

I flipped open my phone. "You talked about cost-benefit a minute ago. I have unlimited minutes on this thing. We can certainly handle the cost of one call." I held the receipt up to the light and punched in the number.

While the phone was ringing, we passed the floor-to-ceiling plate-glass window at the front of the restaurant. A single limo—a white, super stretch model with heavily tinted windows—sat at the curb outside. I tapped Simon on the shoulder. "Didn't you say that you don't use stretch limos?"

Just as a voice on the other end of the phone said hello, a light flashed over our heads. The window exploded. A medicine ball of hot air slammed into my chest and knocked me to the floor.

Outside the shattered window, the mangled hood and roof of the limo cartwheeled from the sky like two huge, wounded birds. They crashed to the sidewalk, side by side, bounced into each other, landed again, and spun several revolutions before nudging together and rocking to a stop in the street. Tires screeched as a taxi swerved to avoid the wreckage. At the curb, flames shot from the limo's passenger compartment, which was peeled open like a sardine can.

I reached up, wrapped my arms around Simon's waist, and sat backward, pulling him to the floor on top of me. To our right a woman screamed. I rolled Simon off me, then crawled beneath the table in front of us. Lifting with my back, I flipped it onto its side. Plates and glasses crashed to the floor. The tabletop was now between us and the window. I tugged Simon's arm, and he moved in behind the table. A cloud of acrid smoke drifted in from the street and settled over the room like a dark fog, burning my nose and throat.

A few feet away Elise stood transfixed, one hand on her forehead. I reached out, wrapped my fingers around her ankle, and jerked. She dropped onto her rear end and let out a high-pitched yelp as if a stranger had just pinched her in an elevator. The sound was so incongruous that I nearly burst out laughing. I dragged her behind the table with us.

Expecting gunfire at any moment, I crawled to my purse, which was on the floor about five feet away. I dragged it back to the table, dug into it, and pulled out my Sig .357. Then I squatted, back to the tabletop, so I was positioned between the table and Simon. I checked the magazine. My ammo was fine.

Throughout the room, people screamed and moaned. I pointed toward Simon and Elise. "Keep your heads down and stay quiet, both of you. We don't want to draw attention. Are you all right?"

Simon nodded. "I'm okay. How about you, Elise?" His voice was steady and so was his hand as he reached out to place it on her shoulder. I was impressed.

Elise nodded, but her face was ashen and her hands trembled uncontrollably.

Simon got on his hands and knees and began to crawl toward a woman at the table next to us who had a bloody gash from her ear to her chin. She was still sitting in her chair, staring straight ahead and moaning.

I grabbed his arm and yanked. "Where do you think you're going?"

"I'm going to see if I can help."

"You're not going anywhere! You're the target!"

He pointed at the woman. "She needs help."

I tightened my grip on his sleeve. "This may not be the end of the attack, and I'm not counting on this table to stop a bullet. I've got to get you out of here." I scanned the room for exits. The only ones were the front door, which was out of the question, and a door in the back with *stairs* stenciled across it in yellow letters.

Simon turned toward me. Blood oozed from a cut on the side of his neck. I picked up a napkin from the floor and pressed it over the cut. "You're bleeding. Hold this tight."

Simon held it there for a few seconds, then pulled it down and looked at it. It was bloody but not soaked. He pressed it back on the wound. "I'm okay. Don't worry about me."

I let go of his sleeve. "We're getting out of here right now. Stay low and follow me." I crawled away from the table, brushing broken glass out of the way with my fingers.

Simon grabbed my leg. "We're not going to leave these people here and run away."

I looked over my shoulder at him. "Oh, yes we are! My job is to protect you, remember?"

He shook his head. "I told you before, I'm not the

president. I'm a preacher. What good am I if I run away from a situation like this?"

I looked around the room. People were scattered about, some sitting in chairs and some on the floor. A number were bleeding from open wounds. Men and women cried. I took a deep breath, turned around, and peeked over the top of the table toward the window—nothing but the burning limo, traffic piling up, and sirens coming closer.

I knelt and faced him. "All right, we'll help anyone we can. But stay down, don't get too far away from me, and always keep something between you and the window. Elise, you stay right here behind this table and don't move a muscle. I don't want to have to worry about both of you."

She nodded and sniffled. I knew she wasn't going anywhere, and I was pretty sure that it would be a long time before she would get over this.

Simon gave me a thumbs-up. He grabbed a napkin off the floor and crawled to the lady at the table next to us. He pulled her gently down, put one hand behind her head, and used the napkin to dab at the blood on her face with the other. He smiled and spoke to her in a low, soft tone. I couldn't make out anything he said, but whatever it was, it seemed to calm her.

Watching Simon with the woman, I remembered something my dad said that last night by the campfire: *When the shooting starts, some men run and some stay and do what they can.* I shook myself. This was no time for daydreaming.

I pulled out my cell phone and dialed 911. "There's been an explosion outside Pascali's on Clark Street. I hear sirens. The police must be on their way. Tell them it was a car bomb."

"Are you inside the restaurant, ma'am?"

"Yes. There are a number of injuries. We'll need ambulances."

"Can you stay on the phone, ma'am?"

"No, but I'll get someone to talk to you." I shoved the phone at a man in a torn gray business suit, who was peeking out from beneath a tablecloth next to me. "This is 911. Talk to her. And don't lose the phone; I'll be back for it." He put the phone to his ear. I crawled over to Simon.

"If anyone was going to come in shooting, they'd have been here by now, but there could be follow-up bombs. Keep your eyes open and remember to stay down." The idea of a follow-up explosion didn't really seem likely. Whoever did this knew we were there and had a great shot at us. For whatever reason, they had taken that shot and missed.

Simon looked around the room, then turned his attention back to the woman in front of him. He had dropped the napkin from the cut on his own neck, which was bleeding again. I picked up another napkin and held it to the wound. "Don't forget, you're bleeding too."

He took the napkin. "Thanks."

I squatted behind him. "You know, this doesn't figure."

"Seems pretty clear to me. The limo driver set us up."

I'd forgotten about Hakim. "Good point. That's not what I was talking about, though. The explosion shattered the window, but that's about it. Look, the broken glass barely made it past the first row of tables. They knew you were here, and they had a whole stretch limo to pack with explosives. But all they did was pop the hood off and break a window. Why wasn't the bomb bigger?"

"You're asking the wrong person."

"Getting the bomb into the car and getting the car to the restaurant were the hard parts. If the bomb had been large enough, we wouldn't be sitting here talking now. Why was the bomb so small?"

"Stupid bomber?" The wind was picking up, and it blew into the room from the street. The woman Simon was helping shivered. He took off his jacket and put it around her.

I shook my head. "Maybe, but I doubt it. A lot of planning obviously went into this thing. I can't believe they wouldn't have gotten the bomb part right. Maybe the bomb was just the right size for their purposes."

He looked over his shoulder at me. "What do you mean?"

"Maybe they didn't intend to kill anybody."

"That makes no sense. Bombs are for killing people. They must have known I was in the restaurant. And we know they want to kill me. Therefore, the bomb was intended to kill me."

"Who wants to kill you?" The woman's voice rose.

"No one wants to kill anyone," he said. "We were talking about a television show." She tilted her head to one side and looked up at him.

I rolled my eyes. He offered a sheepish smile.

"Or it was intended to accomplish something else," I continued.

"Like what?"

"I don't know. Maybe send a message."

"What message?" He lowered his voice to a whisper. "That they want to kill me? We already knew that."

"I don't know what message. Maybe they just wanted to prove they could get to you—to intimidate you. Maybe the message was that if they can get to you, they can get to anyone. Maybe it was a diversion for something else they're doing. I just don't know."

For the first time since the explosion, Simon's face turned pale.

I touched his arm. "What's wrong?"

"Kacey."

CHAPTER
ELEVEN

LATE THE NEXT AFTERNOON, Simon, Elise, and I huddled around a mahogany table with Michael Harrison, Special Agent in Charge of the FBI's Dallas field office. The night before, at about the time we were wallowing in broken glass on the floor of Pascali's, Simon's sister, Meg, had been waiting for Kacey at the baggage claim at DFW airport in Dallas. Kacey never arrived.

Within an hour the Chicago police confirmed that Kacey never boarded her flight at O'Hare. Kacey, her escort Cheryl, and the limousine driver were all missing.

Harrison flew to Chicago that morning, as soon as the Chicago authorities officially designated the case as a suspected kidnapping. We were in the dining room of an executive suite in the Azure Hotel, a room so art-fully fitted with intricately carved furniture and deep, jeweled upholstery that it could have been the setting for an eighteenth-century painting of counts and countesses in powdered wigs. We, however, wore blue jeans—except Harrison, who had already tossed his charcoal suit jacket over a chair and rolled his shirtsleeves up over his broad, dark forearms.

I assumed from the beginning that Kacey was dead. After all, they're called terrorists for a reason. They didn't seem to have anything to gain by kidnapping an evangelist's twenty-year-old daughter. After watching Simon closely, I was certain that he felt the same way. It wasn't just that he was emotionally battered. Who wouldn't be? It was that he was *only* battered. He seemed to have little interest when the discussions turned to the possibility that she'd been kidnapped, as if he were simply going through the motions. The life had left him, and what remained was a mechanical facsimile.

Regardless of our feelings, the FBI seemed convinced it was a kidnapping. Harrison—in his early thirties and already one of the youngest men ever to ascend to Agent in Charge of a major FBI field office—took personal command of the investigation. Though he now lived in Dallas, Harrison grew up in Chicago's notorious Cabrini Green housing project. Thick-necked and solid, with a nose that had been flattened by something blunt, he was, as Dad would have said, a linebacker not a receiver. A summa cum laude economics graduate of the University of Chicago, he had zero tolerance for crime. His recent résumé included a high-profile bust of a Mexican drug runner who killed two elementary school kids in the crossfire of a drug hit. Throughout most of his career he had focused on white-collar economic crime. Since 9/11, though, he had become one of the nation's most respected authorities on Muslim terror groups and frequently consulted with other FBI offices around the country.

Harrison arrived at Pascali's at around 3:00 in the morning. By that time we already knew Kacey was missing, and it was obvious we'd be staying in Chicago for a while. I suggested we move Simon from the Palmer House because whoever set off the bomb almost certainly knew where he was staying. Harrison agreed and arranged to move Simon and Elise to the Azure. We couldn't keep Simon's location a secret for long, but at least this would buy us some time. Harrison arranged for two Chicago cops to guard the hallway outside Simon's suite. Four plainclothes officers guarded the lobby of the hotel. Elise and I checked into the rooms on either side of Simon's.

Now Simon, drawn and unshaven, sat with his back to the table and stared out the suite's expansive row of windows toward Lake Michigan. From time to time he hooked his index finger in the collar of his gray T-shirt and slid it from side to side, as if the collar were too tight around his neck. He'd stretched the collar so much that it was now nearly a V-neck.

Elise hadn't spoken much since the night before. She spent most of the day on the couch in the suite's living area, flipping from one news station to the next. With her blonde curls dangling just to the shoulders of her pink sweatshirt, she looked like a cute but frazzled suburban mom about to drive carpool. I had a hunch she was going to need professional help when this whole thing was over. At the moment she was sitting alone at the far end of the dining room table, drinking too much coffee and sketching something in a spiral notebook with a red felt-tip pen.

A couple of hours earlier, Harrison briefed us on the information the FBI had gathered in the past twelve hours. It was impossible not to be impressed as he strode back and forth next to the table, his tie loosened at the collar, explaining what we should expect if this was, in fact, a kidnapping. Now he leaned back against the wall that separated the dining area from the kitchenette, talking on his cell phone.

I'd just slid my chair back to put on a fresh pot of coffee when the doorbell rang. I went to the door and looked through the peep hole. It was one of the cops posted outside the door. He had a phone to his ear. I opened the door.

"Hey, Michael," the cop said, "the front desk has a delivery package for Reverend Mason. It came over from the Palmer House. What do you want us to do with it?"

Harrison turned toward Simon. "Were you expecting anything?"

Simon scratched his head. "I can't think of anything. Do you know of anything, Elise?"

She looked up from her note pad long enough to shake her head.

"Where is it from?" Simon said.

The cop spoke into his cell phone then looked back at Simon. "West suburbs, Naperville."

"I don't know anyone in Naperville. How could anyone have known I was here?"

"The manager of the Palmer House forwarded it. Someone apparently knew you were there."

Harrison looked at the policeman. "Are we talking about a box or a letter-sized envelope or what?"

"Letter size."

"Get the bomb and biohazard guys over here to check it. In the meantime, have your people take it down to the basement and isolate it so it can't do any damage. They're going to have to open it. Simon. You okay with that?"

Simon waved his hand. "Whatever you say." His voice was so soft that we barely heard him. He turned his chair toward the window.

I shoved my hands in the pockets of my jeans and looked out toward Lake Michigan. A dark bank of clouds moved rapidly toward the Azure, darting and swirling each time the wind rattled the windows. Across Lake Shore Drive the water churned into white caps, making Lake Michigan appear as bitter as the North Sea. I remembered my cab driver's promise of the evening before, that the weather today would be in the fifties and sunny. I wondered where he got his forecast.

Above the narrow strip of beach between the drive and the water, a flock of gulls spiraled downward in slow circles. One by one they landed and pecked at a thick, brown lump that lay motionless in the sand. I couldn't make out whether it was an animal or a bag of trash. I glanced at Simon. He was watching the birds also, his elbows on the arms of his chair and his chin resting on his interlocked fingers. It was a depressing sight on both sides of the glass. I tried to break the trance by pointing to a jogger whose windbreaker ballooned behind him as he ran along the beach, head bowed into the wind. "Intrepid guy there. Reminds me of my dad. Nothing kept him from working out."

Simon looked up at me from his chair. "You must miss him."

I leaned back against the windowsill. "I do."

"Someone you love that much never completely leaves you. I learned that with Marie."

This was not what I had in mind. This conversation was in danger of plummeting into the abyss. Fortunately, Harrison walked over to the window. "I hate to do this to you, but I'd like to go over last night one more time with all of you together. Just in case there was something we missed the first time around."

I was glad for the interruption—not for me, but for Simon. For the next couple of hours we retold the story of the prior day, stopping to focus on every detail with any potential for importance. Halfway through the interview, Harrison received a phone call. They had found Hakim. He had gone voluntarily with the police to

FBI headquarters for questioning. After the call Harrison focused on our brief encounter with Hakim on the drive to Pascali's.

Once Harrison finished with us, there was little to do but sit around the suite and wait. Simon and I remained at the dining room table, talking from time to time, but mostly just staring out the window at the lake. Elise sat on the couch, alternately dozing and watching news reports about Kacey's disappearance.

What would have been a major domestic news story under any circumstances had taken on monumental international proportions because of the media's hype of the war-of-religions angle. FOX and CNN covered the story nonstop. Amazingly—and thanks to the heroic lack of cooperation of the managers at both hotels—reporters hadn't yet figured out where the FBI had moved Simon. Still, we didn't expect our location would remain secret much longer.

Simon had just walked over to the couch and sat down next to Elise when the doorbell rang. It was the same cop as before. When I opened the door he stuck in his head. "Michael, can I see you for a minute?"

Harrison was sitting at a desk in the living area, working on his laptop. He nodded, then got up and went out the door.

After about ten minutes, the bell rang again. When I opened the door, Harrison brushed past me. He carried a cardboard delivery envelope in one hand. "Kacey's alive, but they've got her." He went straight to the dining room table and sat down.

Simon lifted his hands toward the ceiling and closed his eyes. "Thank you, God, thank you!" He moved his chair to a spot directly across the table from Harrison and leaned forward. "Who's got her, and what can we do to get her back?"

Elise came around the table and moved in behind Simon.

"A group called the Storm of Islam," Harrison said. "To our knowledge, they haven't been anything but an obscure Arab-Muslim Internet site until now. There are hundreds just like them. We've got our people researching them."

"How do you know it's them?" Simon said.

Harrison nodded at the package that he'd laid on the table.

Simon looked down at it. "What's in it?"

"There was evidence in the delivery envelope— proof that they've got Kacey. We've put the contents in evidence bags. It's all in the package. I've got to warn you, Simon, it's bad. I think you're going to want to open it alone." He made eye contact with Elise and then with me. I turned to leave.

"It's all right. They can stay." Simon picked up the envelope.

Harrison held up his hand. "I don't think you should—"

Simon turned the envelope upside down and shook the contents out onto the table. A piece of white notebook paper and two zip-top bags fell out. Elise leaned over Harrison's shoulder and squinted to see what was in the bags.

Just as I moved around the table to see, Elise screamed. Simon turned away for a moment, giving me a clear line of sight. In one of the baggies was an emerald ring.

In the other was a human finger.

CHAPTER
TWELVE

SIMON DROPPED THE BAG on the table and put his head in his hands. Elise ran to the couch and buried her head in a pillow. "What kind of animals would do this to a teenage girl?" Simon looked up at Harrison. "They will rot in hell for this."

"I'm sure that's true, but before they get there, I want to make certain they rot in jail. Can you absolutely identify the ring as Kacey's?"

Simon nodded. "I gave it to her for her birthday. If you look inside, there's an inscription. It says *Love, Dad* and has the date."

Harrison used a handkerchief to take the ring out of the baggie. He studied it and put it back in the bag.

"The inscription is there. I'll send the evidence to the lab. We'll be very careful with it, I promise. We'll get it back to you as soon as we can." He looked at me, and I knew he was talking in particular about Kacey's finger.

Simon lifted his head. "No, don't take it yet." He picked up the bag that contained the finger. "Please, can you give me a minute?"

Harrison reached into his pocket and removed a pair of latex gloves. "Sure. Just put these on, please. I understand it's tough, but everything is evidence. I know you want to get her back." He placed the gloves on the table in front of Simon.

Simon picked them up and looked at them for a moment. Then he slid them on.

Elise, her eyes red and swollen, walked from the couch around the table toward the suite's kitchen. Harrison followed her. Before he turned the corner, he said, "Just one more thing."

Simon looked up. "What?"

"I'm going to need you to check your e-mails as soon as possible."

"Why?"

"The note. It says they will e-mail you. That's how we'll learn what they want."

"I can check the e-mails," Elise said. "I'll get my laptop from my room." She headed for the door and looked relieved to be escaping. Harrison went into the kitchen.

I don't know why, because I hardly knew him, but I stopped next to Simon and put my hand on his shoulder. He winced. Then he tilted his head and looked into my eyes. "Thank you," he said. I wanted to cry.

He put his hand on mine. I knew he wanted to touch Kacey, not me, but I was there and she was not, and at that moment the touch of a stranger must have been better than no touch at all. I let him hold my hand—and I did cry. But I cried as quietly as I could, because it was his moment to hurt, not mine. Eventually he nodded, and I understood it was time for me to leave.

As I walked toward the kitchen, wiping my eyes with my fingers, I heard him open one of the bags. I looked over my shoulder. He'd removed Kacey's finger from the plastic bag. It had been cut cleanly, just above the second knuckle. The skin was already darkening. He turned it over and over, studying it from every angle. He nudged it into his palm and touched it lightly, then stroked it with his fingertips, as if it were still attached to her hand and she were sitting right beside him.

I felt guilty for watching, and I started to turn away. Before I did, Simon lifted Kacey's finger and pressed it to his cheek. He held it there for a long time. Then he began to sob.

CHAPTER
THIRTEEN

BY 10 P.M. ELISE had been sitting on the couch for a couple of hours and had barely taken her eyes off the laptop resting on the coffee table in front of her. Simon had been in the bedroom alone since he returned the evidence to Harrison. I sat in an upholstered wing chair, flipping through the pages of one of the hotel's promotional magazines about Chicago. The room smelled like burnt coffee. I wanted a drink of something far stronger.

At the desk in the corner, Harrison hunched over a report that had been delivered to him a few minutes earlier. From time to time he scratched something onto the paper with the hotel's ballpoint desk pen.

Out of the corner of my eye I noticed Elise lean forward and peer at the computer screen. "This may be it!"

Harrison and I hurried over to the couch. Simon rounded the corner from the bedroom. In three long strides he was at the coffee table. Elise stood and moved out of his way. He leaned over the laptop, clicked open the message, and scanned the screen. After a moment he shook his head and toggled the message to the beginning. He read it again, then sat on the couch.

"What is it?" Harrison said. "Is she all right?"

"They have a demand. If I meet it, they say they'll let Kacey go."

Harrison walked around the coffee table and squinted at the laptop. "What do they want?"

Simon rubbed his hand over the bald crown of his head. "They want me to make a statement on international television this Saturday at the Celebration of Hope in Dallas."

"What statement?" Harrison said.

Simon leaned back on the couch. "They want me to deny that Jesus is the Son of God."

FIFTEEN MINUTES AFTER READING the e-mail, Simon paced near the windows of the suite. "If I don't say what they want me to say, they will kill Kacey. If we try to find her and rescue her, they'll kill her." He stopped, and the muscles in his neck strained until they practically throbbed above the neck band of his T-shirt. "What she must be going through . . ." He clenched his fists. "If we find them I swear I will kill them with my bare hands. I will pummel each one of them until they're dead."

Harrison frowned and took a step toward Simon. "I feel the same way, believe me. We're going to do everything we can to—"

Simon spun around and kicked one of the dining table chairs. It smacked against the table and fell backward onto the carpet. "These people talk about religion. This has nothing to do with religion. That's a charade! They're thugs—nothing more than a street gang with a pious-sounding name."

"You're exactly right," Harrison said. "Religion is a tool for them. It's an excuse to do whatever it takes to achieve their political goals."

"But what sort of a tool?" Elise said. "If you go on television and say what they want you to say, it will all come out afterward. Everyone will know. They will be vilified the world over for this, even by Muslims." We all turned and stared at her. She'd hardly spoken all day. She blushed, and her voice lowered. "What can they possibly gain?"

Harrison's eyes narrowed. "You're looking at it from the wrong perspective. These people are fanatics. They don't care how 99 percent of the world reacts."

"But that doesn't answer my question. What do they gain? Any statement by Simon would be meaningless under these circumstances."

"Meaningless to the West, maybe. But with respect to their target audience—the others who think as they do—it would be a public relations bonanza. It would be viewed as a demonstration of our weakness and their superiority." Harrison turned his palms up. "To borrow a political phrase, they're playing to their base."

Elise's voice gained strength. "How can that be? Whose weakness would it demonstrate? Simon's? Why would they care about that?"

He wagged his finger. "Not just Simon—the West, Christianity. To them, we're the enemy. All of us."

What Elise said made sense. I was about to interject that I agreed when Simon threw up his hands. "Would you two stop it?"

Elise's face flushed. She leaned back on the couch, and Simon walked toward her. "This is philosophical drivel. What difference does it make? If I don't do as they say, they're going to kill Kacey. That's the only thing that matters." He turned his back on her and looked at Harrison. "Can we negotiate with them?"

Elise's shoulders drooped. She sank lower into the couch. I wondered whether it was possible for any human being to appear more drained of self-confidence. For an instant I was angry at Simon for treating her so dismissively, but I caught myself. Who was I to judge him under these circumstances?

"We can try to negotiate," Harrison said. "We will try. Maybe we'll even find them before next week—find Kacey and get her back. That's the result we want, but there are no guarantees."

"If you go after her, they'll kill her."

"We wouldn't move unless we felt there was a high probability of getting her out alive."

"High probability? What does that mean?"

Harrison shoved his hands in his pockets. "Why don't we wait and see if we can locate her before we get into a guessing game about whether we can get her out safely? A lot of it would depend on the circumstances. We have no way of knowing what those would be."

Harrison's cell phone rang. He pulled it out of his pocket and held it to his ear. After a moment he nodded. "Yes . . . read it." His eyes narrowed. "Read it again . . . thanks." He flipped the phone shut.

Simon cocked his head. "What was that?"

"We don't have to wait for word of this to get out. They've posted it on their Web site in Arabic. I just got the translation. They want everyone to know exactly what's going on, exactly what their demands are."

"They're lunatics," Simon said.

"You give them way too much credit. They're not crazy. They're no different than any criminal organization. They get their way through murder and intimidation. They're corrupt and ruthless, nothing more and nothing less."

"If Simon does what they say, do you think they will keep their word? Will they really release her?" Elise watched Simon out of the corner of her eye as she spoke.

"Yes, will they make good on this if I do it?" Simon said. Elise appeared relieved that he hadn't snapped at her again.

Harrison ran his hand through his hair. "There's no way of knowing for sure. My strong hunch, though, is that they will. Now that they've gone public with this, they won't have much choice. In their warped world, it would be a matter of honor. They told you they would do it, and I think they will. After we've gotten more research on them, we'll be in a better position to evaluate it, though."

Elise leaned forward, seeming to have regained her confidence. "Then it's great news. You're going to get Kacey back."

Simon stared at her. "Great news? Are you sick?"

Her shoulders sagged again. "That's not what I meant." She squinted up at him, as if searching for a clue to what he wanted her to say. It was painful to watch.

"Don't you understand the significance of what they want me to do?" His jaw muscles clenched with each word.

"Yes, of course. But you will do it, won't you? You just say it one day, get her back, and then go on television the next day and retract the whole thing. Everyone will understand."

Simon scowled at her. She shrank back on the couch. In a voice barely above a whisper she said, "You can't let her die."

Without another word, Simon turned, walked into the bedroom, and shut the door.

Elise's eyes remained fixed on the door. She reached up and straightened her hair, then put her hands back in her lap. A cab horn honked on the street below, and somewhere in the distance a siren blared. I looked at Harrison. He was staring at his shoes. Elise continued to watch the door, but it didn't open. After a few more moments, she straightened her back and stood. Then she picked up her purse from the couch and, without a word, walked out the door of the suite.

Harrison motioned with his thumb toward the door. "Do those two have something going on?"

I shrugged. "I've only known them for twenty-four hours. My read is that she wants to."

He smiled. "Maybe so, but I sure don't think he does."

"Right now it's the farthest thing from his mind, don't you think?"

He shook his head. "Of course. I should never have brought it up."

"I didn't mean to sound self-righteous. I've been wondering the same thing."

Harrison walked back over to the desk where he'd been working.

"Do you think you can find Kacey?"

He leaned on the desk and lowered his voice. "Honestly? She could be anywhere. We'll need a lucky break."

I looked at the bedroom door. Simon was almost certainly praying for Kacey. In fact, millions of people all over the world must be praying for her. On the other hand, millions had undoubtedly prayed for Simon for years and this is where it got him. When I thought of Kacey—how alone she was and how terrified she must be—I felt sick to my stomach. I resolved at that moment that I would pray for her too. My prayers probably wouldn't count for much, but they weren't likely to hurt. And Kacey needed all the help she could get.

CHAPTER
FOURTEEN

BY MIDNIGHT SIMON STILL hadn't come out of his bedroom. With no pressing reason to disturb him, Harrison decided to go back to his room and get a few hours of sleep. As he walked out the door, I hit the mute button on the TV and turned it on one more time to see if the news had picked up the story of the kidnappers' demands.

Just as I was about to click to a news station, Simon walked out of the bedroom carrying a beat-up, green shoe box under his arm. The small amount of hair that he had left on the sides of his head was matted flat. His jeans and T-shirt looked as if someone had wadded them up wet and thrown them in a corner.

When he saw me standing in front of the television, he stopped and rubbed his hand over his head. "I heard the door close. I thought everyone had gone."

"I'm sorry. I'm on my way out." I placed the remote on top of the television. "I wanted to check the news one more time."

"What are they saying?"

"I don't know. I just turned it on."

He stood barefoot in the middle of the floor and looked around the room. He was lean and athletic; his chest and arms stretched against the cotton of his T-shirt. I thought of my father and the way he looked that last night at the campsite. Then I pictured Simon the evening before, how calm he'd remained after the bomb went off.

Dad would have liked this man.

Simon continued to scan the room. His eyes were dark and bloodshot, and he seemed incapable of moving, as if he'd forgotten why he came into the room in the first place.

I stepped toward him. "Are you all right? Can I get you anything before I go?"

He blinked and shifted his weight from one foot to the other. "No, I'm fine. Thanks."

I walked toward the table, where my purse hung from the back of one of the arm chairs. "I'll just get out of your way then. I'm sure you want to get some sleep." I picked up my purse and slung it over my shoulder.

He nodded toward the kitchen. "Is there any coffee left?"

"I imagine so. We didn't drink much out of that last pot."

"Would you mind staying for a bit?"

Surprised, I didn't respond immediately.

He shifted the shoe box to his other arm. "You're probably exhausted. I shouldn't have asked."

"No, a cup of coffee would be good. I'm not sleepy anyway." I dropped my purse onto the floor next to the wall and headed for the kitchen. I looked at him over my shoulder. "You like it black, right?"

He held up a hand. "You sit down. I'll get it." He walked past me, sliding the shoe box onto the table as he went by. "I'm sorry, I didn't notice how you like it."

"I like mine black, also."

I sat down and rested an elbow on the table. The shoe box was inches from my hand. Part of the lid was torn. One of the bottom corners had a hole the size of a dime, where the cardboard had worn through. I resisted the urge to lift the lid and see what was inside.

A few moments later Simon came back from the kitchen and placed a coffee mug in front of me. I picked it up and blew over the top. It smelled strong, burnt. He sat down across from me. Neither of us said anything.

I wondered whether he wanted to talk or just sit for a while. The fear that I'd seen earlier that evening was back in his eyes. He had no one left, and I knew how that felt. I would sit with him all night, and all day, and the next night too if it would help him.

He took a drink of coffee and set his mug on the table. "Do you know how I got to be a preacher?"

"No, how?"

"When I was growing up, my family was not what you would call religious. We went to church once in a while, mostly on Easter, Christmas, Mother's Day. When Marie and I got married, she was more serious about faith than I was. She went to church most Sundays. I stayed home.

"When Kacey was born, I had so much to be thankful for. I still never thought about God, though, or about much of anything except just living my life. We were happy. Our lives revolved around Kacey, and we thought we had everything we needed. At least, I thought we did." He picked up his mug and sipped.

"Then Marie got sick. And then she died. After that, I wanted to die too. But I couldn't. Kacey needed me. She was only three years old. So I kept on living. I tried, really tried, to get back to life, but it was so hard because I missed Marie so much. I kept on living on the outside, but on the inside I was dying more every day.

"About six months after Marie died, I lost my job at the auto factory. We basically had nothing in savings. We'd been a young couple with a kid. We'd poured every penny we had into our house. I'll never forget when I got the notice in the mail saying that we had to move out within thirty days because I wasn't able to pay the mortgage. I wondered how people lived when they didn't have a house or an apartment. I remember lying in bed one night when Kacey was asleep. I put a pillow over my face and screamed into it so Kacey couldn't hear. I was screaming at God. 'Why are you doing this to me? Don't you have someone else to knock around for a while?'"

I wanted to reach out and touch him, hold his hand. But how could I? I hardly knew him.

He turned his palm up. "I don't know why I decided to yell at God that night. It's not as if I'd paid much attention to him in the past thirty years. For some reason, though, as soon as I finished yelling into that pillow, the strangest sense of peace came over me. It was as if he'd just been waiting for me to ask him to help. God moved into my life that night. He moved in because I asked him in. He came in quietly, and he sat with me. I began to talk to him that night, there in my bedroom. And that's how God saved me. He did it very quietly. That's how we talk even today—very quietly."

He shrugged. "I'm sorry, I'm sure you don't want to hear about this. I guess I just wanted to talk to someone."

I leaned forward. "Please, I do want to hear. So how did you end up preaching?"

"That's a little bit tougher to explain." He took another sip of his coffee. "I got some odd jobs around town, things like painting, fix-it stuff. It was enough to get the mortgage caught up and keep us in our house. I wasn't working full time, just a job here and there. I had time to think about things.

"At first the idea of preaching was something that flitted through my mind and was gone. Over time, when the thought came, it stayed longer. At some point I began to consider the details. How would it actually work if I did it? How does a person begin something like that? I finally concluded that God was putting the idea in my head.

"So I raised my objections to him; and I had plenty of them. I'm not an educated man. I'm nobody. Who would listen to me? I would have to go to seminary, and that would take years. How would I pay for it? I had Kacey to think of. How would I earn money for the things she needed?"

I nodded. "Particularly important with a girl."

He smiled. "Yes, you've got that right. Anyway, I sat down and wrote out a list of my strengths and weaknesses. I still have it. On the strength side of the ledger, I figured I was a hard worker, I was sincere, and by that time I felt I really loved God. I had some skills most preachers don't have, but they didn't seem to have much applicability. For example, I was a good athlete. I could dunk a basketball. In high school I'd been a quarterback and pitcher too. I figured that might help me work with youth somehow. I had a good sense of humor, and that could help with kids, also. You get the point. I had very few things going for me. None of them seemed to fit particularly well with being a preacher.

"There were plenty of weaknesses, though. I was still basically unemployed, which is not the best jumping-off point for any new career. I had no college education and no Bible training. I was a single parent, with all of the time demands that go along with that. I had no public speaking experience, and as a matter of fact the thought of speaking in public pretty much terrified me. I didn't have a single connection anywhere in the preaching business to get me started." He took another drink of his coffee and made a face. "This stuff is like mud."

I smiled. "It's been sitting there for hours."

He pushed his mug away. "Anyway, as you can imagine, when I looked over my list, it wasn't a close call. There were practically zero reasons to think I could become any kind of a preacher. So I decided to look for a real job. I answered an ad at a local radio station, hoping to work my way into a sports talk show. Funny, but that's how God started me in my ministry—with a job that I took because I didn't seriously think I could be a minister." Simon chuckled. "God must have realized that my baldness wouldn't be a liability on the radio. I'd been on the radio for a year or so, and someone from my Sunday school class suggested I start working some stuff about faith into my bits on the show. I used real light things at first. People liked it. Before long I was being asked to speak in front of groups. It all snowballed from there."

He leaned back in his chair. "I guess I'm the classic example of how God uses even the bad things in life to accomplish something good. If Marie hadn't died, there is no way I would be a preacher today."

I glanced at the shoe box. He followed my eyes and placed his hand on the lid. "I've been talking to Marie tonight. In the bedroom."

I shifted my weight and scratched at the shadow of a cigarette burn that someone had buffed out of the tabletop.

"Don't worry, Taylor, I'm not crazy." He patted the lid of the shoe box. "This is how I talk to her." He opened the lid. Inside was a stack of envelopes, many of them faded and yellow. Some had been opened and some were sealed. He poured them out on the table. Each envelope had *Marie* written in ink on the front. "I write her letters. I've been doing it since the first Christmas after she died."

When he talked about Marie, the muscles in his face and neck relaxed. I wondered what it would be like to be good enough to have that sort of effect on a man. I couldn't think of anything to say that wouldn't sound inconsequential and stupid. I cursed myself for being just that—inconsequential and stupid.

"You think I'm crazy." He turned the box on its side and raked the envelopes into it. "I shouldn't have shown you this."

"No, stop." I couldn't help myself. I reached across the table and touched the back of his hand. "I don't think you're crazy. I was just trying to keep from crying."

"Why would you cry?"

I waved my hand in the air. "Oh, I cry a lot. It's a real problem."

He turned the box upright and laid the lid crossways over it. "That's hard for me to believe. You seem . . . well . . . pretty tough."

I straightened my back. "I *am* pretty tough."

He smiled.

I wiped at my eye with my hand. "Let's face it,

who wouldn't cry? You've been writing letters to your deceased wife for more than fifteen years. That's the sweetest thing I've ever heard."

"Now you *are* crying. I'm sorry."

"It's okay. Like I said, I do this a lot."

A few of the envelopes were still scattered on the table. He picked one up and ran his fingers over Marie's name. "It's just that sometimes I want to talk to her so much that I almost can't stand it. I lie in bed and close my eyes and think what it would be like if I could touch her hand one more time. Sometimes I can feel it— her skin on my fingertips. I want to reach out and hold her . . . but I open my eyes and she's not there."

That did it. I got up and picked up my purse from the floor. I pulled out a tissue and sat back down at the table.

He nodded at the letters. "This is the closest I can get to her, and it helps. So I write."

I wiped under my eyes with the tissue. "I can't imagine anyone loving me that much." I could have kicked myself for saying it; this was not about me. I crumpled the tissue and shoved it in the pocket of my jeans.

He waved the envelope that was in his hand. "Tonight I talked to Marie about Kacey. I asked her what I should do." He leaned back in his chair and looked up at the ceiling. "That's the issue, isn't it? It's a matter of who I love and how much. I think I must have loved Marie too much, and now she's gone. I must love Kacey too much, because she's gone too."

"What do you mean, you loved them too much?"

"I think I loved them more than I love God. Maybe that's why they're gone." He dropped the envelope back on the table.

"Why would God be angry that you loved your wife and daughter? Isn't that what you're supposed to do?"

He didn't answer.

"Wait a minute. I know that you're the preacher here, but that's not the way things are supposed to work, is it? I thought God *wanted* us to love each other."

He leaned forward and put his elbows on the table. "He does, but not more than we love him. 'Anyone who loves his father or mother or son or daughter more than he loves me is not worthy of me.' That's straight from Jesus' mouth. You can look it up in the Bible."

"I'll take your word for it. I wouldn't be able to find it anyway. Surely that's not meant literally, though. If it were, God would seem petty and jealous."

"You want jealousy? 'I, the Lord your God am a jealous God.' You can find that in the Ten Commandments."

"That's in the Ten Commandments? Okay, fine. Even if it is, that was two thousand years ago. It was a different time."

"Was it? Do you think I'm the first one ever to be put in this position? The Romans forced Christians to watch as their wives and children were tortured. But those people didn't deny Christ. At least some of them didn't. Do you think that people back then loved their families less than I love Kacey?"

"I don't know, but what difference does it make? That was then. This is now. Maybe more was required of them because of the circumstances." I cradled my coffee mug in my hands, but it smelled so bitter I couldn't bring myself to take a drink.

"Really?" He narrowed his eyebrows. "How were their circumstances so different? They stood by their faith when it was under attack by people who wanted to wipe it out. They died, and their wives and children died. Eventually even the Romans began to sympathize with them. What those Christians did changed the world. If they hadn't been willing to suffer, to allow their families to suffer, who knows if Christianity would have taken hold? They accomplished something that in the big picture was more important than an individual life."

"Fair enough, but Christianity is here now. It's established. That sort of thing isn't necessary anymore."

He leaned back in his chair. "Remember what Hakim said? There are billions of people in the world who don't know Jesus. A billion of them are Muslims. Are we supposed to ignore them because we're comfortable suburban Christians, half a world away? Are their souls unimportant?"

"Hakim may have been involved in kidnapping Kacey. I'm not sure he's the guy you should be quoting."

He shook his head. "I've been thinking about that. I can't believe he was involved in this. If he was a terrorist, wouldn't he have had the bomb in *his* car? Besides, I doubt that Muslim terrorists are infiltrating seminaries. Even if he was involved, though, it wouldn't make what he said any less true. What about the people he talked about, the people of Lebanon, the Middle East? Who is responsible for saving them?"

I crossed my arms. "That's a bit parochial, isn't it? Who says they need to be saved? They've got their religion, and we've got ours." I should have blushed when I said that. I didn't really have any religion to speak of— but this was an argument, not a confession.

He turned his head away, and his neck flushed. When he turned back, he said, "Look, I don't even know what *parochial* means. I'm no philosopher, and I'm not a college professor. All I know is that I believe that if they don't accept Christ, their souls will be lost. There's no other way to put it."

"And they believe that if you don't believe what they believe—Muhammad and Allah and all that— you're the one who will be lost. Who's to say you're right and they're wrong?"

He shrugged. "Only God will say. I can't force them to believe what I believe, and it's not my duty to force them. But it is my duty to tell them so they can decide for themselves. If I don't do my best to tell them, how will God judge me if I *am* right?"

"Fine, but what does that have to do with Kacey? You can still preach to anyone you want. Kacey doesn't have to die for that. You don't think God wants Kacey to die, do you?"

He stood, walked to the window, and looked down toward the street. "No, I don't think God wants Kacey to die. But I also don't think he wants me to go in front of a hundred million people and deny that Jesus is the Savior of the world. Can't you see? Carrying the Word to those people has to start somewhere with somebody. Maybe this is what everything has been for—the crazy rise of my ministry, the fame. Maybe it's all been building to this moment, this sacrifice. This could be the purpose that God has for my life. If it is, and I let him down now, hasn't it all been for nothing? I would have done more harm than good with my life."

"What do you think Marie would want you to do?" I glanced at the box of letters on the table. "Do you think she would want you to let Kacey die?"

He turned. "Do you think *I* want Kacey to die? I'd rather they torture me! And, no, when Marie was here on earth, I know she would have told me to save Kacey. Knowing what she knows now, though . . . I don't know. She's with Jesus. She knows the secret, the answer to the mystery."

For once I agreed with Elise. I thought the decision was simple. The terrorists told him exactly what he had to do to get Kacey back. He didn't have to climb a mountain. He didn't have to put himself in danger. He just had to say a few words that no one in the world would believe were true. I figured he got a lucky break. But now I at least understood what I couldn't have imagined before—how Simon could agonize over whether to save his own daughter's life.

He put his elbows on the table and grasped his head in his hands. "Why couldn't they have kidnapped me? I would gladly die in Kacey's place. But it's not me, it's

Kacey, and I love her so much. Do you see what I mean? I love her too much."

I walked around the table and put my hand on his shoulder. "You've been put in a horrible situation. A situation no human being should ever have to be in. But one thing I know with certainty is that you don't love Kacey too much. I've never been a religious person, but I believe in God. It doesn't take a theologian to tell you that God wants you to love Kacey every bit as much as you do. Even a person like me knows that."

He lifted his head and looked into my eyes. It occurred to me how inappropriate this scene would seem if someone were to walk in. The two of us alone in a hotel room—after midnight. Maybe I should take my hand from his shoulder? But it wasn't inappropriate, and I couldn't move. He needed a human's touch. He needed Marie's touch, and Kacey's touch, but he couldn't have them. So I left my hand where it was, and I wanted to do even more. I wanted to hold him close and comfort him.

In hindsight, I guess that was the moment I first began to wonder what I really felt for Simon Mason.

"What do you think I should do?"

I couldn't believe he was asking me, of all people. I couldn't even manage to live my own life. But I was glad that he asked. It had been a long time since my personal opinion had mattered to anyone. "I don't know what you should do, because I don't have the faith you have. I know what *I* would do, though. If Kacey were my daughter, no power in heaven or earth could keep me from saving her. If it required my soul to be damned, then it would be damned."

He moaned.

"Simon, if you say the words, no one will believe you mean them. Not one person on earth. Not even God. If he loves you, there must be some sort of dispensation for this, because in this situation his requirements are just too difficult. You're only a human being."

"Only a human being. Funny, but that's exactly what I said to Marie in my letter tonight. I'm just a human being, and what God expects me to do is too hard. Does he really expect me to sacrifice my own daughter for him? Who could do such a thing? But who knows? Maybe he'll save me yet. When he asked Abraham to sacrifice his son, he stopped the knife before Abraham could bring it down. Maybe he'll stop the knife for me, also. I can only pray. Because what kind of parent would I be if I let my own daughter die? And what kind of preacher would I be if I denied Jesus?"

"I'm so sorry this is happening to you."

He moved away slightly, just enough that my hand fell away from his shoulder. "Thank you for talking to me. I didn't want to be alone. I think I'll go to bed now." He got up, gathered the remaining letters into the shoe box, and walked toward the bedroom.

"Simon?"

He turned back toward me.

I cleared my throat. "I'll pray for Kacey tonight. And I'll pray for you too."

He smiled. "Thank you," he said and walked into the bedroom.

When the door closed behind him, I sat down at the table and pulled my sweatshirt up to cover my face. I didn't want Simon to hear me when I cried. I don't know how long I sat there at the table like that, but before I got up to leave, I lowered my head. "God, you know what kind of person I am, and you have no reason to listen to me. But you've got so much reason to listen to this good man who loves you so much. And you've got so much reason to help Kacey. Please help them."

I raised my head and looked around the room. I didn't know what I was looking for. Maybe I was expecting God to swoop in and pat me on the back. Nothing happened except that I felt a little bit of the tension unwind in my shoulders. I supposed that was part of the bargain with praying. A person received some small amount of comfort. It helped me to think that with the millions of prayers going up for Simon and Kacey, they might receive some small comfort too. I picked up my purse and walked out the door.

CHAPTER
FIFTEEN

BY THE TIME I awoke the next morning, word of the terrorists' demand was on every one of the major networks and all over the Internet. Police had found Cheryl, the intern, in an abandoned warehouse outside West Chicago. She was tied up but otherwise okay. The limousine driver had disappeared, and the FBI believed he was in on the kidnapping. The police were interrogating employees of the limo service.

Unfortunately, Cheryl could provide little useful information other than that the attackers wore black ski masks. In the meantime the FBI confirmed Simon's instinct about Hakim. They questioned and released him, convinced he had nothing to do with the kidnapping.

The search for Kacey focused on a giant triangle, with vertices at Chicago, Rockford, and Milwaukee. The FBI admitted, though, that the kidnappers could have doubled back and taken her south of the city. The potential search area was so huge and the leads so few that they were looking for luck more than anything else.

Simon, Elise, and I were to meet Michael Harrison at 11 a.m. I had an hour to kill in my hotel room, so I made a pot of coffee, propped two pillows against the headboard, and sat down on the bed to watch the news. It was the top of the hour, and as I flicked from station to station, Simon and Kacey were the lead story everywhere. I settled on the Instant News Channel, where anchorwoman Summer Harcomb moderated a discussion with an imam, a Baptist pastor, and a rabbi.

"This is not Islam, and these criminals are not Muslims." The dark-bearded imam's voice rose as he spoke. "The Brotherhood of Midwestern Muslims condemns this heinous terrorist act in the strongest terms. We are asking all Muslims in the Chicago area to cooperate with the authorities in their effort to find Kacey Mason and bring her back to her father."

The rabbi pushed his glasses up with his index finger. "I am happy to hear that you condemn the atrocity these animals have visited on this poor young woman," he said in a gravelly voice. "I only wish that you were as vocal in your condemnation of suicide bombers who target innocent Jews on the streets and in the cafes of Israel."

The camera moved to the pastor, a younger man with thinning blond hair and eyebrows that moved when he spoke. "Millions of people around the world—"

From off-camera the imam's voice interrupted him. "Wait just one minute, please, Reverend Hale." The camera swung to the imam, who was wagging his index finger in the air. "I want to address the statement that was just made. We have been crystal clear on this point, and I want all Americans to understand this. We condemn all terrorist acts, whether against young girls in the United States or innocent civilians in Israel. I want to repeat what our organization has said many times: There is no justification for violence targeting innocent civilians anywhere. None." He slapped his palm on the table.

Summer nodded. "You've made the same statement on this program several times."

"Ah, but we must pay close attention to the words that the imam uses," the rabbi said. "Notice that he refers to *innocent* civilians. And I would like to ask him to clarify that statement. Does it apply to *all* civilians, sir, or just to the ones deemed by these fanatics to be innocent?"

The imam tapped his index finger on the desk, next to a copy of the Quran that rested in front of him. "All civilians, period. That is our position and always has been."

The pastor held up a slender hand. "One thing I think we can agree on is that our prayer at this time is for Kacey Mason's safe return, and for these criminals to be brought to justice."

Summer leaned forward. "Yes, thank you, Pastor Hale. I wanted to get your views—the views of each of you gentlemen—on the nightmarish situation that Reverend Mason has been placed in. Put simply, wouldn't God forgive him for meeting the kidnappers' demands? I mean, everyone will know that any statement he makes is coerced."

"Nightmare is the right word, Summer," the pastor said. "I know Reverend Mason personally, and my heart goes out to him. I can't even imagine the agony he is experiencing."

"Well, let me ask you this way then: What would you do if faced with this situation? Could you allow your own child to die to make a point about faith?"

"First of all, it is not just making a point about faith, as you put it. The Bible is clear that Christians are expected to love our Lord more than material possessions, more than friends, and even more than our families."

"Yes, but what would *you* do, sir?"

The pastor cleared his throat. "I can't answer that question. My children are much younger . . . It is almost unimaginable that I could allow one of them to die if I had the ability to stop it. On the other hand, it is no small thing for a Christian—and particularly a spiritual leader like Simon Mason—to renounce his faith in Christ. I can only pray that I will never face the choice he is facing."

Summer turned to the rabbi.

"God is both just and merciful," the rabbi said.

"Whatever choice Reverend Mason makes, we must believe that the God who made heaven and earth is big enough to find a way to comfort this man and redeem him."

"Yes, Allah is merciful," the imam said. "And we need to remember that there is still hope that Kacey will be found before Reverend Mason must make his decision."

Summer turned to the rabbi. "I'll put the same question to you that I put to Pastor Hale. If you were in Reverend Mason's position, what would you do?"

"I don't know. Who could possibly know? Our God is a God of life, not death. I pray that he will have mercy on Kacey and on our brother, Reverend Mason."

She looked at the imam. "Imam?"

"I do not know what Reverend Mason will do, and I sympathize with him as he faces a terrible decision. I know, however, that no matter the circumstances, no matter the sacrifice, I would never deny Allah. Never."

"Then you believe that Reverend Mason should allow Kacey to die?"

"Only Reverend Mason can make that decision. I will not presume to think for him or speak for him."

"But in the same situation, you would let your own child die?"

"Allah allows me no choice."

Summer brushed back her blonde hair. "This is, indeed, intense." She placed her hand to her ear. "All right, we've got a caller who has an interesting point. Let's go to Peggy, from Alton, Illinois. Hello, Peggy. What do you think Reverend Mason should do?"

A woman's voice crackled over the speaker phone. "No father could allow his child to die like this, and the God that I know would not expect it. No one will believe that Reverend Mason is really denying Jesus, and he will not believe it in his own heart. That's what matters, what's in his heart."

Summer nodded. "What's in his heart . . . that's an excellent point, Peggy." She looked at the pastor. "And what about that, Pastor Hale? If Reverend Mason says the words the terrorists demand but doesn't believe them in his heart, do the words really matter? Is he really denying his faith?"

"The thing that makes this so difficult, Summer, is that words *do* matter. I wish it were as easy as the caller suggests, but when a leader of the stature of Simon Mason speaks, people all over the world listen. This is not the average guy walking down the street."

"How ironic," she said, "because much of Reverend Mason's appeal throughout his career has been that he seems to be just an average guy, someone to whom ordinary people can relate. Now I'm sure he would give anything to be able to disappear into the crowd, as the rest of us can do. Then his words would not have the effect that they may have next weekend, whatever he decides to do. Let's face it, though, he's become too well known for that to be a possibility."

The camera cut back to the rabbi just as he was taking a sip from a blue Instant News Channel coffee mug. He lifted his hand in a stop sign and smiled.

"Sorry, we caught you in midsip, Rabbi," Summer

said. "It's happened to me many times. We'll come back to you in a moment."

The camera panned back to Reverend Hale, who leaned forward and clasped his hands. "I want to remind people that the Apostle Peter denied Christ publicly— not once, but three times. And, of course, Christ forgave him. Peter became an indispensable leader of the early church. He eventually suffered greatly for his faith and was martyred. As legend has it, he asked to be crucified upside down because he did not feel worthy to die the way Jesus died. In any event, there is clear precedent that even a person who publicly denies Christ can be forgiven."

"So, as is often the case, there is instruction in church tradition." Summer touched her earpiece. "Well, they're telling me we're out of time. I want to thank you, gentlemen . . ."

The imam held up his hand. "One moment, Ms. Harcomb. I would like to ask—and I'm sure that Reverend Hale and Rabbi Stone will join me in this wish—I would like to ask all people of faith the world over to offer prayers for Kacey and Simon Mason during this terrible ordeal."

The other men nodded.

I turned off the television and leaned over my laptop to check the Internet, clicking from one news site to the next. Virtually every major newspaper in the world had an editorial piece about Simon's dilemma. Most took no position on the decision that he should make but instead condemned the terrorists and sympathized with him and his agonizing situation. A number of papers did, however, offer advice. The *Post*, the *Times*, and several leading European papers urged Simon to say whatever words would save his daughter. Each assured him that no one would believe he was truly renouncing his faith. The *Times* even instructed him that no loving God could hold him to account for his decision.

I worried that Simon was not going to do what the terrorists demanded. That, in fact, he couldn't do it. As horrible as the consequences would be, I was beginning to understand how he could make such a decision. I had been around two presidents and had seen firsthand the burden borne by men under great responsibility. They were among the few people on earth whose decisions regularly resulted in one person dying and another living—the men and women who sometimes had to sacrifice individual lives for the benefit of a larger group, or a larger principle.

Simon's situation was not that different. His actions influenced millions, perhaps hundreds of millions of people, and that influence could alter the fate of souls. Who would want such responsibility?

I got up and walked into the bathroom. Maybe the authorities would find Kacey and free her. Maybe he would never have to decide. I leaned over the sink and splashed water on my face. When I peered into the mirror, the eyes that looked back at me were dark and swollen. My head hurt, and I wished I hadn't emptied my room's mini-bar of bourbon after I left Simon the night before. But I'd needed something to calm me down. Who wouldn't under these circumstances?

No matter how bad I felt, though, I knew that Simon felt worse. I pictured him standing in his wrinkled jeans in the living room of his suite. How alone and lost he'd looked. I wished I could see him again right that moment, that I could talk to him and hold his hand. I wished that I could do more to comfort him.

More than anything, though, I wished that some miracle could make a man like Simon want to be comforted by a woman like me.

his Dallas office. He hoped that the event would somehow trigger a significant lead. We all knew, though, that there was virtually no chance of rescuing Kacey.

Simon was going to have to decide whether to meet the kidnappers' demand.

My first night back in my apartment, I slept restlessly and woke to the unsettling feeling that my bed was bouncing across the floor. I punched my pillow and tried to burrow to a more peaceful place. Within a few moments the window above my bed rattled so violently that I pulled the pillow over my head in case it shattered. Then the rattling stopped.

I sat upright and ran my tongue across my lips—stale bourbon—and as I recalled, lots of it. My head throbbed. I resolved not to have a drink for at least two weeks. The rattling started again. I leaned over and peered through the slats of my plantation shutters. Several stories below, three men in orange hard hats and fluorescent vests were bending over, looking into a hole in the sidewalk. Another worker rode a jackhammer that bucked him like a mechanical bull. The sunlight streaming through the shutters made my head feel even worse. I pulled the slats closed.

I turned toward the ostrich egg alarm clock next to my bed. The red numbers blinked 4:00. The power must have gone off during the night. I grabbed my watch off the nightstand. It was ten o'clock.

I swung my feet off the bed, hopped down, and threw on a pair of jeans and a sweatshirt that lay in a wad on the floor. Simon had talked about visiting a chapel at a neighborhood Methodist church that morning. With the press stalking him, visiting his own church was out of the question. He hoped to slip out of his house somehow.

The pastor of the Methodist church offered instructions on how to find an out-of-the-way entrance that would lead Simon to the chapel. If I hurried I could be there in ten minutes. I didn't know if Simon had made it, or whether he would still be there if he had. The least I could do, though, was try to support him on what was going to be the most difficult day of his life. I grabbed a bottle of Tylenol out of the bathroom and downed three of them dry on my way out the door. As I jogged through the parking garage to my car, I shoved a stick of gum in my mouth.

When I pulled my Camaro into the massive parking lot of the Methodist church complex, there was not a single car in sight. The grounds stretched for acres. The campus consisted of a number of gray stone buildings that, judging by the slightly different shadings of the stone, had been added one at a time over the years. According to Simon's description, the side entrance I was looking for would have a small, blue awning over a single door. I walked a considerable distance and peeked around a number of corners before I finally spotted it.

The morning was already developing into the type of shining March day that forces Yankees to admit there is something for which they envy Texans. Unfortunately, my hangover was brutal, and the bright sky was not helping. By the time I ducked under the awning and walked down three narrow steps to the door, my head was pounding and my forehead damp with sweat.

The building seemed to be the original sanctuary, although it was now dwarfed by a newer, more elaborate structure a few hundred yards to the west. The door and doorknob appeared to be original equipment. I grabbed the knob and turned it. It wobbled so dramatically that I wondered if it would fall off in my hand. The door swung open.

Inside the dim building my eyes took a few moments to adjust. I was in a hallway so narrow that two adults could not have walked side by side. The cinder-block walls were glossy gray, and a strong scent of fresh paint suggested a recently applied coat. The air was cool and damp. The ceiling was so low that a tall man would have to duck to avoid the teardrop light fixtures hanging, like stalactites, from the ceiling every fifteen feet or so. As I made my way down the hall, my sandals tapped on the slate floor. The sound echoed off the close walls, reinforcing the unsettling sensation that I was moving deeper and deeper into a cave.

I rounded a corner and arrived at a medieval-looking oak door with a darkened brass plate above it, engraved with the words *Martinson Prayer Chapel*. I turned the knob and eased it open. It creaked as it swung. I half expected Vincent Price to greet me on the other side.

The lights in the chapel were off, but the small room was illuminated in an ethereal way by sunlight that streamed through red and yellow and blue stained-glass windows. The chapel consisted of two short rows of straight-backed pews, separated by a narrow aisle. In the front, a plain wooden altar looked out over the room from the middle of a raised chancel. The altar was quite old, judging by the number of nicks and gashes that were apparent even from where I stood.

Near the front, in a hooded blue sweatshirt, Simon sat hunched over in the middle of a pew. I watched him for a few moments. He couldn't have made himself look any smaller, sitting alone in that tiny chapel. He didn't move. I assumed he was praying and hadn't heard the door creak. As I watched him sitting there, I wondered whether he'd fallen asleep. I decided that my coming had been a bad idea. Just as I turned to leave, I heard him say my name.

By the time I turned back, he was standing in the aisle. He pushed the hood back and motioned toward the pew. "Will you sit with me?" The filtered light from the windows glinted off the bald crown of his head, and for an instant his face seemed to glow.

"Of course." As I approached him, he stepped to the side and let me slide into the pew. He sat next to me.

He smiled. "Like my outfit? The security guards created a diversion in the driveway, as if we were going somewhere in the car. All of the cameras scrambled to get in position. I took off out the back door and jogged over here."

"You should be a politician."

He nodded toward the beat-up altar. "This place doesn't seem to get much use, but it must have at one time."

"If not for the stained glass, it would have all the ambience of a dungeon."

He chuckled. "You hit it on the head. It's the stained glass. You could put stained glass in a parking garage, and it would still create the sense that God was nearby. These sorts of prayer chapels aren't built much anymore. They're viewed as an unnecessary expense. It's a shame. Sometimes people need a small, quiet place."

I wasn't qualified to respond, so I simply sat there looking at the altar.

He rubbed the top of his head. "You know, I just kept praying that it would never come to this—that something would happen—that God would never actually make me choose. After all, how can it be that a man could end up in this situation? Now it's here, though, and I've got to choose: God or Kacey. Today is my last day with one of them."

I turned and looked at him. In the bending light, in profile, the lines in his forehead and around his eyes were deeper, sharper than I'd ever noticed. A shadow cut a dark, diagonal slash across his cheek. "I don't believe that this is your last day with either God or Kacey."

"No offense, but it doesn't matter what you believe. That's part of the cruelty of it. It doesn't matter what you believe, or the anchormen, or the preachers, or the editorial writers, or the people watching on television, or whoever. It's not a group decision. It's just God and Kacey and me. No one else decides; no one else pays."

I touched his arm. "You're a good man, Simon. When

I met you, I was prepared to believe you were a fraud. But you're not. You love God and you love Kacey, and I just don't see how that can result in something bad. I hadn't prayed since I was a kid, but I've prayed very hard for you for the past few days. I don't know if that's a plus for you or not, but I know I'm not the only one."

He put his hand on mine. "You judge me too kindly because you don't know me well. I have more flaws than you think. But I appreciate your prayers. I really mean that. I'm glad you're praying. I guess that shows that every situation, no matter how bad, has some good results." He loosened his grip. I wanted to reach out and pull his hand back to mine.

"Somehow, something good will come of this," I said. "It's just hard for us to see right now. Something like this could not happen to a man like you unless there was a purpose."

"I'll agree that any purpose in all of this is hard to see."

"So what are you going to do?"

"Please don't ask."

"I'm sorry. That was presumptuous of me."

He rubbed the back of one hand with the fingertips of the other, as if trying to scrub something off it. "It's all right. I just can't make myself tell you. If I'm going to die inside, I may as well die only once. That will be tonight."

A tear edged from the corner of his eye. He wiped it with a finger. At that moment I knew what decision he'd made.

"I'm sorry. I'm sure I'm less of a man than you thought."

"No, you're one of the few real men I've ever met." My neck grew warm.

He looked into my eyes and smiled. "Thank you again." He clapped his hands on his knees. "Well, I've been praying all morning, and we can't stay here all day, I suppose." He stood up and stepped out into the aisle. I got up and followed him down the narrow hallway and out of the church.

Outside Simon shaded his eyes with his hand and gave a slight wave. "I'll see you tonight."

"Yeah, I'll see you."

He jogged down the sidewalk and around the corner of the building.

When I arrived at my car, I opened the door and slid into the driver's seat. I put the key in the ignition, but rather than starting the car, I leaned my forehead against the steering wheel. Kacey was going to die, and as horrible as that was, it wouldn't be the end. For Simon it would only be the beginning. He was about to enter a living hell. There must be something that I could still do to change things.

I had to try.

CHAPTER
SEVENTEEN

THE DALLAS CELEBRATION WAS such an obvious target for terrorists that the City of Dallas had imposed its strictest security measures ever for a nonpolitical event. We checked everything from the limousine drivers to the microphones. I had to be at the Challenger Airlines Center hours before the program to coordinate with the police and the FBI.

After my talk with Simon at the chapel, I went home to change clothes, then grabbed a burger at a drive-thru. As I was chewing my burger, I had an idea. On my way to the auditorium, I stopped at FBI headquarters for a talk with Michael Harrison. After much cajoling, I left his office with an envelope in my pocket.

In it was something that I hoped might save Kacey.

As I drove toward the arena, I called to check on Simon. Elise answered the phone and told me that he'd remained in his room the whole afternoon. She'd been even more protective of Simon than usual lately, at least when it came to me. She didn't volunteer to let me talk to him, and I didn't press the issue.

I spent the afternoon at the arena working with the police and the volunteers from local churches. Around 5:30 I stepped outside for some air. The day had been unusually warm for late March, and many of the pedestrians around the arena wore shorts. I looked down at my black wool pants and shook my head. At some point the law of averages had to work in my favor in the appropriate-dress department, but it sure hadn't yet. Under the circumstances, though, I couldn't work up a good lather of self-criticism. My inadequacies didn't even register on the radar screen of the day's problems.

I walked around the outside of the arena, and the evening was so calm that the south breeze barely ruffled the sleeves of my white cotton blouse. In contrast to the tranquil weather, the streets surrounding the auditorium had the feel of a circus just before the lions enter the ring. Television technicians marked their territories. They prowled the sidewalks next to vans from which satellite dishes extended like giant ears. Reporters moved in tight semicircles around blue-jeaned camera operators whose hoisted equipment protruded from their shoulders like metal appendages. Occasionally, the more prominent reporters received last-minute grooming from attentive assistants—a licked finger applied to an errant hair, a calculated tug on a crooked tie. Scattered amongst the packs of television workers, street vendors barked at roaming herds of pedestrians, hawking everything from hot dogs to "Free Kacey" buttons.

In its morning editorial, the *Times* speculated that, except for Neil Armstrong's first step on the moon, Simon's statement might be watched by a higher percentage of people with television sets than any live event in history. The *Dallas Morning News* reported that the best seats to the celebration were bagging up to a thousand dollars on Internet auction sites. Several prominent Las Vegas bookies speculated that it was one of the most heavily wagered events of all time. Kacey was the prohibitive favorite.

My phone beeped in my pocket. It was one of the security guards I'd assigned to ride with Simon in a police-escorted convoy. They were five minutes from the arena. I jogged back into the building and hurried toward the underground tunnel where I would meet his car.

When Simon arrived, I opened the door for him. He stepped out, carrying his tattered Bible, and wiped a palm on his leg.

I touched his elbow. "How are you doing?"

"Is there a room somewhere for me? This is the first time we've done anything here since it opened. I don't know my way around." His eyes moved from me to the car to the tunnel entrance and back to me. He shifted his Bible from one hand to the other. I needed to get him to a place where he could at least try to calm down.

"I'll show you." I turned and headed into the building, looking over my shoulder at him as I walked. "Where's Elise?"

"I asked her to ride over with the others."

When we arrived at Simon's dressing room, I punched the security code into the keypad and swung the door open. Although I'd checked the room out earlier, I went in before Simon and took another look around. It was the size of a very large family room but furnished in a hip, minimalist way—black and white leather and stainless steel. Along the wall to the left, a long narrow table overflowed with an assortment of fruits, cheeses, breads, cold cuts, and soft drinks. A door off the wall to our right opened into a cavernous marbled restroom. I opened the door and checked it out. Everything appeared in order. Looking at Simon in his yellow chamois shirt and corduroy slacks, I wondered how out of place he must feel in this room that was obviously designed with rock stars in mind. I wasn't sure this was the setting he needed right now.

I nodded toward the table of food. "Can I get you anything? Have you eaten?"

"Thanks, but I haven't had much of an appetite." He sat on the couch, crossed one leg over the other, then uncrossed it and leaned forward with his elbows on his knees.

I got a bottle of water anyway and handed it to him. "Would you like some company? I can stay."

"Thank you, but no." He smiled. "You haven't stopped praying for me, have you?"

"No. I doubt if my prayers do you much good, though."

"You say things like that too often, Taylor. You're a better person than you think."

I felt my neck warm and wondered how he could give my feelings even a moment's thought under the circumstances. I didn't know what to say, so I turned to leave. Then I paused and turned back to him. "Have you got your cell phone with you?"

"Yes."

"If you need anything, just call."

"I will."

I remained in the doorway for a moment.

"Is anything wrong?"

I stuck my hand in my pocket. "On the way over here this afternoon, I stopped off to see Michael Harrison. I hope you won't be angry. He gave me something that I thought might help you tonight." I handed him the envelope.

He tore off the corner. Kacey's ring dropped into his hand. He moved it from hand to hand, then held it in his palm and caressed it with his index finger.

"I thought about it and knew that if I were in your position, I would want something of Kacey's with me. It just seemed wrong that you didn't have it tonight. Michael agreed."

"I'd like to be alone." He spoke without taking his eyes off the ring.

I turned and walked out the door.

TWO HOURS LATER Elise and I stood at the stage entrance as Simon's song leader, Donny, prepared to pull back the side curtain and walk out to address the crowd. Every seat in the auditorium was occupied. A hum of voices rose from the floor of the auditorium. The stage was surrounded by more cameras than the playing field at the Super Bowl.

Elise looked at her watch, then at me. "One of us had better go get him."

"Let's give him a couple more minutes."

Under the circumstances the program was drastically shortened. The plan was for Donny to lead the auditorium in one song and a prayer for Kacey and Simon. Then Simon was to go out onto the stage and make his statement. No one knew what he intended to say, whether Kacey would live or die. A father's nightmare was a television producer's dream.

At exactly 7:30, a network person in a black silk shirt held his headset tightly to his ear. He pointed at Donny and held up three fingers, then two, then one. He waved toward the stage. Donny pulled the curtain aside and walked to the podium. No band played, no choir sang. The only backdrop was a video screen picture of a giant Jesus, floating in a cloud, his arms outstretched to the audience.

When Donny arrived at the glass pulpit, he said, "I would like for you to join me in a song and then a prayer for Kacey and Simon Mason." With no musical accompaniment, he began to sing "I Need Thee Every Hour." Jesus disappeared from the video screen, replaced by the words to the song. At first the crowd seemed taken aback by the lack of musical accompaniment, so Donny sang solo. Soon a few voices near the front joined in, then more. Before long the auditorium filled with the most sorrowful and beautiful a cappella song I'd ever heard.

About halfway through the song, just as I was about to go get him, Simon walked up. He clutched his Bible in one hand. Elise hugged him. The rings beneath his eyes seemed even darker than they had before. I wondered whether he'd slept at all the past few days. He looked my way and nodded but said nothing.

When the singing stopped, Donny's prayer echoed through the silent auditorium: "God of love and mercy. Two of your children, Simon and Kacey Mason, are suffering. They have done nothing to deserve this horror that evil men have thrust upon them. We ask why, oh God, you would allow this to happen? How long will you tolerate the senselessness of terrorism? How long will you wait before exacting a price for evil? Bless Simon and bless Kacey, Lord. Hold them near in this time of trial. Guide them and give them strength. In the name of Jesus, we pray. Amen."

Donny looked toward the stage entrance. When he saw Simon, he turned and walked off the opposite side, leaving the stage empty. The picture of a floating, open-armed Jesus flashed back onto the screen overlooking the stage.

Simon cleared his throat, then stepped through the stage curtain and walked toward the podium. The silence was cavernous—not a whisper, not a cough. Not a sound of any sort except the clip-clap of Simon's loafers on the wooden floor. If I closed my eyes, I could imagine the auditorium empty.

When Simon arrived at the pulpit, he placed his Bible on it and looked out at the crowd. His eyes focused on the front rows, then swept deliberately around the auditorium, taking in each section. He opened his Bible and lowered his eyes to it, standing perfectly still for at least a full minute, as if reading a passage. Then he picked something off the page—something that caught the light and glimmered. It was Kacey's ring.

He held the ring between his thumb and index finger, then closed his hand around it. Looking at the audience he tightened the hand into a fist. With his other hand he reached into his pocket, pulled out a handkerchief, and wiped his forehead. He placed the handkerchief on his Bible and leaned forward slightly.

"Many of you have sons and daughters of your own." Though he spoke softly, his words boomed off the walls of the auditorium. "You know what the love of a parent is—what it feels like—how you can love your child so much that it hurts physically. I know that you understand how much I love Kacey." The muscles in his forearms flexed beneath his rolled up sleeves as he gripped Kacey's ring with one hand and the podium with the other.

"I have given much thought and prayer to my faith and to Kacey during the past week. In fact, I have thought and prayed about nothing else but Kacey and my faith. I have determined that there is one thing that I simply cannot do, no matter the consequences." Opening his hand, he lowered his eyes to Kacey's ring. He ran his other hand over his head. Gripping the pulpit again, he looked back at the audience.

"I cannot let my little girl die." He coughed and cleared his throat, "So I am here tonight to tell you that it is no longer my belief that Jesus is the Son of God."

A woman in the back of the auditorium wailed. A wave of whispers washed from one end of the building to the other. Cameras flashed.

Simon lowered his eyes again to the ring. He leaned toward the microphone. "Jesus is not the Savior of the world, and Jesus is not my Savior."

The woman wailed again. Simon's shoulders sagged. He bowed his head and stood there in front of the crowd.

A man near the front shouted, "God knows you don't mean it, Simon! And we do too!" Someone near the man applauded. Others near him clapped, also. The applause edged tentatively back from the front few sections but never took hold. Soon the auditorium was silent again.

Without raising his head, Simon picked up his handkerchief, turned, and walked back across the stage, leaving his open Bible on the pulpit. The auditorium exploded again with camera flashes.

As Simon approached the stage curtain, our eyes met. He shook his head from side to side and tightened his fist around Kacey's ring, then he brushed past us and walked down the corridor toward his dressing room.

No one around me moved. I glanced at Elise, and she turned away. In the audience, some stood at their seats; others sat, but no one moved to the aisles. A smattering of whispered conversations built to a low rumble.

I looked at the pulpit. It was wrong for Simon's Bible to be there. Wrong for him to leave it behind. I pulled the curtain aside and hurried onto the stage, half running toward the pulpit. As I reached the center of the stage, many in the audience looked toward me, perhaps thinking I was going to speak. When I arrived at the pulpit, I looked down at the open Bible. The page was dog-eared, and Simon had underlined a passage in red. I picked the Bible up and shoved it under my arm. Then I turned and ran off the stage.

When I reached the stage entrance I met Elise's eyes, but I moved past her without a word. I expected her to follow and hoped this wouldn't turn into some sort of petty competition to determine who could best comfort Simon. I decided that if she followed I would let her go to him, and I would stay outside his dressing room. As I walked down the long corridor, I looked over my shoulder. She wasn't behind me.

Despite the pain I knew Simon was feeling, I was relieved at what he'd done. A faith that required the sacrifice of a child made no sense to me. At least Kacey had a chance now. He had given her that. We could only wait to see whether the kidnappers would keep their word. If Simon could get her back, the worst would be past. He could begin to put his life and his ministry back together. Surely God would be merciful enough to forgive him and help him with that.

As for the immediate future, it never occurred to me that the remainder of Simon's evening would involve anything more than sitting and waiting—waiting to see if Kacey would be freed. After all, this was a kidnapping, and that was the logical next step.

But the world that surrounded Simon Mason was a big one, and logic didn't always rule.

CHAPTER
EIGHTEEN

APPROACHING SIMON'S DRESSING ROOM, I slowed to a walk. I had no idea what I was going to say to him, and it made sense to give it some thought before I knocked on the door. Roger Ferrell, a security guard with whom I'd had a brief fling a couple of years earlier, stood up from a folding chair next to the door, raised a giant hand, and waved. I'd stopped using Roger for security jobs as soon as I got to know him. He was too irresponsible to be trusted. Somehow he had convinced someone at the Challenger Airlines Center that he was up to the job of guarding Simon's dressing room. That hadn't pleased me, but it wasn't my call.

Roger's charcoal sport coat barely contained his arms, which were as big around as my thighs. "Tough night, huh, Taylor?" His jacket flapped open for an instant, exposing a holstered Beretta M9. Between his body and his gun, he had plenty of firepower. I hadn't dated him for his brains. I wondered whether he'd somehow miraculously developed the sort of judgment that ought to accompany a weapon with that much muzzle velocity.

As I stopped and pondered what to say to Simon, I nodded at Roger's gun. "You like your Beretta?"

He opened his coat and drummed his fingers on the pistol. "It's what the Army Rangers use. You know your guns, don't you?"

"I had a good teacher. You weren't Special Forces, were you?"

"No, but I think it's cool. Once you shoot one of these, you don't want to use anything else."

I rolled my eyes.

"What?"

"Nothing." I motioned toward the door. "Is he in there?"

"Just went in. Looked pretty grim. I heard his talk—" Before he could finish, something slammed against the door from inside the room.

"What the—" Roger grabbed the knob and rattled it.

Something crashed, and glass broke. Then someone shouted. I couldn't make out the words or the voice. "Simon?" I shouted.

No response. Something slammed against a wall again, this time farther into the room.

I punched in the code and tried the door. Nothing happened. Roger looked at me. I pointed to the door. "Break it down."

He stepped back and heaved his body into the door. The frame shattered, and Roger fell face first into the room, shards of splintered wood raining to the floor around him. I hopped over his legs, took two steps, and stopped.

A huge, fat man in a red Hawaiian shirt had Simon pinned against the opposite wall. The man's back was toward us, and his massive legs were spread and bent at the knees as he pressed his weight down on Simon. In his right hand he clutched a broken juice carafe. The jagged glass glinted in the light, so close to Simon's face that the last remaining drops of orange juice dripped down his cheek. Something red was also dripping. It looked like blood. It mixed with the juice, streaking Simon's face red and orange. A vein in the side of Simon's neck glowed bright purple as he strained to prevent the man from driving the glass into his face.

To my left Roger popped up on one knee, pulled out his Beretta and pointed it at the Hawaiian shirt. I spun and swung my fist down on his forearm. It was like hitting a granite counter top. "You'll kill them both!" Pain shot up to my elbow, but I moved the gun far enough off line to stop him from firing.

Wheeling back to my right, I ran straight toward the fat man, brought my leg back, and kicked it up between his spread legs. He howled and dropped to his knees. The carafe flipped into the air, descended end over end, and crashed to the floor next to his feet.

Just to Simon's left was a glass end table with a brushed-stainless-steel lamp. I lunged toward it, grabbed the lamp by its neck, and yanked the cord from the wall. Turning, I took two giant steps and swung the lamp like a baseball bat. The thick base of the lamp slammed into the side of the fat man's head. He collapsed from his knees to his stomach and lay there like a beached whale. Within seconds, a bloody red circle was expanding on the floor beneath his hair.

I stood over him, sucking air in rapid gulps, and waited. His eyelids fluttered, but he didn't move. I kicked his side hard. He still didn't move.

By that time Roger was on his feet, mouth hanging open.

"That Beretta of yours would have gone right through him and killed Simon too," I said.

He looked at his gun, then back at me. When he finally moved his lips, he said, "I think you killed him."

I tossed the lamp to the side. "Maybe."

"Is he breathing?"

"I don't know. And frankly, right now, I don't care." I turned and looked at the shattered door. "How did that guy get in here? Where were you?"

His face flushed. "I don't know. I only left for a few—"

Before he could complete his sentence, a man in a green golf shirt and thick black glasses stuck his head through the opening where the door used to be.

I scowled at Roger, then pointed at the man at the door. "Simon Mason's been attacked. Go find a doctor."

The man looked at the shattered pieces of door frame scattered around the floor. When he saw the man at my feet, his face turned pale. He covered his mouth with his hand.

I waved my arms at him. "I said, get a doctor. *Now!*"

He turned and ran away.

Roger took a step toward the door. "I'll go too. We don't even know who that guy is."

I scowled again, knowing full well why he wanted more than anything to get out of that room. He'd probably been under the stairwell with some young thing when elephant man slipped into the dressing room. "Okay, but leave me your gun." I motioned toward the Hawaiian shirt. "I left mine in a locker behind the stage, and I'm not taking any chances on this guy waking up."

He handed me his Beretta and hustled out the door. I shoved it in the waistband of my pants and walked over to Simon. He had slumped to the floor, his back still to the wall. The front of his shirt looked as if he'd fed it through a paper shredder. I grabbed it and ripped it away. An ugly red gash ran diagonally from his shoulder halfway across the middle of his chest. The bleeding was slow, and the cut did not appear to be deep. I wadded his shirt and pushed it onto the center of the wound. "Can you hold this?"

"Yeah." He moved his hand up and took the shirt. "How is it? It hurts like heck."

"I think it looks worse than it is. It's a shallow cut."

He lifted the shirt and tried to look. "Ouch. That was a mistake." He smiled and pushed it back onto the wound, then leaned his head back against the wall.

For an instant a picture of Dad lying in the dirt flashed through my mind. Without thinking, I dropped to my knees and pressed my head against his.

He pulled back from me, eyes wide, but I didn't care. I must have looked frantic. When he saw my face, his expression softened. "I'm okay."

I've thought many times about what he said next, because it showed that he already understood me better than he should have. He squeezed my arm. "Don't worry, Taylor. I'm not going anywhere."

He shifted his weight and tried to stand. His leg gave out beneath him. "I was afraid of that. I twisted my ankle when that guy put his weight on me." He put his hand to his head and slid back against the wall. "I'm a little dizzy too. Basically, I guess I'm a total wreck."

"Just stay where you are. You don't need to go anywhere. Help will come to you." I pulled my cell phone out of my pocket and speed-dialed Elise. "Simon's been attacked in his dressing room. Get some help and get over here."

"Attacked? Who?"

"I don't know. He's hurt. Just get over here as quickly as you can." I hung up and turned to Simon. I motioned toward the fat man on the floor. "Do you know him?"

"Never seen him before. Blond hair—not exactly your classic Arab terrorist."

"Could be just a nut." I got up, went over to the table against the other wall, and pulled a bottle of water out of an ice bucket. I took it to Simon and twisted off the top. "Need a drink?" I handed him the bottle.

He took a gulp.

"How did he get in?" I asked.

"I don't know. He was hiding in the bathroom. I didn't hear him until he was on me. I was lucky to grab his hand. By the way, remind me never to make you mad."

I smiled. "You've had some day. How does it feel to be the most threatened man in America?"

He touched the cut on his chest with his fingertips and winced. "It doesn't matter, as long as they let Kacey go. Do you think they'll keep their word?"

"Yes, I do."

I went over to where I'd dropped his Bible and picked it up. Stepping back over the Hawaiian shirt, I held the Bible out to Simon. "You left this on the pulpit."

"I left it there on purpose."

"You shouldn't have. What you did tonight . . . I want you to know that I think you're very brave." I hadn't told a man that since the night my father died.

He waved his hand in the air and laughed. *"I'm* brave? You're the one who laid out Godzilla over there."

"I was lucky his back was turned. He would have been too big for me to handle." The Bible still in my hand, I turned my back to the wall and slid down beside him.

He handed me the bottle of water. I tipped my head back and took a long drink.

"I don't know why I fought so hard to live. Thirty seconds before he attacked me, all I could think about was how much I wanted to die."

I gave him back the bottle. "Life is funny. We can take it pretty lightly until it's about to be snatched away. Most people just want to know that when they die, they're doing it for something that's worth it." I nodded toward the Hawaiian shirt. "Letting him slice you in two with a juice bottle doesn't qualify."

He poured water on his hands and rubbed them together to wash the blood off. Without looking up he said, "You've got an awfully good head on your shoulders for someone so young."

My face became warm. "It seems as if I've never felt as young as I should."

Still rubbing his hands together, he looked at me out of the corner of his eye. I changed the subject.

"The police will be here any minute. I guess we'll both be answering some questions. Here, give me that water." I took the bottle and poured water onto his torn shirt, then gently wiped the blood and orange juice from his face. "There, now you'll be ready for the photographers. They'll be right behind the police."

"Oh, great. I can't wait." He tilted his head back against the wall. "You know, the guys who took Kacey, I would like to kill them. Every one of them. I want to do to them what you did to this guy."

I shook my head. "I'm glad you don't have the chance."

"What?"

"I said I'm glad you don't have the chance." I set the Bible on the floor and pulled my knees up to my chest. "I know what I'm talking about. I killed a man once for revenge."

"You're telling me you murdered someone?"

I took a breath and let it out. "Yes. The man who was responsible for my father's death."

"That was self-defense, not murder. I read the clippings on the Internet before I contacted you."

"It was murder. He was too hurt even to stand up. He begged me not to kill him. I pointed the gun at his head—not six inches away. I pulled the trigger. It was an execution."

"I don't care, Taylor. He deserved what you did to him. That's justice, not murder." He put his hand to the side of his head. He probed it with his fingertips and winced.

"That's what I told myself for a long time. Maybe it's true. All I know is that I still think about him. I see his face at night. It's no small thing to take another person's life. My father told me that once, and he was right." I nodded toward the floor. "I'll think about this guy too, if he dies. Right now I can't muster any sympathy for him, but later I'll wish I had. So, for your sake, I'm glad you don't have the chance to kill them. It wouldn't help."

"Maybe not, but it sure seems like it would feel good." Simon touched his hand to his head again. When he pulled it away, it had blood on it. "That guy really busted my head against the wall." He chuckled. "I'm bleeding from so many places, I guess I didn't notice this one."

"You were busy."

"Yeah, you too. Thank you for what you did. I guess I picked the right security chief." He took a drink from the water bottle. "Things are beginning to ache. I suppose that's a bad sign."

I smiled. "It's a better sign than being dead."

I had the strangest feeling sitting there with him, just the two of us. Of course, Hawaiian Shirt man was there too, but he didn't count for much right then. For the few moments before half of Dallas swarmed the room, it was really nice—a good kind of warm—despite the circumstances. I'd lived my entire adult life without experiencing what it was like to have a real man want me around. But Simon was a real man. A good man.

He wanted me there; I was sure of that.

I didn't want it to end.

Within seconds, though, police and medical personnel poured through the door. The reporters wouldn't be far behind. A few moments later the medical personnel were nudging me away from Simon as they knelt to work on him. I stood and walked to the door. When I turned back toward him, he was still looking at me. He smiled and gave me a thumbs-up just before a medical technician dabbed something on the cut on his chest.

A policeman standing by the shattered door motioned for me to come over. I would be answering quite a few questions, I was sure. Nevertheless, I felt strangely relaxed as I walked over to him. Despite how awful the day had been, for the first time in a week I had the feeling that things were going to get better.

CHAPTER
NINETEEN

AT 4:30 THE NEXT morning, Simon's cell phone rang. Thinking it was an alarm clock, I reached over to slap the snooze button, but my hand hit only air. I had the strange sensation that I was sitting up. I opened one eye and saw Simon several feet away from me, stretched out beneath a white sheet. I jumped to my feet, then realized where I was and slumped back onto the daybed next to the window.

We were at Parkside Hospital where Simon was admitted the night before. Among other things, he had suffered a concussion from bouncing off the walls of the dressing room. The police determined that the guy in the Hawaiian shirt was an auditorium employee who believed Jesus had instructed him to assassinate Simon. I was relieved to hear I hadn't killed him, although he was now looking forward to several reconstructive facial surgeries. All to be performed in a prison hospital. That seemed fair to me.

The doctor asked that someone wake Simon every two hours because of his concussion. I volunteered so quickly that the doctor raised an eyebrow. Trying to keep myself from blushing, I sighed, as if bearing a heavy burden. "Security," I said. He gave me an understanding nod before instructing a nurse to wheel in a daybed. Fortunately, Simon was half asleep during the exchange.

Simon's phone rang again. I checked my watch's alarm: ten minutes to go before his next wake-up. After the second ring, he rolled over but his breathing remained steady and slow. I must have been half asleep too, because it was the third ring before it occurred to me that it could be the kidnappers. The working assumption had been that information from the kidnappers would come by e-mail since that was the way it had come before, and e-mail was so difficult to trace. The FBI had thrown an electronic blanket over Simon's e-mail account. But who else would be calling him at 4:30 in the morning? I swung my bare feet back onto the floor, grabbed the phone off the stand next to Simon's bed, and shoved it toward his face. I nudged him. "Simon, your phone. It might be them."

He sat upright, then grabbed his head and moaned. He slid back down to the pillow but still managed to take the phone and hold it to his ear. He pushed the button.

"Hello," he said, his voice raspy. He moaned again, more softly this time.

The next couple of minutes consisted of a series of short questions and grunts, with Simon still lying on his back. He motioned to me to get him a pen and paper. I dug them out of my purse, and he scribbled notes. "Heberlin or Heverlin Road? Look, I'm in the hospital. How can I—okay, okay, I've got it."

He flipped the phone shut and laid it on the nightstand. "Kacey's alive."

I wanted to wrap my arms around him. Instead, I walked over to the bed and patted him on the arm. "I'm so happy for you."

"If I could sit up, I would hug you."

He wasn't going to have to raise that issue more than once. I leaned over and put my arms around his neck. "How's this?" I enjoyed the hug so much that I might still be there clutching his head to my chest if he hadn't squeezed my arm and tried to sit up.

I pushed him back down. "You'd better stay where you are."

"I can't." He leaned up on his elbow. "I have to go get her."

"Get her? Where is she?"

"They're taking her to a spot in the country, outside Elgin, Illinois. Three-thirty tomorrow morning. I've got to be there to pick her up. They said no police or they will kill her." He reached over the side of the bed and searched for the buttons that controlled the recline. "How do you get this stupid thing to sit up?"

I held down one of the buttons with my finger. The bed hummed and gyrated until he was semi-reclining, with his knees elevated slightly above his feet. "I don't get it," I said. "Why don't they just let her go—drop her off someplace? This sounds like a trap."

"They said they don't trust the cops. They think the police would kill her for propaganda."

"Kill her? That's crazy."

He leaned forward and massaged his temples.

"Does it hurt?"

"Yeah, but I'll be okay." He lay back on his pillow and closed his eyes. "We're not dealing with people who think normally here. They sound crazy because they *are* crazy."

"You told them you're in the hospital. Don't they understand that you can't possibly go to Illinois?"

"They don't care about my problems. They said I could go or I could send someone else, but no police and only one person." He sat up and slid his legs over the side of the bed. When his feet hit the floor, he grimaced.

I reached out and steadied him. "Look, even if your head would let you go—which it won't—you've got a sprained ankle. It would be impossible for you to handle crutches, fly to Chicago, and then drive a car to some place out in the country. You'd kill yourself, and who knows what they'd do to Kacey if you didn't show up? Let me go get her."

He shook his head. "I can't. This is dangerous. Who knows what they'll do? You said yourself it might be a trap."

"Think about it, Simon. It wouldn't matter if you were in perfect health. You still couldn't go. There are two FBI agents sitting outside the door of this room, and at least fifty reporters outside your window. There is no way you could leave the hospital and fly to Chicago without anyone knowing it. You'd never get out of the parking lot."

He lay back on the bed again. "I hadn't thought of that."

"You're paying me to think. I guess this is one of the rare instances in which you got your money's worth."

"You're laughing, but I'm not paying you nearly enough for what I've gotten so far."

"Don't you remember my catchy motto? 'Dallas business's choice for tough security assignments.'"

"Quit joking, Taylor. This is dangerous. I don't want anything to happen to you."

After hearing that, I would have walked through fire for him. "You don't really have any options. Give me the directions. You can pay me more money later if it will make you feel better." I stuck out my hand.

He rested his head on his pillow. "My head is spinning. I think I might throw up."

I picked up the metal bedpan off the cart next to his bed and set it beside him. "I've thrown up in front of plenty of people. Don't worry about it. As soon as you're feeling okay, though, I'll be needing those directions."

CHAPTER
TWENTY

I NEVER IMAGINED WHAT it would be like to be in a slasher movie until I found myself creeping along an Illinois farm road at three o'clock in the morning in a rented SUV. The sky was impenetrably black. A light mist coated the windshield, and I hit the wiper switch every minute or so as I squinted to see the low-slung wooden road signs.

I found Heberlin Road without much trouble. Then I wound for miles through fallow cornfields, leaning forward and peering through the windshield each time I came to a crossroad. The odor of fresh manure seeped in through every seal and gasket of the SUV.

The road narrowed as I got farther from the highway, and I wondered if the pavement would eventually end, leaving me fender deep in mud. I crossed a gravel farm road that ran parallel to a wooded creek. The SUV rattled over a narrow wooden bridge. As I came off the bridge, two rows of craggy cedar elms, one on each side of the road, arched their limbs above me like disfigured old men stretching up to touch fingertips. The creepy canopy made the asphalt road even darker and harder to follow.

For company I turned on the radio. An oldies rock station was playing a Doors song, "People Are Strange." It was too spooky. I smacked the knob and turned the radio off. If I was this jumpy, I figured that Kacey must be nearly catatonic. I resolved to worry more about her and less about me.

About ten feet after I emerged from the trees, I came to another farm road, which veered to the right. I squinted through the mist and made out the sign: Woodburn Road. This was the spot. I turned onto the road, pulled up about a hundred yards, and stopped. My headlights reached far enough to show me that the road continued for about another hundred yards before curving around some trees and out of sight to the left. I looked at my watch: 3:15. Pulling the glove box open, I felt for my Sig Sauer, checked the magazine and the safety, and placed the weapon on the console beside me.

I killed the headlights but debated whether to leave the car running or turn it off. If I left it running, my chances of making a quick getaway were better, and I would have the additional benefit of heat. Although the temperature outside was well above freezing, the air was damp and chilling. On the other hand, if I turned the engine off, I had a better chance of hearing someone coming. After a few seconds I realized that if the kidnappers wanted me dead, I had almost no chance of staying alive anyway. They chose the ground. They undoubtedly saw me coming. In fact, they were probably watching me at that very moment. No reason not to do what made me most comfortable. I left the car running and turned the radio on, keeping the volume low.

The oldies station was playing "Yesterday." A tiny light on the bottom of the rearview mirror cast a dim glow onto the console, illuminating my pistol. I kept glancing at the gun, as if worried that an unseen hand might reach into the car and snatch it away. I checked over my shoulder every thirty seconds or so. The trees behind the car were close enough that an elephant could have snuck up on me. Nevertheless, I found comfort in maintaining some semblance of a three-hundred-sixty-degree lookout.

The station played the *Kill Bill* version of an old Zombies song, "She's Not There." Just as I turned to look out the back window again, something smacked against the roof of the SUV. I jumped about a foot, grabbing my Sig Sauer from the console and looking from window to window, checking the perimeter as best I could. Nothing but darkness.

I hit the radio button, killed the heater, and listened. The only sound was the hum of the idling engine. I released the safety on my pistol. My brain inventoried all of the harmless things that could have hit the roof: a small tree branch carried by the wind, a dead bird . . . I really couldn't think of anything else. It wasn't very windy, and what were the odds on the bird? My stomach rumbled. If I wanted to find out what *did* hit the car, I would have to get out and look. That struck me as a stunningly poor option.

I continued to listen, my neck swiveling to cover the windows. I cursed the inventor of the SUV—way too much glass. Several old camp stories found their way forward from my brain's deep-storage vaults. Each one seemed to end with a dead girl near a car on a dark country road.

Ultimately I determined that sitting in the car and torturing myself over whether something was on the roof was worse than getting out and dying. I gripped the door handle.

Should I ease out and peek above the SUV, or throw the door open and jump clear before turning to look? I opted to jump clear and spin back toward the car as soon as I got my feet under me. That way maybe I could at least create an advantage with surprise.

I braced my right foot against the base of the console and stared at the door. Leaning toward the door handle, I prepared to yank and dive. My head was so close to the handle that my breath fogged the chrome. I hadn't realized how silent the night was until I began to imagine how loud it would sound when the door handle popped the door open. I would have to move fast. I tightened my grip on the handle and counted: one, two . . .

Something banged against the passenger door behind me. Before I could react, the door swung open. I spun and pointed the gun—directly at Kacey's face. She lunged into the front seat and threw her muddy arms around my neck. Then she pulled back. "Where's Dad?"

I reached across her, slammed the door shut, and punched the auto lock. "First, where are they?" I scanned the windows.

"They drove off as soon as they let me out on the other side of the creek. I waded the creek and ran through the woods."

"Are you okay?"

"Yeah."

I stretched my arm across her chest and pushed her back to the seat. "Hold on." I threw the SUV into reverse and mashed the accelerator. We squealed backward all the way to the intersection, where I spun the car ninety degrees, threw it into drive, and stomped the accelerator again.

Kacey looked at me, eyes wide. She grabbed her seatbelt and buckled it.

We shot back across the bridge. I checked her out of the corner of my eye. She was clutching the sides of her seat. "Don't worry, I know how to do this. I have no intention of letting those guys change their minds."

A few minutes later, when we were back on the highway, I eased my foot off the accelerator and handed her my cell phone. "Punch eight. It's a speed dial to your father's hospital room. He's waiting to hear from you."

"Hospital?"

"Only a hospital could have kept him away. He's had some excitement too, but he's fine."

As she talked to Simon, I pulled the Internet directions to the Elgin Police Department from my pocket and held them up to the tiny dome light. We were just a few minutes away. I wadded the paper and dropped it on the floor.

When we pulled into the police station parking lot, Kacey flipped the phone shut. I turned off the car and looked at her. Her clothes were coated with mud, and she was missing a shoe. Her face and neck were covered in wet brown splotches. I reached out and gently lifted her left hand. A filthy gauze bandage covered her missing fingertip.

"I'm fine."

I wiped mud from above her eye. Suddenly I began to cry.

She touched my hand. "I said I'm fine. Are you?"

I waved my hand in the air. "Oh, I'm okay. I do this sometimes. I'm just really happy that you're alive." I swiped my sleeve across my face, spreading mud over the bridge of my nose. Her hug had made me nearly as muddy as she was.

She laughed. "We look great. I sure hope there are photographers in there, don't you?"

"You bet. Let's make our entrance." I pulled the key out of the ignition.

As we walked in the front door of the station and headed for the intake desk, clumps of mud dropped behind us like bread crumbs. The cop at the desk was hunched over a computer, typing. He looked up at us and his mouth dropped open.

"This is Kacey Mason," I said. "Have you got a shower around here?"

Without taking his eyes off us, he picked up his phone and punched a button. "Sam, you're never going to believe this."

BY THE TIME WE got cleaned up, several Chicago police officers and two FBI agents had arrived at the station. They questioned us for a few hours, trying to gather every detail that might matter to their investigation. Then they put us on a charter flight to Dallas with the understanding that Michael Harrison and the Dallas FBI would want to talk to us again after Kacey saw her father.

Late that afternoon Kacey and I turned the corner into Simon's hospital room. She ran across the floor and practically leaped into the bed. Even from the doorway I could see him wince as she squeezed against the wound on his chest. He gritted his teeth but didn't complain. His face was pure joy.

"I was scared to death I'd never see you again," he said. Are you all right?" He looked at her finger. She had a new bandage, compliments of a Chicago police doctor.

"I'm fine. The doctor with the police said the terrorists did a good job on it. I asked him if he thought I should send them a thank-you note."

Simon's eyebrows narrowed. "You're really okay?"

"If you're worried that I'm going to be messed up or something, I'm not. I've got half a finger less than I had a week ago, but I'll survive."

"I just want you to know that you don't have to act tough around us."

"I'm not. I was terrified, believe me. I was asleep when they did the finger. They had a doctor—or he acted like a doctor—and he put me out. I didn't know what they were doing. When I woke up part of my finger was gone." They gave me pills for the pain, so it wasn't as bad as it could have been.

"Did they . . . do anything else to you?"

"Don't worry, Dad, they didn't touch me. They hardly even talked to me." She pointed at the bandages that were visible above the neck of his hospital gown. "How about you? I heard you got beat up."

He smiled. "He mugged me. Taylor laid him out, though."

"I heard that too." She smiled at me. "Pretty cool, Taylor. Can you teach me to do that?"

I looked at Simon, and he nodded. "Sure. I can teach you some things. You're a good athlete. You'll learn quickly."

She held up her hand. "Good, because nobody's ever going to do this to me again."

CHAPTER
TWENTY-ONE

THAT EVENING THE HOSPITAL staff brought another bed into Simon's room. Kacey and Simon went to sleep around 10:30, but not before Simon received a call from the vice president expressing his and the president's happiness that Simon had gotten Kacey back safely. The Dallas police stationed two officers outside the door to replace the FBI agents. They both poked their heads around the corner when Simon cleared his throat and said, "Hello, Mr. Vice President."

Once Simon and Kacey were settled for the night, I drove to my apartment to clean up and get something to eat. When I returned, I pulled the only available chair over from the nurse's station and joined the policemen outside Simon's door. The chair was straight-backed, and the night promised to be long and uncomfortable. I nodded my appreciation when a sympathetic nurse with a round face and a green hair clip offered me a pillow and cotton blanket.

The hospital wing was a rectangle with rooms around the outside and a nurse's station in the center. From where the policemen and I sat, we could see the television at the nurse's station but could not hear the sound. A flushed anchorman with unnaturally thick black hair sat in front of a photo of Kacey. He held several sheets of typing paper in his hands and stared earnestly into the camera. His lips moved above a scrolling ticker that carried a quote by the Elgin police chief. One of the nurses reached up and changed the channel, then changed it again. Simon and Kacey were the story on each station.

I scanned the hallway that surrounded the nurse's station. Everything was quiet. The hospital had a no-media policy on patient floors, and I hoped their security team knew how to enforce it. It didn't require much imagination to envision photographers trying all sorts of schemes to reach Simon's room. I didn't want a tussle with the press tonight.

Just before 1 a.m., my chin was drooping to my chest when I heard the elevator doors open at the end of the hall. I shook my head and sat up. Elise stepped out of the elevator and looked around. When she spotted me, she frowned and strode down the hall, her blonde curls bouncing. By the time she was within ten feet, she was already wagging a finger and scolding me for not calling her to let her know what had been happening. I glanced at the door to Simon's room and held a finger to my lips. "Keep it down; it's a hospital." She lowered her voice but continued her assault.

The reality was that with all of the excitement I just hadn't thought to call her. Neither had Simon and Kacey, a circumstance she chose to overlook. In the meantime Elise didn't say a thing about my risking my life to bring Kacey back. Since Simon and Kacey were asleep, Elise made me promise to tell them she would return in the morning. She pivoted on the heels of her tan loafers and stomped back to the elevator.

I squeezed out a few hours of neck-wrenching sleep and was happy to hear Simon rustling in his bed around six. He must have hit the call button, because within a few minutes a nurse clip-clopped into the room pushing a white cart. I heard her say something about a fever. The doctor entered soon after, and before long they had Simon hooked up to an intravenous antibiotic for an infection in his chest wound. The doctor made it clear that Simon would not be leaving until the next day. Maybe not then.

Thankfully, the antibiotic worked quickly. Later in the morning Simon was already feeling much better. He stood up on his crutches and made his way into the bathroom to shower and shave. Kacey stayed with him, while I made a run to their house to pick up snack food, playing cards, and clothes.

By the time I got back, Simon had his bed in the sitting position. The three of us ate junk food and played spades on his food tray. If it weren't for the antiseptic smell of the place, it would have been like a little party in the den.

Around noon Elise stuck her head in the door. She saw me and scowled. Did the woman make a conscious decision to do that every time she saw me, or had it become a reflex thing, like breathing or blinking? When she saw Kacey, she ran over and wrapped her arms around her. "Are you all right, honey?"

"I'm okay. Dad's the one who's a mess."

Simon gave her a weak smile. "What a wimp, huh?"

"You shouldn't be sitting up, should you?" Elise looked at me as if I'd planned every ill-conceived moment of Simon's after-care program. "I would think they should both be resting, not playing cards."

I shrugged and popped a cheese puff into my mouth.

Kacey jumped in. "It was my idea, Elise. We were getting bored just lying around. Dad doesn't want to watch TV."

"Too bad. You're on every station."

Simon shot her a look. "I'm sure someone is recording it for us. I want to spend some family time before we have to deal with the media."

Elise flushed. "Of course." She was off to another great start with Simon.

I wasn't eager to listen to another of their awkward conversations, and this time I had a way to save her. "Oops, that reminds me—" I dug my hand into my purse—"I brought my other phone for you. It's loaded with music." I handed it to Kacey.

Her face brightened. "You're a life saver—I guess that's literally true, right, Dad?"

"You better believe it."

Elise moved to the corner of the room and sat in a chair directly beneath the television, which hung on brackets from the wall. She folded her arms across her chest and may as well have clucked her tongue. I tried hard not to wish for the television to fall.

Kacey put the phone's earbuds in and hit the menu button. "I guess I'll be buying a new one of these," she said. "The kidnappers weren't courteous enough to gather my things for me before they put a bag over my head."

I smiled. "My stuff's probably not exactly what you would choose to listen to, but I've got some Beatles and some other oldies you might like. If you've never heard The Doors or Blind Faith, you might like them. My dad listened to them when I was growing up, so I kind of got hooked."

"I like guitar."

"Then you're going to love the Allman Brothers Band. I've got a lot of their stuff."

Elise stood. "There are a million reporters outside. They're asking when someone's going to talk to them."

We all turned and looked at her. She sat back down and put her hands in her lap. "I was just wondering if you ought to say something to them, Simon.

Michael already read them a statement from the FBI's perspective."

Simon shook his head. "I'm not talking to them today; and probably not tomorrow, either."

"Of course not today, you're sick. But perhaps we could issue a written retraction of your statement at the Challenger Airlines Center. That would buy some time until you're ready to do a live retraction. Letting people share in your reunion with Kacey might help put the whole thing in perspective, help them remember what was at stake."

Kacey cocked her head. "What statement?" She looked at Simon, her brow furrowing. "What did you say, Dad?"

Elise put her hand to her mouth. "Hasn't anyone told you? It's been all over the news. I assumed you knew."

"She hasn't seen any TV," I said. "We were with the police the whole time in Chicago. I didn't think it was my place to discuss it with her."

Simon set the cards on the food tray and frowned at Elise. She froze. "We haven't had a chance to talk about it yet. Thank you for bringing it up, though."

Kacey looked at Elise, then at Simon. "What are you guys talking about?"

Elise got up and walked over to Kacey. She knelt beside her and put her hand on her knee. "Honey, your father had to—"

"Elise, please run downstairs and let the press know that I'll talk to them tomorrow morning, here at the hospital," Simon said. "If you go right now, you can probably catch them before they scatter for lunch."

Elise blinked several times. "Oh, you changed your mind?"

"Yes, I changed my mind."

Her shoulders sagged. "I understand. I'll take care of it." She picked up her purse and walked out the door.

Despite the way Elise treated me, it was still painful to watch her interact with Simon. I could understand why he wouldn't want to encourage her feelings for him, but I didn't see why he couldn't be a little gentler.

Kacey put the phone in the pocket of her jeans. "Is anyone going to tell me what happened?"

I got up. "I'll go out in the hall for a while so you two can talk."

Simon waved me back. "No, please stay."

"All right." I sat in the chair Elise had vacated, crossed my legs, and wondered why he wanted me to be part of such a personal conversation.

Simon picked up the deck of cards and shuffled them in his lap. "The kidnappers made a demand. I had to meet it to get them to let you go. Did they say anything about it to you?"

"No, they barely talked to me the whole time. What was the demand?"

He continued to shuffle the cards, his fingers moving more and more quickly.

She reached over the bed rail and touched the deck. "I think the cards are shuffled now, Dad. What was the demand?"

He set the cards back on the tray. "I had to deny my faith in Jesus, and I had to do it on television."

She blinked hard. "And you did it?"

"Yes."

She rubbed the back of her neck. "Elise said something about the Challenger Airlines Center. What was that about?"

"That's where I made the statement, at the celebration in Dallas on Saturday. Listen, you're alive, Kace. That's all that matters."

"It's *one* thing that matters; it's not *all* that matters."

"It's all that matters to me."

Kacey got up and went to the window, which overlooked a courtyard where many of the media had set up their equipment. She stood with her arms folded for a few moments. Then she turned and faced Simon. "I want to talk to the press."

"What?" Simon looked at me.

I raised an eyebrow but kept my mouth shut.

He propped himself on one elbow. "Why would you want to talk to the press?"

"I had a lot of time to think during the past week. There was nothing else to do but think and pray and be scared. One of the things that I thought about was how I would describe what happened if I ever got out of there. I would like to do that."

"I'm not sure that's such a good idea," Simon said. "You don't have any experience with the press. What would you tell them?"

"That the guys who took me are cowards; that they didn't have the guts to talk to me or let me see their faces. I want to tell them how they did this." She held up her bandaged hand. Her face flushed. "I want to tell them what kind of people did this to me—and to you. I'm sorry, Dad. I'm so sorry." She covered her face with her hands.

"Oh, Kace, come here." He held out his arms. She moved over, sat on the edge of the bed, and leaned into him. After a few moments he eased her away and looked her in the eye. "You don't have anything to be sorry about. You didn't do anything. They're criminals. They did this; you didn't. I don't ever want you to feel a bit guilty about this." He pulled a tissue out of a box on the end table next to his bed and handed it to her. "I still don't think talking to the press would be such a good idea, though."

I stood up. "I think you should let her do it."

They turned and looked at me as if they had completely forgotten I was in the room. I'd never seen Simon really lose his temper, but I figured that if he was ever going to, this was a likely time. He tilted his head to one side and frowned. An explanation was called for, and fast.

"Kacey went through a lot. If she wants a chance to tell people about it, I think it's great. Number one, it could help her deal with everything. Number two, any chance we get to expose these people for what they really are, we should take it. Besides, what's the press going to do to her? She's a twenty-year-old kid who just survived a kidnapping. They'll handle her with kid gloves." I waited for the explosion.

Simon leaned back on his pillow. He ran his hand over his head and squinted at the ceiling. After a few moments, he turned toward us. "You're right, Taylor. If you really want to do this, Kace, I'm okay with it."

I exhaled.

"I do want to."

He wagged a finger at her. "It won't do any good, though, if you lose your temper. Can you keep your composure? Because if you can't, this will be a disaster."

"I can do it."

"We'll have to clear this with Michael," I said. "We need to be sure it won't affect the investigation. There may be information Kacey shouldn't give out. I'll call him."

I pulled out my cell phone and made the call. Within minutes I had the okay from Michael. His only instructions were that she stay away from information about specific locations and times.

Simon picked up his cell phone and punched a number. "Elise? Kacey is going to talk to the press with me tomorrow, so you can let them know. I'm sure that will increase attendance by about fifty percent." He paused. "Yes, nine o'clock would be great. Then I can check out of this place. Thanks."

He clicked off the phone. "She's going to set something up outside if the weather is okay. There isn't any place in the building that could handle all the press for something like this."

Simon turned to Kacey. "Just be yourself and you'll be fine. I'll sit next to you. If you decide you want to stop at any time, you just let me know and I'll end it. We can go over some things tonight, like sitting up straight and keeping your voice loud enough."

Kacey nodded. "I guess I'll stay at the house tonight. This cot isn't the most comfortable."

"By yourself? I don't think that's going to happen. Why don't you stay with Meg?"

"I'll have to wake up early to get ready for the press conference. I won't have all of my stuff at Meg's." She looked at me. "Can you stay at our house with me tonight?"

I was taken aback and didn't know what to say. Simon spoke up. "It's okay with me if it's okay with you."

"Well, you've got the police outside your door here, Simon, so I guess you'll be fine. Sure, I'd be happy to do it. Kind of like a sleepover, right, Kacey?"

She pumped a fist. "Yeah, let's trash the place."

"Funny," Simon said.

Kacey got up. "I'm going to the bathroom." She grabbed the overnight bag I brought her, walked around the corner, and closed the door behind her.

Simon looked at me and raised an eyebrow. "What do you think?"

"She's got a lot of guts. You'd think she just came back from a tough day at school rather than a kidnapping."

"Do you think this is real, or is she holding things in?"

I shrugged. "She's got to be holding things in to some extent. No one could be this composed after something that traumatic. I guess only time will tell whether it's a problem. She's a tough kid. She's got a lot of her father in her."

He rolled his eyes.

"I'm no psychiatrist, but I think that telling the story at the press conference might help her."

Kacey came out of the bathroom. Her dark hair was brushed and shiny, and fell smoothly over her shoulders. "How's this look for my first press conference?"

I smiled. "You're gorgeous. But you might be getting ready a little bit early since it's not until tomorrow morning."

Simon frowned. "If you're going to do this, you have to be serious. If you go out there acting like a princess, they'll eat you alive."

"Give me some credit, Dad."

He smiled. "I do, honey. Believe me, I do."

CHAPTER
TWENTY-TWO

THAT NIGHT KACEY AND I stayed up too late watching a romantic comedy. We ate buttered popcorn and ridiculous amounts of candy. The next morning we were up early fixing her hair for the press conference. I never had a brother or sister, and I have to admit that it was one of the most fun things I'd done in ten years. We laughed like middle-school girls and spent a full hour picking out just the right outfit. We settled on a blue skirt, white camisole, and yellow crop sweater with three-quarter length sleeves. She was gorgeous and wholesome, the perfect combination for the press conference. I was sorry when it was time to leave.

The hospital was shaped like a giant letter *E,* with the long back side of the *E* in front. The press conference would take place in a courtyard tucked between two of the wings. The building faced east, and in the early morning sun most of the courtyard was in the shade. The air was dry and cool as Kacey, Elise, and I walked out the side door. Behind us a nurse pushed Simon in a wheelchair, his sprained ankle wrapped in a blue boot. Kacey slowed her pace and shivered. I had on a white cotton cardigan, which I took off and draped over her shoulders. We laughed about instantly ruining the "look" we had worked so hard that morning to create.

"I'm not sure I'm really cold," she said. "It might just be nerves. Besides, I'd rather freeze to death than cover up my outfit. This is my first time on TV." She pulled the sweater off and held it out to me.

"You'll be fine. You're going to be sitting in the shade, though, so why don't you hang onto the sweater in case you need it?"

She rolled it up and carried it in one hand.

At least a hundred reporters, photographers, and camera operators stood on the grass, chatting in clusters of two and three. A rope separated them from a long folding table set up with a row of microphones. When the press saw Kacey and Simon, the photographers surged toward the rope, clicking as they moved. The television camera operators slung their cameras onto their shoulders and trotted to the front, twisting and slide-stepping for position.

Elise stopped next to the table and spoke to a tall, freckled young man with thick red hair. He wore a hospital ID card on a cord around his neck. He pointed toward the rope and shouted, "Let's keep this organized, folks. We'll have a few minutes for photos. Then Reverend Mason and Kacey will take some questions."

Elise tapped him on the shoulder. He leaned over and she whispered in his ear. He straightened and opened his mouth to speak but stopped, wrinkled his forehead, and leaned over to her again. They whispered some more. Then he held up his index finger. "Correction. Only Kacey will be taking questions today. Reverend Mason will have a separate press conference tomorrow morning at his house." Elise had talked it over with Simon, and they had agreed that Kacey was likely to have an easier go of it if Simon was not fielding questions with her.

It was the time of year in North Texas when spring nudges the remaining traces of winter from the landscape for good. Azaleas lined the back wall of the building with dark pink flowers. The lawn was still mostly brown and dormant, crunching beneath our shoes as we walked. But sprigs of new Bermuda poked through here and there, speckling the courtyard with patches of green.

I stopped short of the table while Kacey and Elise made their way to the folding chairs. They sat behind the microphones. The nurse wheeled Simon next to Kacey. On the press side of the rope, the hospital had lined up ten rows of chairs in a setting that reminded me of a high-school assembly. Within a few minutes the physician who had examined Kacey hurried across the lawn in his blue scrubs to join them at the table.

After an introductory statement by the doctor and about ten minutes of questions for him, Elise held up a hand. "Dr. Sabbathia has to get back to surgery. Thank you, doctor." He nodded and got up. "Now, Kacey will take a few questions. Please remember that she's just a college student and she's been through a lot more in the past week than most of us will ever experience."

Several reporters shouted questions at once. "Let's take them one at a time, please," Elise said. She pointed at an Asian woman in the front row.

"Kacey, I think I speak for everyone here when I say that we're happy you're safely back with your father." Several people clapped and before long all of the press members were standing and applauding.

Kacey blushed. As the applause continued, her eyes filled with tears. She turned to Simon and wrapped her arms around his neck, which led to even louder applause and some whistles. Flashes flickered all over the lawn.

Elise beamed. I knew that she was picturing the next morning's front page—either that, or some future family photo with herself in the mom's slot.

I mentally kicked myself for being catty.

When the applause quieted and everyone took their seats, Kacey dabbed at her eyes with my sweater. She looked at Simon and he nodded. She leaned forward to one of the microphones. "Thank you very much. I've always heard that the press can be tough, so I wasn't expecting that." That drew a laugh. She leaned into the mike again. "I guess people are too hard on you guys." They roared.

The red-headed hospital employee stepped over to me and nudged me with his elbow. "You'd think she was a pro."

His blue-green eyes had some sparkle, and he appeared to be about my age. I nodded. "She's pretty amazing."

"By the way, I'm Jason." He held out his hand. I shook it. His handshake was so limp it was like squeezing a peeled banana. That was that.

"I'm Taylor," I said as I turned my back on him.

When the laughter quieted, the reporter went on. "Can you tell us what happened the night of the kidnapping, Kacey?"

Kacey folded her hands on the table in front of her. "I was in a car with Cheryl Granger on the way to O'Hare. A few minutes after we left the Mid America Center, our car pulled onto a side street. It was very dark—no street lights at all. Another car swerved in front of us, and we had to stop. Three men in black ski masks jumped out of the car in front of us and pulled open the doors on both sides of our car. Two of them dragged me out. They grabbed me under the arms and carried me to the front car where they pushed me down into the floor of the back seat. Someone put a hood over my head, and I couldn't see what happened to Cheryl. I was glad to hear that she's all right."

A short, stocky man in the second row leaped to his feet. "Did they hit you or abuse you in any way?"

"They were very rough and held me on the floor by putting their feet on my back. Then, of course, there's this." She held up her left hand. In a move that was savvy beyond her years, she'd removed the bandage in the hospital room so the stub of her finger was exposed above the second knuckle. The skin flap over the stub was discolored. Several reporters gasped.

Others shouted more questions. Elise pointed to an older woman in a cotton dress in the back row.

"Where did they take you, Kacey?"

"I don't know. We drove for what seemed like a long time. At first I tried to count the seconds in my head because I thought it might be important to know how far we'd driven. That didn't work so well. I was still on the floor. It was very dark. I was too scared to keep counting. I prayed a lot, and that calmed me down some.

"Then the car stopped. They dragged me out again, just like the first time. They shoved me onto the floor of another car. Then that happened one more time after we had driven a while longer. At one point the hood was pushed so tightly against my face that I couldn't breathe. When I tried to move, the one with his foot on my head pushed me down even harder. That was the scariest time of all. I thought I was going to suffocate." She took a drink from one of the bottles of water the hospital had lined up on the table.

I watched her closely, amazed at her poise. The reporters were captivated. Though we were outside, there was complete silence except for the occasional chirping of a single bird in a tree near the building. Every eye was on Kacey as she set the bottle back on the table—every eye, that is, except Simon's. He stared down at his hands. A vein in the side of his neck had grown larger and larger as she described the way the kidnappers manhandled her. I wasn't sure how long he could take this.

"I was able to move my head enough to find a space where I could get air," she continued. "Finally the car stopped. They pulled me out again. They squeezed my arms so hard that I have bruises right here." She pointed to her upper arm, just beneath her shoulder. "They carried me down some stairs into the basement of a house or a duplex or something. They took the hood off my head, and there was a man waiting there. He was tall and thin and wearing a mask just like the rest of them. They pushed me down on a couch. The tall one stuck a needle in my arm. Then everything went dark."

"How did they do that to your finger?" This from a man in the back.

"When I woke up, I was lying in a small bed, with just a sheet and a thin yellow blanket. Two masked men stood over me, looking down at me like I was some sort of insect in a jar. That was another really scary moment. I wasn't in any pain yet, though. I guess because the anesthetic hadn't worn off. They didn't say anything about my finger. They just stared at me. That was when I cried. I thought for sure they were going to kill me. The first time I saw what they had done to my finger was when I lifted my hand to brush the hair from my eyes. I think I passed out then."

"So they cut your finger off while you were knocked out?"

"Yes. I didn't know what had happened until I actually saw it."

A young reporter in the third row with a notepad in his hand jumped up. "After that, did they treat you well?" Several in the crowd groaned.

Kacey paused for a few seconds until everything was quiet again. Then she leaned to the microphone. "We got off to such a bad start that it's tough for me to be objective about that one."

The lawn exploded with laughter. The reporter turned bright red and sat down. I looked up at the highest floors of the hospital. Patients stood at a number of the windows. In one window a woman held a hand-scrawled sign that read: *We love you Kacey.*

Jason nudged me again. "What timing! Is she too young to run for office?"

I didn't respond.

A trim, pretty woman with auburn hair stood up in the back row. I turned to Jason. "She looks familiar. Do you know who that reporter is?"

"Katie Parst, *Dallas Morning News.* She's the one who's been doing the series about organized-crime extortion rings in Dallas. She's a gutsy one."

"Kacey, what did they tell you about why they took you?" Parst said.

Kacey sat up straight. "That's the thing I most wanted to tell everyone. These men who took me, they didn't talk to me at all. They just motioned with their hands. Any time they were in the room, they wore masks. I never saw their faces. I saw their eyes, though. Their eyes were cold. Every one of them had cold eyes. Not one showed even an ounce of sympathy for me. I was nothing to them. Not a person, not even an animal. I was just something they needed to use to get what they wanted, whatever that was." She shivered and pulled my sweater over her shoulders. She glanced at me and I gave her a thumbs-up. My sweater had managed to ruin her outfit after all. She started to laugh, then quickly covered it by coughing into her hand.

No one spoke for a few seconds. A man cleared his throat. An older gentleman in a cardigan sweater, standing off to the side, raised a finger in the air. "Kacey, what are your feelings about what your father had to do to win your freedom?"

Simon's back stiffened. He placed his palms flat on the table.

Kacey brushed a hair from her face and spoke deliberately. "My dad is a great man, and I don't mean just because he's kind of famous." A few of the reporters chuckled. "He loves me and would do anything for me. I feel awful that he had to do that, because I know he would never have done it to save his own life. But he did it for me. He made an incredible sacrifice to save my life." She turned toward Simon. "I love you, Dad." Tears edged down her cheeks.

Simon put his arm around her shoulder and hugged her. Flashes fired.

Elise stood. "Kacey's been through a lot. That will have to do it for today. Thank you everyone." She walked over to Kacey and helped her with her chair. Kacey stood, then leaned over and hugged Simon again. The flashes flickered again. A nurse moved toward Simon, but Kacey grabbed the handles of his wheelchair and pushed him back across the lawn toward the hospital door. The entire press corps stood and applauded. I applauded too.

"They love her," Jason said, as I turned to follow them.

"We *all* love her," I said over my shoulder.

CHAPTER
TWENTY-THREE

IMMEDIATELY AFTER THE PRESS conference, Simon checked out of the hospital. Since my car was already there, I volunteered to drive Kacey and him home while Elise finalized the preparations for Simon's press conference the next morning.

"I'll bet you're glad that's finally over," I said as I pulled away from the curb.

Simon leaned forward and rubbed his forehead with his fingertips. "It's not over. It will never be over."

I eased the car to the stop sign at the hospital exit and looked at him. His face was pale and his forehead was damp with sweat. For a second I wondered if he was having a heart attack. I glanced in the rearview mirror.

Kacey already had her ear buds in and was scrolling through songs on my phone.

"Are you all right?" I said to Simon in a low voice.

He didn't answer.

"Simon, are you okay?" I checked the mirror again. Kacey was still focused on the phone.

"I'm all right. Please just get me home."

We drove in silence. Each time traffic would allow, I checked on him from the corner of my eye. His color returned to normal, and he didn't seem ill. Nevertheless, I was relieved when we pulled into his driveway.

Simon and Kacey lived in a modest ranch-style house in North Dallas, largely hidden from the road behind a thicket of live oaks. If not for the unusually large lot, the house could have been picked up and dropped into any number of neighborhoods in the area without attracting attention. Simon's sister, Meg, met us at the door in blue jeans and a cotton sweater. More thickly built than Simon, she had the same engaging smile and an air of matronly authority that was reinforced by slightly graying hair.

Meg had prepared a brunch of scrambled eggs and bacon and had a bowl of batter for French toast waiting by the stove. After kissing Simon and Kacey, introducing herself to me, and then kissing them again, she helped Simon to a chair. She leaned his crutches against the wall behind him. The rest of us sat at the table.

"Sadie will go crazy when she sees you two," Meg said. "Are you ready?"

Simon smiled. "I'll brace myself."

Meg left the room and a few moments later we heard paws scrambling on the tile. Simon's golden retriever, Sadie, burst through the doorway and practically leaped into Simon's lap, her tail wagging frantically. Simon winced when she bounced off his chest. She darted over to Kacey, licked her on the face a few times, then flew back around the table to Simon.

"Wow, she *is* excited to see you." I lifted a wedge of buttered toast to my lips, but before I got it into my mouth, Meg said, "Simon, would you say grace? Then I'll put Sadie in the laundry room so we can eat in peace."

I cleared my throat and lowered the toast back to my plate. "Sorry."

Meg waved her hand. "No need. Every family's different. We pray before we eat. Simon?"

He sat with his head bowed over his plate. "Will you do it, Meg?"

She cocked her head to the side and looked at him. He still didn't raise his eyes from his plate. "Of course." She bowed her head. "Lord, we thank you for bringing us all back together safe and sound. And thank you for this food. Amen."

Kacey grabbed a grape and popped it in her mouth. "Aunt Meg's the best at table prayers. Gets right to the point and then shuts it down. Some people would have dragged that one out forever with everything that's happened to this family in the past few days."

Meg wagged a finger at her. "You think you can say anything now, just because you've been kidnapped?"

Kacey laughed. "You got that right. I figure I've got a get-out-of-jail-free card for at least a month for this one."

I had to appreciate a family resilient enough to joke about a kidnapping. I glanced at Simon. He was still leaning over his plate, swirling his fork in his eggs. Meg watched him, too, although she kept up a lively conversation with Kacey.

I needed to talk with Meg, and I had to do so before the day was finished. Because I needed some insights, and very clearly, Simon wasn't talking. Not to me. Not to anyone.

I SPENT THE AFTERNOON inspecting the house and neighborhood to develop a security plan. For the next few nights I intended to cover the front of the house from my car, parked just down the street. One of my security specialists would cover the back of the house. I'd checked with Michael Harrison, and the FBI believed that the security risk from terrorists had dropped dramatically since Kacey's return. As Michael put it, the terrorists already got what they wanted from Simon. They had moved on.

According to the FBI, Simon's biggest risk was that some deranged Christian would take a shot at him—similar to what happened at the Challenger Airlines Center. Fortunately, that was a much easier risk to prepare for, since it would come from an amateur.

Toward the end of the afternoon, I rang Simon's doorbell. Meg answered the door. She took my hand and steered me to the left into the living room, a long rectangle at the front of the house that extended about twenty-five feet from a bay window and built-in love seat. The walls were pale green and framed in white dental molding. The room was sparsely furnished, except in the center where a few tightly grouped pieces surrounded a carved stone fireplace. In short, it was an otherwise beautiful, southern room that looked as if it had been furnished in about fifteen minutes by a forty-four-year-old widower.

Meg led me to a cream-colored upholstered couch that faced the fireplace. We both sat. She smoothed a wrinkle out of her sweater with her hands. "I'm worried about Simon," she said in a low voice. "He spent the whole afternoon in his room."

I crossed my leg. "I noticed that he's been quiet since we left the hospital. Was he sleeping? He must be exhausted."

"No, that's what worries me. He was talking. I heard him through the door. He wasn't on his cell phone, because he left it on the kitchen counter."

"Are you sure Kacey wasn't in the room with him?"

"She was watching a movie in the family room."

"Maybe he was praying."

She turned her palms up. "Maybe. But the one thing I heard him say several times was Marie."

I smiled. "I think that's a good thing."

"What do you mean?"

"Has he ever told you that he talks to Marie?"

She raised an eyebrow. "You mean *his* Marie?"

"Yes."

"No, he's never told me that. Is that what he told you?"

"Yes. He talks to her when he's got a problem that he's working through." I thought back to our conversation in the Azure Hotel. "He asked me if I thought he was crazy."

"I don't mean any offense by this, but I'm surprised he told you something like that when you've only known him for a short time."

"No offense taken. I was surprised too. He was under a huge amount of stress at the time. I think he just wanted someone to talk to, and I happened to be there."

She brushed at her sweater again. "Is there anything . . . going on between you two?"

I shook my head. "No."

"Would you like there to be?" She put her hand to her cheek. "Oh, my, that wasn't very subtle, was it?"

"I don't mind your asking. Honestly, I don't know."

"I see." She studied my face. After a few moments she clasped her hands in her lap. "Well, can you stay for dinner? I didn't have to talk to Kacey long to figure out that she idolizes you. Having you around can only help her, especially if Simon's not himself."

That was not what I expected. "I'd be happy to stay.

I'm planning on spending the night out front in my car anyway."

She put her hand on my arm. "I want to thank you for all you've done for Simon and Kacey. I understand you're a very brave woman. If it weren't for you, they might not be here at all."

"We've been pretty lucky. It could have been much worse."

"But because of you, it wasn't. God sent you to watch over them. I'm sure of that."

My eyes widened. "I'm afraid you've got the wrong woman, Meg. I can assure you I'm not the type of person God would pick to be anyone's guardian angel."

She smiled. "You're forgetting that millions of people were praying for someone to save Simon and Kacey, and there you were. So God obviously did pick you. You're selling yourself short. You might not see that, but God can." She stood. "We'll be eating around five since we didn't really have any lunch. Please make yourself at home. You can come into the family room and watch television if you'd like. I think Kacey is still in there."

I got up and moved toward the front door. "Actually, I think I'll go back to my apartment and pick up a few things. I'll be back in about an hour, if that's okay."

"That's fine. Just come on in when you get back. You don't need to ring the bell."

As I walked to my car, I considered Meg's guardian angel theory. It made me chuckle, but something about it brightened my day too. I wasn't accustomed to thinking of myself in positive terms, so it was nice to know that someone else might.

I also thought about Meg's question: Why would Simon confide in me? And why would he let me into his inner circle so quickly? It would be different if he'd indicated a romantic interest in me. But he hadn't. I shook my head. Why did I constantly search for mysteries around every corner? After all, I was his security chief, and I'd probably saved his life. That should be enough to explain it. Nevertheless, I'd always been a realist, so as I pulled into the parking garage of my apartment building, I couldn't get past the sense that there was something about Simon I was missing.

CHAPTER
TWENTY-FOUR

AT DINNER SIMON ATE in silence while the rest of us made small talk. Every effort to include him in the conversation went nowhere. Afterward, we all moved to the family room to watch television while we devoured Meg's homemade chocolate chip cookies.

The family room and kitchen were one big room in the back of the house. The only thing separating them was a long, granite-top breakfast bar with low-backed stools on the family-room side. Both rooms looked out on the backyard through picture windows that ran nearly the length of the back wall, except where a bay window on the family-room side created a small breakfast nook.

Kacey and I sat on a tan leather couch facing the TV. Simon sat in a matching leather easy chair to our left, his ankle elevated on an ottoman. He thumbed through a copy of the *Sporting News* and occasionally glanced up at the television. Meg sat in an upholstered arm chair to our right.

The local news led with Kacey's press conference. The anchorman referred to her as "courageous" and "spunky" and ran a lengthy clip that included her clever answer to the question of whether the kidnappers treated her well. Meg laughed and patted her niece's leg. "You're a real star, Kace."

Without cracking a smile, Kacey said, "I'm just glad they used a clip from before Taylor's cardigan ruined my outfit."

I burst out laughing, and Kacey followed suit. Simon and Meg looked at us as if we were crazy. When Kacey finally stopped laughing, she said, "It also would have helped if the wind hadn't been blowing my hair in my face. I looked like I was swatting at a spider web through the whole thing."

"Don't be ridiculous," Meg said. "I didn't notice that, did you, Simon?"

I gave Kacey a sideways smile. "We could always rewind it and see."

"Great idea," she said. "Give me the clicker, Dad. We'll do an instant replay analysis of my hair during my first press conference."

Simon pointed the clicker at the television. "I can handle that. Here we go."

We watched the clip again, running it forward and backward over and over. Although Kacey's hair really hadn't been blowing around in any significant way, she'd taken a few swipes at loose strands as she spoke—just enough to provide us with several good laughs. Simon joined in with some good-natured teasing, and it was nice to see him come out of his funk for a few minutes.

After ten minutes or so, Simon put the clicker down. "Okay, that's enough. Seriously, though, Kace, you did a great job. And you looked just the way you usually do: beautiful. You gave some really clever answers too. Overall, I give it an A-plus."

"Spoken like a true dad." Kacey grinned.

"I really mean it. In this case I'd have said the same thing even if I weren't your dad."

Meg nodded. "He's right. You were great, Kace."

She stood and gave an exaggerated curtsy. "I want to thank you all, and most of all I want to thank my fans, without whom it would never have been possible."

Simon peeked around the corner of the magazine that he'd picked back up. "You already thanked all of your fans. We're sitting right here."

"Clever, Dad, clever." She pulled out the new cell phone she'd bought that afternoon and checked her text messages, then flipped it shut. "Rachel left me a message about the press conference. And she said she posted some pictures from their trip to Florida. I'm going to my room to check them out."

After a few minutes Meg got up. "I think I'll go sit with Kacey and look at Rachel's pictures." She headed down the hallway, leaving Simon and me alone in front of the television.

"One more press conference tomorrow morning and you may be able to get back to your life," I said.

He tossed his magazine onto the coffee table. "I suspect it'll be a couple of weeks before they decide we're old news and move on to something else. I'm looking forward to that."

"How's your ankle?"

"It hurts some. Not too bad, though. I've had sprained ankles before from basketball. It should heal pretty quickly."

I stood. "Can I get you some coffee? I don't think Meg unplugged it."

"Yes, thanks. Black, please."

I walked over to the kitchen and poured us each a mug. When I came back, I handed his to him and sat at the end of the couch, next to his chair. I took off my shoes and folded one leg beneath me. "What now? How long before you get back to preaching? If you ask me, you should take a long vacation."

He sipped his coffee but said nothing.

"Sorry, it's none of my business."

He set his mug on the end table between us. "It's not that it's none of your business."

"Well, then?"

"You have a gun in your car, don't you?"

I stopped my coffee mug just short of my lips. "Yes, why?"

He sat back in his chair. "Go get it, bring it in here,

and shoot me." He saw the expression on my face and shook his head. "I'm kidding."

I frowned. "Are you?"

"Honestly? Right now, I don't know."

I took a sip. The coffee was hot and stung my lip. I rested the mug on my knee. "Anyone would be depressed after all you've been through. It'll pass. You'll feel different a couple of weeks from now."

"I don't know about that."

"Maybe what you need is to get back to your usual schedule. Once you start preaching again, you'll feel better."

"Now *you're* kidding, right?"

"No, I'm not kidding. What made you think I was?"

He looked away. "I can't go back to preaching."

"I don't mean tomorrow—after you take some time off."

"I can never go back." He squinted as he spoke, as if someone were sticking a needle into his stomach each time he opened his mouth.

He seemed incapable of being objective, but I wasn't sure how to reason with him. "I don't understand. Why can't you go back? It's what you do. People need you."

"Who would ever listen to me again?" He crossed his arms. "Look, I'm guilty of the most public denial of Jesus since the Apostle Peter. Millions of people all over the world watched me turn my back on him. *I* wouldn't even listen to me now. Why would anyone else?"

"Simon, you are so wrong on that. You'll be more popular than ever. People will listen to you who never would have listened to you before. You were well known before, but now you're the most famous person in the world." I blew the steam from the top of my mug and took another sip, more carefully this time.

He shook his head. "It's not about being famous. It never has been."

"Okay, I didn't mean that to sound the way it did. What I meant was that you can reach even more people than you did before. Think of all the good you can do. Fame is a way to reach people. That's what you want to do, isn't it?"

"Even if I could reach them, even if they would listen, I could never preach again. I despise myself. How can I stand up in front of people and talk about faith when I've denied mine? I'm not willing to be that much of a hypocrite." He leaned back in his chair. "I'm a fraud and I don't see any way to get back to where I was. It's as simple as that."

I pulled my leg from beneath me and leaned toward him. "Don't say that. It's not true. You're a good man who was faced with an impossible situation. You did the best you could. No one could have done any better."

"You're wrong, Taylor. Others *have* done better—in many ways. I'm supposed to be this big-shot leader of the faith, and I've done more harm than I could ever make up for if I lived ten lives. You would be hard-pressed to find anyone who hasn't done better than I have." He stood up and hobbled over to the fireplace.

"Do you think you should be up on that ankle?"

"I'll sit back down in a minute. It doesn't hurt to get the blood circulating."

"If it had been your own life at stake, I imagine you would have been happy to die for your faith. But it wasn't your life; it was Kacey's. So don't judge yourself so harshly. You did what you had to do to save your daughter. There was no other way."

"I would do the same thing again. But that doesn't mean I don't despise myself for it. I basically told God that I love my daughter more than I love him. That's the bottom line."

I turned my palms up. "Is that a crime? Would you have felt better if you had let her die?"

"No, I would have despised myself for that too. You're not a Christian. You just don't understand how serious it is to do what I did."

"Hey, I'm a Christian. Just not a good one."

He put his hands in his pockets and leaned back against the fireplace mantle. "I didn't mean that. I just meant that you don't have the background to understand the seriousness of this."

"So what you're saying is that no matter what you would have done, you were doomed?"

"I suppose that sums it up."

"You're not being fair to yourself."

"Fairness has nothing to do with it. I'm just telling you how it is."

"So that's it? If you don't preach, what are you going to do?"

"I don't know. I'll have to think about it."

I set my mug on the end table. "You *should* think about it, and for at least a month or so. You may not feel the same after some time passes. You're still only a couple of days past one of the most extraordinarily difficult situations a man could ever face. This probably isn't the best time to make a life-changing decision."

He nodded. "That we can agree on. I'm not going to do anything rash. I'll give it some time. But right now, I don't see myself ever going back to preaching. Maybe I can coach or something."

A door closed in the hallway. A few moments later Kacey and Meg walked into the room.

Simon smiled. "Look who's back. Someone call the Entertainment Channel."

"What are you doing standing up on that ankle?"

He gave his sister a sheepish look, then hobbled back to his chair and sat down.

Meg put her hand on Kacey's shoulder. "As much as this one wants to act like Superwoman, she's not. We've been talking. She's feeling a little scared about staying in her room alone tonight. I offered to stay, but she doesn't think I would be much help if a terrorist crawled through the window."

Kacey smiled. "No offense, Aunt Meg."

"None taken, honey."

Kacey looked at me. "Would you mind sleeping in my room again tonight? You've got your own twin bed. It can be practically like home."

I glanced at Simon. "I don't know, Kacey. Your father

asked me to keep an eye on the outside of the house for a while. I can't exactly do that from inside your room."

"Can't some of your other people watch the house for a few nights?" Simon said.

"I suppose so, sure. But what about the tabloids? Don't get me wrong, but they could have a field day with a young single woman staying overnight at your house."

"Not if I'm here," Meg said. "I'll stay for a few nights until Kacey settles in. That should satisfy them."

Even though I tossed out some quick objections, in reality I was thrilled. "It's okay with me, if you're all right with it, Simon."

He shrugged. "Honestly, right now I don't care much what they write about me. If it will help Kacey, it's fine with me."

I ran my hand through my hair. "Let's see, I'll need to run home again to get some things for the night. I can be back in an hour. Robert is out front watching the house. I'll just ask him to stay. I'll have my cell phone on if you need me."

"We can put on some popcorn again." Kacey grinned.

"Nothing I'd like better."

As I walked to my car, I debated for about thirty seconds whether staying at Simon's house was a wise thing to do. For the rest of the drive home, I daydreamed about the impossible:

What it would be like to stay there for a long, long time.

CHAPTER
TWENTY-FIVE

THE NEXT MORNING AT nine, Kacey and I sat on the love seat in the living room and watched through the bay window as Elise walked out onto the front stoop. Simon followed her on his crutches. In one hand he held a folded sheet of yellow legal paper that contained the notes he and Elise had been working on since 7:30. Reporters and camera operators packed the yard, having jockeyed since before sunup for any open spot they could find among the live oaks.

At the front of the stoop stood a loudspeaker microphone flanked by several television microphones. Elise stepped up to them. "Thank you all for coming. Reverend Mason is going to make a brief statement.

I think you can understand that he and Kacey have been through a lot. As you can see, he's still dealing with his injuries. He will not be taking any questions."

Simon used one crutch to pivot over to the microphones. He looked out at the crowd and gave a weak smile. "Thank you for coming today." He unfolded the sheet of legal paper and looked at it for a few moments. Then he folded it back up and put it in the pocket of his corduroy pants. He cleared his throat and leaned toward the microphones.

"Saturday night I did something I felt I had to do to save Kacey's life. I understand that my actions and the things that I say can influence people who look to me for leadership in issues of faith." He leaned back on his crutch and ran his hand over his head. "I've never felt worthy of the attention my ministry received, but for whatever reason, God blessed me and my preaching. I've been able to reach many people around the world, and I hope I've done some good. But Saturday night I did something that I am sure caused great harm, aside from the effect it had on me.

"To save my daughter's life, I denied my faith in Jesus. I did it with words only; I did not deny him in my heart. I would never deny him in my heart. Jesus is my Savior. He died for my sins and the sins of all of us. He rose from the dead so that we can live forever. His love conquered evil. Evil men can still cause us pain. They can still do cruel things and cause us to suffer. They cannot, however, win. Because evil has already lost. Jesus made sure of that. Evil is doomed, in this world and in the next.

"I am sorry for what I had to say to save my daughter's life. But I am incredibly happy to have Kacey back home and safe." He paused and looked over at the window where Kacey and I were watching. Then he leaned into the microphone again. "Kacey is the light of my life. Jesus is the light of the world. Thank you again for coming."

He steadied himself on his crutches, turned, and walked back into the house.

CHAPTER
TWENTY-SIX

ONE THING I LEARNED from my experience with Simon is that boring is good.

After his press conference we had a brief interlude of easy, calming, boring, everyday life. During that time I learned that I love boring. In fact, I had been looking for it all of my life, I just didn't know it. In many ways boring is what family life is all about. It's the presence of loved ones and the absence of crisis—a real blessing, to my way of looking at things.

The day after Simon's press conference, every news channel in America ran a clip of him leaning on his crutches and saying, "Kacey is the light of my life. Jesus is the light of the world." Editorial pages applauded him for his handling of the ordeal. Then, just as he predicted, within a couple of weeks the news world moved on to the next big story. Even the tabloids lost interest, running only an occasional photo of Simon walking Sadie down the street, or Kacey sipping a latte in the Starbucks near the SMU campus.

Though the Mason story faded fast from the news, it had a much longer shelf life in the entertainment industry. Because of the publicity from the kidnapping, Simon's previously published books locked down six of the top ten spots on the *Times* nonfiction best-seller list. A handful of publishers and movie producers contacted Elise with proposals for books and movies about the kidnapping. Agents clamored to sign Simon and Kacey. The Masons would be financially sound, even if Simon never returned to preaching.

As for me, I grew comfortable in the Mason home. They kept asking me to stay longer, and I was happy to do it. Kacey and I loved being roommates. For some reason I was the only one who made her feel secure, and she seemed convinced that my life possessed an element of glamour that I, for one, had never noticed. I was concerned that she'd romanticized my self-defense capabilities to the point where she thought I was indestructible. I explained to her that if the huge man in the Hawaiian shirt hadn't had his back turned to me, he probably would have overpowered me. I'm not sure she believed me. I'm not sure I wanted her to. It's intoxicating to have someone look up to you. She was the closest thing to a little sister I'd ever had.

It soon became apparent that Kacey had more emotional fallout from the kidnapping than she'd initially let on. In addition to her fear of being alone, she had little appetite and was losing weight quickly. Despite her protests, Simon insisted she see a faith-based psychiatrist every week. In return for going, she extracted Simon's promise to let her learn to shoot a gun. He assigned me to teach her.

I bought her a used Ruger Mark III, twenty-two-caliber pistol. Since she'd decided to take a leave of absence from SMU for the remainder of the semester, we had plenty of time to practice. We went to the range three times a week. She quickly demonstrated natural talent—a steady hand, a cool head, and a serious competitive streak. Even when she was just beginning, it was obvious she wanted to become good enough to beat me.

The days I spent at the Mason house were my happiest since Dad died. Having lived alone for so long, I was initially anxious that having someone around all the time would drive me crazy. What I found was the opposite. I felt I'd become part of the Mason family: Meg as the mother, Kacey as the daughter, and Simon as . . . well, his role with respect to me was less clear. I wasn't sure whether he viewed himself as a father, a big brother, or something else.

Many evenings, while Meg was at her house and Kacey was in her room, Simon and I lounged in the family room with a Rangers baseball game unfolding on the television. I would read a magazine while he watched the game. Sometimes he headed out to his wood shop in the corner of the garage for an hour or two. I would hear hammering or the faint buzz of an electric saw, but he always came back for the last couple of innings.

Simon liked having me around, I was certain of that. Our relationship, though, hadn't moved beyond a certain easy comfort at being together. On many subjects we thought alike, from our contempt for tardiness to our geekish penchant for solving math problems in our heads. But each time I thought one of our talks was about to lead to something more, he pulled back. I attributed his standoffishness to his feelings for Marie, and I was jealous of her. No one can compete with a ghost. I wondered if Simon wouldn't benefit from a few sessions with Kacey's counselor. After all, at some point didn't a man have to let go?

As for Elise, she had faded to the background—somewhat bitterly, as far as I could tell. To Simon's discredit, when it came to her emotional attachment to him, he had a tin ear. It seemed inconceivable that he hadn't recognized it, but he was, after all, a man. In my experience that meant nothing was to be assumed in the feelings department. Whether Elise blamed me for his indifference, I was never entirely clear. We didn't spend a lot of time chatting.

After a month or so, Meg began to nudge Simon back toward his ministry, but to no avail. He shuffled around the house for days at a time, doing nothing but watching baseball and reading newspapers and magazines. Granted, in the beginning it was difficult for him to leave the house without photographers and reporters hounding him. As time passed, though, those problems evaporated. Soon his choice to stay at home all day was just that—a choice. Meg, however, had no intention of letting her brother quit on his life. She came up with a plan for what she termed an "intervention."

She invited an old family friend—Thomas Carston, the long-time minister at the largest Baptist church in Dallas—over for coffee to talk things out with Simon. She asked me to attend, which I thought odd. When I asked her whether my presence would be appropriate, she said Simon insisted. That set me thinking in earnest about what exactly our relationship was.

The morning of the meeting with Reverend Carston, I pulled Simon's Bible out of the corner of Kacey's closet. I had wedged it there the day I moved into the Mason house. It was the Bible he left on the podium at the Challenger Airlines Center. I'd fantasized that, at just the right moment, I would hand it to him and say the one thing, the right bit of wisdom, that catapulted him back into his ministry. Most of these fantasies ended with Simon pulling me toward him in gratitude for having shown him the way back, not just to his ministry, but to love and companionship and . . . what?

I wasn't sure.

In these visions I never made it all the way into his arms. The image always blurred to nothing just at the point where our feelings for one another would have become unequivocally clear. I was content, though, with the thought that dreams of any sort are rarely perfect.

Despite the incomplete nature of mine, I filled many hours picturing that emotionally pivotal moment.

Standing in Kacey's closet, I flipped slowly through the Bible's pages as if I were about to say good-bye to an old friend. Though I'd never opened it to read, Simon's Bible had kept me company by stimulating visions of a life I long ago abandoned any hope of finding—a life with a family of my own. A life that did not include the word *alone.*

As I closed the Bible and turned to leave the closet, I allowed myself one final image of Simon pulling me toward him. I was so focused on my fantasy that I forgot to pay attention to what I was doing. I slammed my funny bone into the door jam. To keep from yelping, I bit my lip. The Bible slipped out of my hand and bounced off a shoebox before coming to rest on its side, propped against a teetering stack of romance novels that Kacey kept on the floor.

I shook my tingling arm and bent to pick up the Bible. When I lifted it off the carpet, my finger touched something sticking out of the binding. A row of stitches had torn free from the bottom seam, and the corner of a folded sheet of white paper poked out.

I pulled the paper free. Judging by the way it was folded, it appeared to be a note. I leaned around the corner of the closet and peeked into the room. It was empty. I reached up and twisted my bangs with my fingers. Large black letters showed through the paper, so how secret could it really be? After all, by simply holding it up to a light, I could read it without even opening it. I looked out the door one more time—still no Kacey. Leaning back against the closet wall, I slid down to the carpet and crossed my legs Indian style. I unfolded the paper.

The single page of plain white stationery contained only one sentence, written in heavy black marker:

I KNOW ABOUT THE BOY.

CHAPTER
TWENTY-SEVEN

AFTER I'D SAT IN the closet for fifteen minutes trying to arrive at all of the possible explanations for the note, the doorbell rang. I stood up, folded the paper, and stuck it in the back pocket of my jeans. With the Bible in my hand, I walked into the family room. Simon was sitting in his favorite chair in the corner, reading the sports section of the *Dallas Morning News*.

Meg led Carston into the room and offered him a cup of coffee.

"No thanks, but I'll take a glass of water if you don't mind."

"Simon? Kacey?" she said.

Simon pointed to a glass on the end table next to him. "I've already got lemonade."

"I'll have a cup, please."

While she was getting the drinks, Meg pointed at me. "Tom, this is Taylor Pasbury, Simon's security chief. Taylor, this is Tom Carston, pastor of Fourth Baptist Church downtown."

"How do you do?"

I nodded. "It's a pleasure."

Carston pointed at Simon's newspaper. "Reading about the Rangers, I see. That's a gutsy undertaking any-time, but especially when they've started the season so slowly."

Simon stood up, walked over to Carston, and held out his hand. "Call me a dope, but I'll never give up on them."

Carston took his outstretched hand and shook it. "Okay, you're a dope."

Simon laughed. "We've always got the Cowboys." He motioned toward the couch. "Have a seat. I under-stand that you're here to save me from myself."

"I told Meg we should meet on the golf course. It would be easier to save you there. She vetoed the idea. I have a strong suspicion that she doesn't play."

"You've got that right," Meg said from behind the breakfast bar. She walked back into the family room, handed me my coffee mug, then walked over and placed Carston's glass of ice water on the coffee table in front of him. She sat next to him on the couch.

I sat off to the side, at the breakfast table next to the

windows. I blew steam from my coffee and waited to see what would happen. Meanwhile, I was so conscious of the tiny bulge that the folded note made in my pocket that it might as well have been a tennis ball. I set Simon's Bible on the table.

Carston rubbed his hands together. "As much as I would like to talk baseball, I think it would be better for us to get right to the point. Meg tells me that you've decided to stop preaching. That seems like a bad idea to me."

Simon crossed his leg. "Well, to begin with, she's not exactly correct."

Carston looked at Meg, who raised an eyebrow. "I'm glad to hear that. What do you mean 'not exactly correct'?"

Simon picked up his lemonade. "I've given this a lot of thought and prayer. I'm thinking about taking my ministry in a totally different direction. It's a direction I think I've been called to."

"What direction is that?"

"I want to become a missionary." Simon tipped his glass, as if toasting Carston, and took a drink.

"What sort of missionary?"

"To Muslims."

Meg's mouth fell open.

Simon smiled at her. "Yes, Meg, I said Muslims. You know, Muhammad and all that?"

"Very funny. Where are you going to find these Muslims—in Iran?" Her laugh was decidedly nervous.

A drop of condensation slid from Simon's glass onto his pant leg. He brushed at it, then put one hand under the glass. "Actually, you're not far off. I would like to go any place they are—any place that will let me in, that is. In fact, there are areas in the U.S. that have large Muslim populations. I've been researching on the Internet. Dearborn, Michigan, for example."

Carston leaned forward. "Aside from where you will find these Muslims, I'm interested in hearing why you've decided God is calling you in that direction."

Simon turned toward me. "Taylor, do you remember that limo driver in Chicago—the seminary student from Lebanon? Hakim."

"There's not much that I'll forget about that night."

"Do you remember what he said?"

"He asked you when you were going to go to Lebanon to preach."

Simon turned back to Reverend Carston. "I don't think it was an accident that we had that conversation just before all of this happened. I'm convinced this is all part of God's plan for my life. It's a way to make something good come from this thing that I've done."

Meg threw up her hands. "*What* thing that you've done? You were put in an impossible situation and you saved your daughter's life. You retracted what you said, and now it's over."

"Look, Meg, I don't really want to get into a discussion about all of that. I feel the way that I feel about what I did, so let's just leave it at that. I'm convinced, though, that God wants to use this whole situation for a purpose."

"Fine, but does that purpose have to involve Lebanon?" Meg said. "Do you know what's been going on over there? You would be committing suicide to go there and try to convert Muslims."

Simon shook his head. "It doesn't have to be Lebanon. I said it could be here in the U.S. I don't know yet. Don't worry. I'm not looking to get myself killed."

I watched his eyes as he spoke, and I wasn't so sure. But I decided to sit this discussion out if I could.

Simon immediately dashed that plan by turning toward me and nodding at the Bible on the table. "That's my Bible, isn't it? The one you picked up from the Challenger Airlines Center?"

I held it up. "Yes. I figured you might want it back today."

"When you picked it up that night, did you notice what it was open to?"

"No. The page was dog-eared. I remember that. Even if I'd read it, I wouldn't have known what it was."

He pointed to the Bible. "Find the page. It's a passage I read over and over in the days leading up to that evening."

I opened the Bible and flipped the pages until I found the one with the corner folded over. "Here it is."

"Read it."

My neck became warm. Within seconds it would resemble a fire hydrant. It was time to punt. I got up, walked over to Reverend Carston, and handed it to him. "I'm no Bible scholar. Maybe you should read it."

He chuckled as he took it from me. "You know, Taylor, you don't have to be a theologian to read this thing. You should stop by Fourth Baptist sometime. We have plenty of programs to help people get comfortable with the Bible."

I was mortified already and the conversation was only a few minutes old. I gave him a lame smile and crept back to my chair.

"Now, let me see what we've got here." He spoke with the confidence of someone who spends much of his time with a Bible in his hands. He pulled reading glasses out of his shirt pocket and leaned over. Placing his index finger on the page, he glanced up at Simon. "The underlined part?"

Simon nodded.

"It begins at John twenty-one, verse fifteen. *'When they had finished eating, Jesus said to Simon Peter—'*"

Simon held up his hand. "You don't need to read it out loud."

Carston smiled. "Sorry, I misunderstood you." He bent over the Bible again and ran his finger over the page, occasionally moving his lips. When he finished reading he looked up at Simon. "Jesus asked Peter three times if he loved him, and Peter told him three times that he did."

"Why did Jesus ask him that?"

Carston rubbed his earlobe between his index finger and thumb. "Before Jesus was crucified, Peter denied three times that he knew him. Peter had been afraid that if he admitted he knew Jesus, he would be arrested too. This verse is after the resurrection. Now Jesus is basically beginning Peter's rehabilitation by giving him a chance to start over. That's why he asked him to restate his faith publicly, and why he asked him three times—because that was how many times Peter denied that he knew him."

"That's right. Jesus was giving Peter a gift that he desperately needed. He had let Jesus down terribly. He'd been afraid and denied him. Jesus was giving him a chance to redeem himself. He was asking Peter to commit. In verse 18 he even tells Peter, in so many words, that if you do commit, you'll eventually have to die for your faith."

Meg raised her hand. "Excuse me—what does this have to do with your becoming a missionary to Muslims?"

"Without Peter the church might not have survived in those early days. Jesus needed leaders with total commitment. Guilt is a remarkable motivator. If Peter hadn't denied Christ, if he hadn't felt the shame and guilt, who knows whether he would have been committed enough to risk death every day by spreading the Word? Who knows if he would have been willing to die for what he believed? The same thing happened with the Apostle Paul. He persecuted the Christians before Jesus appeared to him on the road to Damascus. Who knows whether he would have been willing to suffer the things that he suffered to build the church if not for the guilt that he must have felt from that? He eventually died a martyr also."

"Are you implying that Jesus wants you to die?" I said. They all turned and looked at me. My neck grew warm. I reminded myself that as the spiritual leper of the group, I needed to keep my mouth shut.

Simon shook his head. "No, I'm just saying that I've done something as awful as any Christian could ever do. I'll spend the rest of my life trying to make up for it. Maybe God is using my guilt in the same way that he used Peter's and Paul's. Maybe that's why we just happened to run into a Lebanese limo driver on the night all of this began—a limo driver who put the idea of preaching to Muslims into my head. Do any of you doubt that Muslims need to hear about Jesus?"

Meg crossed her legs. "Just a hunch, little brother, but I don't think they're interested."

"You could say that about any group that missionaries have reached over the years. How can they know whether they're interested until they hear the story?"

Carston tilted his head back. "'How can they believe if they have not heard? How can they hear without someone preaching to them?'"

"What was that?" Meg said.

"I'm sorry. The verse just came to me. It's Romans 10:14. I didn't mean to interrupt."

Meg frowned, then turned back to Simon. "Look, this is crazy. You'll get killed. Preaching to Muslims in the Middle East is not like preaching in Ecuador or Samoa. You know that."

"Yes, I do know that. Does the fact that it's dangerous make it any less important? Besides, you're getting too hung up on the Middle East part of this. I may never leave the U.S."

Carston took off his reading glasses and pointed them at Simon. "You know, old pal, an outsider looking in and listening to what you're saying might conclude that martyrdom *is* what you really want out of this."

"That's a little dramatic, don't you think, Tom?" Simon leaned back in his chair. "There's a difference between doing something that has identifiable risks, and going out and looking to die."

"Maybe, but if you have the notion that you are going to stand outside of mosques in the U.S. and preach to Muslims, you will most certainly be in some danger. If you try to do it in the Middle East, you may very well die. That is, if you can ever get there in the first place. It's not as if you're unknown. I'm not sure any of those governments would even let you in."

"I've thought about that—about whether I would even be allowed to try to preach in those countries. On that score, I've got an idea that I've been bouncing around in my head. I don't know if it could work or not."

"What is it?" Carston picked up his glass of water and took a drink.

"Something like a debate."

Carston hesitated, then lowered the glass back on the table. "A debate . . . about what? With whom?"

"Maybe *debate* isn't the right word. I'm thinking about something more like a public dialogue with a prominent imam—the principles of Christianity versus the principles of Islam. That's simple enough, wouldn't you say? I'd venture that most Christians don't know much about Islam, and most Muslims don't know much about Christianity. Maybe it's time to let the ideals of the two religions compete openly."

Carston rubbed his earlobe again. After a few moments, he nodded. "I get it."

Meg, who had been standing beside the couch, spun toward him. "What do you mean, 'I get it?' I didn't ask you over here to *get it*. I asked you over to reason with him."

He held out a hand. "Now, calm down, Meg. We are reasoning. All I'm saying is that I understand what Simon is suggesting. There is a certain theological symmetry to it."

She squinted down at him. "This is not some classroom discussion at the seminary. My brother is talking about getting himself killed!"

"Most missionaries expose themselves to danger," Simon said. "If they didn't—if they hadn't—Western civilization wouldn't exist. What you're saying, Meg, is that all of that is fine as long as someone else's brother, husband, wife, or daughter, is taking the risk."

"Now you've got it right. I don't want my brother exposing himself to that level of risk, and I don't care about all of your talk of missionaries and saints. By the way, you haven't mentioned Kacey. You still have a twenty-year-old daughter, you know. Have you thought about her? You couldn't exactly take her with you."

Simon leaned forward. "Of course I have. That's the rub in this whole idea. It's the one thing that's holding me back, the one thing that makes me think of doing something else, or going just halfway."

"What do you mean, halfway?"

"Like I said, I may start here in the U.S. There might be a little bit of risk in that. I'm sure there are some radicals out there, but they're a tiny minority in this country. I don't think it would be all that dangerous. And doing that would help me get my feet on the ground with this thing—figure out the best approach. In the meantime, though, I could contact Hakim in Chicago. At the least I'd like to discuss this Lebanon idea with him."

Carston stood and put his hands in his pockets. "I'm sorry, Meg. I don't think I've been much help. As crazy as this sounds, I can't tell you that Simon is wrong. If anything, I'm a bit ashamed that I haven't got the sort of commitment necessary to do the same thing. When I look at the world and what's happening around us every day, it's clear to me that this is the most pressing missionary opportunity that exists."

Meg's mouth fell open and she shook her head. "I don't believe what I'm hearing."

Simon chuckled. "We can do a team thing if you'd like, Tom."

"Thanks, but I'm pretty sure my wife would wring my neck before any terrorists got to me." He looked at Meg, who scowled. "I guess I should be going now." He turned to leave but stopped and turned back. "One thing, though, Simon: If this really is about martyrdom, if you have some cockeyed notion that you need to become a martyr to redeem yourself—well, you know it doesn't work that way. Don't lose sight of grace. It applies to famous televangelists just as much as anyone else. If you've asked for forgiveness, you've been forgiven. You don't need to—you can't—earn anything better than what God's grace can give you."

Simon nodded but merely said, "Give Cynthia my best."

CHAPTER
TWENTY-EIGHT

AFTER REVEREND CARSTON LEFT, I could see that Meg wanted to talk to her brother, so I excused myself and spent the next hour in Kacey's room, listening to downloaded songs on my phone and wondering about the note in Simon's Bible. When I went back out to the family room, Simon was in the kitchen making a peanut butter sandwich.

He pointed toward the peanut butter jar with his knife. "Want one?"

"Yeah, thanks." I opened the refrigerator and pulled out a bottle of water.

"Would you grab me a soda, please?" He spread the peanut butter on a slice of bread. "Open faced or closed?"

"Open is the only way." I closed the refrigerator door.

"Agreed."

I handed him the soda can, and he handed me the sandwich. I walked over to the breakfast table, balancing the sandwich on the palm of one hand.

"Where's Meg?" I lifted the bread carefully with both hands and took a bite.

"She went home for a while. She's got a family, too, you know."

"You're lucky. She really loves you and Kacey." I worked my tongue through the peanut butter on the roof of my mouth.

"In some ways I think this whole thing has been harder on her than on Kacey and me. She worries so much." He folded his sandwich in half and took a giant bite. Half of it disappeared.

"Why do you bother making it open faced if you're going to fold it in half?" I took another bite.

"Haven't you ever folded a slice of pizza?"

"No."

"Then you wouldn't understand." He took a drink of soda.

I stuck my hand in my back pocket and touched the note from his Bible. "Did you get your Bible back when Reverend Carston left?"

"Yes, he left it on the couch. Have you had it all this time?" He shoved the rest of his sandwich in his mouth.

"Yes."

He took another drink of soda, then put the can on the table. "I'm glad you didn't let me leave it at the auditorium."

"I figured you would want it."

He looked at me for a few moments. "Do you have anything that belongs to me?"

I shifted my weight in my chair. "I think I might."

He held out his hand. I reached into my pocket and pulled out the note.

"Is that something you really thought I would want you to read?"

I placed the note in his hand. "No, I assumed you wanted to keep it private." There was a time when I would have concocted a lie at this point. Now I didn't even consider it. "I read it anyway."

"And you want me to tell you what it's about." He sat down with one hand resting on the table.

"Do I want you to tell me? Sure. It's not self-explanatory. But do I *expect* you to tell me? Not really. If it affects your security or Kacey's, you should tell me. Otherwise it's none of my business."

"It has nothing to do with keeping us safe."

"How do you know that?"

"Now you're just trying to convince me to explain the note." He picked up his soda and drained the rest of it.

"That's not true."

"It doesn't matter."

"Fine." I folded my arms.

He opened the note and focused on the page. "I should fire you."

"I can't disagree with you on that. I hope you won't, though."

He folded the note again, took a deep breath, and let it out. "A year or so before Marie got sick, I had an affair. I have a son. At least I think I do. That's what this is about."

I leaned back in my chair. "You're kidding me."

"It would take an unusual sense of humor to kid about that, wouldn't it?"

"But, the letters in the shoebox."

"They're real. I did love Marie, and I still do. Do you want to hear the explanation?"

"That's up to you. You certainly don't owe me."

He tapped his index finger on the side of the soda can and studied it, as if the words he needed could be found in the ingredient list. He didn't look at me when he began to speak. "She had an affair first; I was paying her back. It's as simple as that."

I shook my head. "This is the most incredible thing I've ever heard. I mean, coming from you."

"Well, it's the truth."

"How can you act as if you're still in love with her?"

"It's no act. I miss her more than I can describe. No offense, but you're very young, Taylor. You've seen a lot in your life, but you've not seen marriage from the inside. It's different than you might think. At least, it was different than I imagined. In some ways marriage is a much stronger thing than I thought, in other ways more fragile. Marie and I had our problems, but we got over them. Then she got sick. When I told you how much I loved her, how much I still love her, I meant it."

"You said you *think* you have a son. Don't you know for sure?"

"No. There's never been a blood test or anything. I do believe that it's true, though. I believed it then, and I believe it now."

"Where is he?"

"He lives in a suburb of Houston. He's eighteen years old."

"Does he live with his mother?"

"No."

"Then who?"

Simon looked away. "He's been adopted."

I folded my arms.

"I know what you're thinking," he said.

"No, you don't."

"You're thinking that you're disappointed in me, that I should have taken him in, that I'm not the man you thought I was."

I leaned forward. "I stand corrected. You do know what I was thinking."

He stood up, walked to the picture window, and looked out into the backyard. "Fair enough. It was all very complicated, though. If I'd taken him in, I never could have saved my marriage. Then Marie got sick, and taking him became impossible. He was with his mother. I had no reason to think she was going anywhere. It wasn't until much later that she abandoned him. I didn't know she'd left him until after my ministry took off.

To have the affair come out would have ruined me and everything I'd worked for. Anyway, he was with a foster family by then, and they eventually adopted him."

If he hadn't had his back turned, my face would have showed him what I thought of that explanation. "Have you seen him?"

"Just pictures. I've been able to get news about him from time to time, mostly from the newspaper." He turned, and his eyes brightened. "I understand he's quite a baseball player."

"Does he know about you? That you're his father?"

"Not as far as I know."

"How about the note? Who wrote it?"

"Two days before the FBI called me about the terrorist threats, I found the note folded under the windshield wiper of my car."

"Did you tell the FBI about it?"

"I didn't see any reason to. It had nothing to do with Kacey."

I waved a hand in the air. "Well, that's one *heck* of an assumption to make."

"I *know* it had nothing to do with Kacey."

"How?"

He crossed his arms. "Because the day after I found it, I talked to the person who left it."

"Who was that?"

"I don't know. A man called me on my cell phone. He said that if I didn't give him two hundred thousand dollars, he would give the story to the press."

I raised an eyebrow. "What did you do?"

"I told him I had to think it over—that it would not be easy to come up with that kind of money quickly. He gave me a number to call in five days. He said someone would give me instructions on where to leave the money. I was going to tell you about it when I hired you, but then Kacey got kidnapped and everything else seemed insignificant. I never made the call."

"Who knows about this?"

"Only Elise. I told her right after I talked to the man."

"Have you heard from him since?"

"No." He smiled. "I guess he had the unluckiest timing of any extortionist in history. I think the kidnapping must have scared him off. Elise thinks so too."

"Who could have known about the boy?"

"Just his mother, and anyone she might have told."

"Do you think she's in on it?"

Simon came back to the table and sat down. "That was the first thing I thought, of course. But it doesn't make any sense. After all this time, why would she just now decide to do this? Someone else must have found out. I just don't know."

"Was it a one-night stand?"

"More like six or eight nights. It never meant anything from my end. It was strictly revenge. It may have meant more to her, I don't know. She was older than I— a difficult woman to read. Brilliant and difficult."

"Who is she?"

He stood up again and crumpled his soda can in his hand. "It doesn't matter. I don't know where she is.

I'm not even certain she's alive." He walked to the waste-basket in the corner of the kitchen and tossed the can into it.

The garage-door opener rumbled. "That's Kacey," he said.

"Does she know?"

"No, and I don't want her to know. Someday, maybe, I'll tell her. I've trusted you with this. Please don't tell anyone, and especially not her."

"I wouldn't stay in business very long if I went around blabbing all of my clients' secrets."

"Of course, it's just business."

I felt terrible for having put it that way, then I felt stupid for feeling terrible. After all, *he* was the one who abandoned his son. On the other hand, Marie had been the first to cheat. That must have crushed him. I wanted to comfort him, and I wanted to kill him. I wasn't certain which to do.

One thing *is* certain now, though: If I'd known in that moment that he was still only telling me half of the story, I would have done something. Comforted or killed him. One or the other. But I didn't know. And before I found out, something happened that turned my focus away from the Masons and back to me.

Kacey was improving every day—and I was about to lose a roommate.

CHAPTER
TWENTY-NINE

IF A PERSON HAS been blind for most of her life and has the chance to see again, but just for a few weeks, should she take it? Or is the pain of blindness worse if the memory of sight is fresh?

For a month I saw what it was like to be part of a family. Though Kacey, Simon, and Meg weren't my real family, they were the closest thing I'd had for a long time. As confused as I was about Simon, I was still in no hurry to go back to being alone. But Kacey's psychiatrist concluded that she was ready to take the next step to overcome her fears.

It was time for me to leave the Mason house.

As I prepared to move out, I felt blinder than ever. It's hard to describe what it's like to be alone—not just for an afternoon or for a week, but as a permanent condition. I'm sure that it's difficult for people with families to understand how hopeless, how utterly dark, loneliness is. After all, even a dysfunctional family provides occasional comfort.

The easiest way for me to explain the kind of loneliness I'm talking about is with an example from my senior year in college. I lived in an apartment complex that bordered a pond. It was a small, shallow pond, not far from a creek that ran along the edge of a narrow woods. Like most college towns, College Station, Texas, was fertile ground for planting apartment complexes. In my neighborhood the apartments ran thick and stark right up to the pond. Then the buildings stopped and nature took over for nearly a mile until the bricks and mortar regrouped on the other side of the woods. In a sense, the thirty-yard strip of grass between the sliding glass back door of my apartment and the pond was the border between civilization and nature, at least in my little part of the world.

The pond was beautiful in a simple, wild sort of way. It had frogs and turtles and bugs, and kids from the subdivision down the road frequently fished from the bank. Several families of ducks lived near the water.

I lived in the apartment complex for three years, and each year the duck families added to their numbers with the spring hatch. Even in this relatively protected nature sanctuary, life was difficult for new hatchlings. A mother might start the spring with up to a dozen young, but usually only three or four would survive to become adults.

My last year in the apartment, several weeks after Easter, I looked out my sliding glass door one evening and saw Patsy, the research assistant who taught my economics lab. She was a bookish woman, with narrow shoulders and big, round glasses. She was standing near the pond with a loaf of white bread in her hand. I went outside to say hello. As I approached, three fuzzy ducklings, nearly full-grown but obviously very young, waddled near the water a few feet from Patsy's feet. They were picking up pieces of bread that she'd dropped onto the ground, lifting their bills toward the sky, and jiggling their heads until the bread dropped down their slender throats.

After exchanging hellos, we talked about the unusually mild spring weather and watched the ducklings gobble the offered bread. Eventually I nodded toward them. "Where's the mother?"

Patsy looked at me and wrinkled her forehead. "There is no mother."

I shoved my hands in the back pockets of my jeans. "How can there be no mother?"

"They're Easter ducklings."

"What do you mean, Easter ducklings?"

"People use live eggs for the Easter egg hunts at their kids' Easter parties. The guests take them home and keep them warm because the kids are excited about them. It seems like such a cute idea. Then they hatch. Pretty soon it's not so cute to have ducklings making a mess in the backyard. So people dump them at places like this."

"Real duck eggs? I thought Easter eggs were hard boiled."

"Not these. It's the latest thing."

"How do you know about this?"

"My daughters came home from a party with real duck eggs a couple of years ago. I called the mother who threw the party and chewed her out. We took the eggs back to the farm where she got them."

I looked around the pond. Two duck families paddled in tight formation. One mother had six ducklings, the other had four, all much smaller than Patsy's Easter ducklings. "Will the other ducks take them in?"

"Not a chance. They're on their own."

"How can they possibly survive without a mother?"

She dropped more bread on the ground.

One of the ducklings, the yellow one, was the leader of the three. Larger and more daring than the others, he waddled to the water's edge, stuck his bill beneath the surface, and came up shaking his head from side to side, water splashing in all directions. Then he turned and looked at his brother and sister, as if checking to make sure they were okay. The other two watched him intently. After a few quacks, the smallest sat down, curled into a ball, and tucked her head into the brown, fuzzy feathers at her side. Soon her other brother, a black one, stretched his neck and sat down practically on top of her. They huddled there, a few feet from the cattails, each moving with the other's breathing, neither willing to move away from the other's touch. They watched their yellow brother as he continued to explore at the edge of the water.

"They haven't got a chance."

Patsy shook her head. "Probably not. I've been bringing them food for the past two days." She wadded the empty bread bag into a ball and put it in her pocket.

"If they can get through the first couple of weeks, maybe they can survive," I said.

"Maybe. Well, I've got to go."

"See you at class." I turned and walked back into my apartment.

The next morning I grabbed a dinner roll from the pantry and went out to the pond as soon as I awoke. At first I didn't see the ducklings, but then I spotted the black brother and the brown sister. They were still huddled together in a tight ball, about two feet from the cattails. I didn't see the yellow one anywhere.

I walked around the pond looking for the yellow duckling. There was no sign of him. Finally, I walked back to where the smaller brother and sister were huddled together. About five feet away from them, under a thin pond cypress, I found a flattened cluster of yellow feathers and a picked over skeleton. As I watched, the two remaining ducklings stood, shook themselves, and stared at the water. Before long they waddled to the bank and gently dipped themselves before settling into the water and paddling in tight circles, never straying more than a few feet from the bank.

I wondered whether their brother had died defending them, or if that was just my effort to make the whole thing into a Disney drama. I tore up the dinner roll and tossed the pieces onto the ground. The ducklings quacked tentatively, paddled onto the bank, and gobbled the roll chunk by chunk. Then they walked in circles for a few moments before plopping down so close to one another that they appeared to be a single, two-toned duck with two bills. Out on the pond the other duck families paddled about, the mothers in the lead, paying no attention at all to the two orphans.

That evening I walked to the pond again. The two ducklings were still huddled next to each other but were fifteen feet or so from where I'd left them that morning. They looked up at me expectantly. I dropped pieces of bread for them to eat.

The next morning the black duckling was gone. The smallest, the little brown one, waddled back and forth from the roots of the pond cypress to the edge of the water, quacking the entire time. She never got in the water, and I wondered whether she was too afraid to do it without her brothers around. I walked around the pond but found no sign of the black duckling. I fed her some bread and went to class.

That evening when I went to the pond, the brown duckling huddled alone, her back pressed tightly against an exposed root of the pond cypress. I brought her pieces of bread again, but she ate little. I sat on the grass beside her and cried.

When I finally left to go back to my apartment, she was still there huddled against the tree root, waiting for night to come.

There is nothing worse than being alone.

Nothing.

CHAPTER
THIRTY

I MOVED OUT OF Simon's house on a Friday morning and slept the entire afternoon in my apartment. Around five o'clock I ordered a pizza and ate it in front of the television, still in my pajamas. I almost poured myself a bourbon, but I got a diet soda out of the refrigerator instead. It had been more than a month since I'd had a drink, and going cold turkey hadn't been hard at all while I was at Simon's.

Now, however, I was alone again, and things weren't going well. I sat on the floor and watched a rerun of *Everybody Loves Raymond*. I ate the whole pizza. When I finished, I turned the sound down and looked around my apartment. Expensive furniture, a minimalist theme, a sparkling view of the Dallas Arts District skyline—all the things that had made me feel hip and young now seemed cold and depressing when compared to the warm boredom of family life.

On the television the muted characters worked their mouths, gave exasperated looks, laughed, mugged, and ate together. Even with no sound it was obvious they were a family. I tossed the empty pizza box across the floor and went back to bed until ten the next morning. When I awoke, I shuffled around the empty apartment for a couple of hours, then felt tired and went back to bed again. This time I slept until five. That's what depressed people do—they sleep.

That evening I decided enough was enough. At around nine o'clock I put on a short, tight cocktail dress and walked a block down McKinney Avenue to a bar called Purple. It had only been open a few months, and the *Morning News* was calling it the hottest new place in the city. I figured that getting out of the apartment was just what I needed, and a drink or two might raise my spirits.

I'd gone to plenty of bars alone during my life. The thought didn't trouble me at all. I had never, though, seen anything like Purple. It was already dark outside, but my eyes required several minutes to adjust when I stepped through the triangular entryway. Once I could make out my surroundings, it became apparent where the bar got its name. Nearly everything in the giant room was purple: the walls, the floor, the ceiling, the furniture, the clothing on the employees. To top it off, a flashing purple light came on every ten minutes or so and bathed the entire bar in an eerie, throbbing glow.

The place was an epileptic's nightmare.

When the purple light was on, the customers' faces became iridescent and their teeth took on a radioactive gleam. Even the aquarium behind the bar had purple water, though the tropical fish were various shades of yellow and orange. I couldn't help but wonder whether a long-term market really existed for this theme.

Making my way around several clusters of Dallas's young and beautiful, I headed straight to the semi-circular chrome bar that enclosed one end of a raised dance floor. The dancers' hips twisted and thrust at eye level as I climbed onto a low-backed stool. I ordered a bourbon, straight up.

I hadn't been at the bar for ten minutes before a wavy-haired lifeguard-type in a tight designer polo made eye contact from a nearby bar stool. I turned in the opposite direction. By the time I turned back he was standing so close to me that his thigh touched my knee. I moved my leg away.

He leaned against the bar. "My radar is pretty good, and it tells me that you like to dance." He looked directly into my eyes. I felt like I was being hit on by a sales trainer for a surfboard company.

"Actually, you're wrong. I don't like to dance." Just as I was about to tell him to get lost, I noticed that my glass was nearly empty. I'd been viewing the situation wrong-headedly. This guy was not an irritant; he was an opportunity.

I picked up the glass. "I like to drink, though. Will you buy me one?"

His eyes lit up. I suspect that he was imagining an opportunity also. "Sure. What are you having?"

"Bourbon, straight up."

He waved at the bartender. "One bourbon, straight up. And get me a chocolate martini."

It figured. I hated him.

He held out his hand. "I'm Rob."

I wasn't certain, but his fingernails appeared to have been manicured. I didn't take his hand, I just let it dangle there until he dropped it to his side.

"I'm . . . Kristin."

"Hello, Kristin. I dated a girl named Kristin in high school. She was hot—like you."

Even the bartender rolled his eyes at that one. He placed our drinks on the bar. Rob held up his purple martini glass and said, "To Che."

I sipped my bourbon. "Who's Che?"

"Che Guevara."

So, Rob was not only a pretty boy but a pro-Communist pretty boy. The sun was really rising on my world. "You're a student of Cuban history?"

"Not really. I saw *The Motorcycle Diaries*, though. He's been my hero ever since—living free, riding around on motorcycles, standing up for what he believed in."

I couldn't take it any longer. "You're exactly the type of guy whose head he had a tendency to put a bullet in, you know that, don't you?"

He shrugged and picked up his chocolate martini.

"I don't really like politics. I just think he was cool, that's all."

I swallowed the last of my bourbon and put the glass back on the bar. "You're not from Texas, are you?"

"No."

I held my glass up and tipped it. A few drops of bourbon landed on the floor. "Uh-oh, I'm empty."

He waved at the bartender. "Another bourbon, please."

In a couple of minutes the bartender was back. I drank the whole thing down. "Do you want to dance?" I said.

"I thought you didn't like to dance."

"Look, do you want to dance or not?"

"Sure."

I was definitely feeling the bourbon now. "First, shake my hand."

"What?"

I held out my hand. "Shake."

He grabbed my hand firmly enough, but his palm was so warm and moist that I wanted to head straight for the soap dispenser.

"What was that all about?"

I shook my head. "Doesn't matter. Let's dance." I grabbed the sleeve of his polo and dragged him up the stairs to the dance floor.

He apparently had seen *Pulp Fiction* in addition to *The Motorcycle Diaries*. He thought he had a twist thing going on. One song was all I could take. We went back to the bar, and I downed another bourbon. Despite my contempt for him, he was starting to look cuter.

"Read any good books lately?" I asked it primarily to torment him.

"I don't read much. No time."

Now *there* was a real shocker. "What keeps you so busy?"

"You know, work, working out."

"Sales?"

"How did you know that? You're some sort of fortune teller or something, right?" He laughed. He had good teeth.

Bourbon always did help me to see positives.

"You caught me. I'm a for-tul-tel . . ." I slowed down and forced myself to focus on the words. "A for-tune tel-ler."

He waved at the bartender to get me another bourbon, then he moved so close to me that his cheek was touching my hair. "Since you're a fortune teller, maybe you can tell me what's going to happen with you and me tonight." He lowered his voice. "This place is pretty loud. If you wanted to, we could get out of here."

I looked at my watch. The numbers swam a bit, but I got them in focus. Almost eleven. "I'll be right back. Bathroom break." Before I left, I poked him in the chest with my finger. "I'm going to call you Robby Boy, how 'bout that?" I can't recall his response, but I'm certain by that time he didn't care what I called him, as long as I was good and drunk.

I grabbed my purse and headed toward the *Women*

sign on the far side of the bar. When I got to the bath-room, it occurred to me that Simon must be sitting at home waiting for me to call. I also realized that I had many important things to say to him—things I'd some-how left unsaid up to that point in our relationship. I pulled my phone out of my purse and pushed the speed dial for his house. The low battery message blinked. I put the phone to my ear and got nothing. I stuck it back in my purse.

Leaving the bathroom, I practically sideswiped a curvy purple pay phone that looked like something out of *The Jetsons*. I pulled out my cell phone. The screen still worked. I hit the speed dial again for Simon's number. Then I swiped my credit card through the pay phone and dialed the number that I got from my cell phone screen. It required about five attempts before I could induce a ring on the other end.

By that time the bourbon was slugging me hard. So much so, I must have pulled the wrong speed-dial num-ber. Michael Harrison answered the phone. Who knows what I said before I realized I was talking to him and not Simon. And why he was at his office at 11 p.m. on a weekend is a question that only he can answer. In fact, he probably did answer it, but I don't remember. In any event I must have made it clear to him that a surfer was about to take me back to his apartment, and that with the help of quite a few bourbons I was feeling pretty okay about it.

Michael has subsequently assured me that he tried hard to talk me out of leaving the bar. Failing that, he managed to get me to tell him where I was. The next thing I remember is staggering out of Purple, Robby Boy in tow, heading down McKinney Avenue toward his place. Or mine. I'm not sure which.

We hadn't gotten fifty feet before Michael pulled up to the curb, the lights flashing on his unmarked car. He blocked an entire lane of traffic on one of the busiest streets in Dallas (which, I recall, made a big impression on me at the time). He jumped out and stepped in front of Robby Boy, who immediately puffed out his chest. Michael flashed his badge. There was no trouble after that. Michael got me into his car, and I somehow convinced him that I simply had to talk to Simon. He called ahead to Simon's house and took me there.

I have thanked Michael several times for what he did for me that night. Each time I thanked him, I was more embarrassed than the time before, which is probably a good sign with respect to the direction my life has taken. What conclusions he drew about me and my request to go to Simon's house, I don't know. We've never discussed it. But at least he cared enough to take the time to leave his office and save me from Robby Boy—or save Robby Boy from me. I've put him on my very short list of good guys. I do know that he drove me to Simon's house and walked me to the door. Then he left without so much as a thank you (at the time) from me.

There are only a couple of things I remember about Simon that night. First—and this irritated the heck out of me—he kept putting a finger to his lips and shushing me until he could get me into his car to drive me back to my apartment. He didn't want Kacey to see me in that condition. I'm so grateful for that now. Second, despite the fact that I was sloppy drunk, he was kind to me. He later told me that he concluded that I had a problem more chronic than a single night of too many bourbons.

There is really nothing else to tell about that evening, because there is not a single other thing that I remember. The next afternoon, though, Simon came back to my apartment and had a talk with me.

That part I remember well.

CHAPTER
THIRTY-ONE

WHEN THE DOORMAN CALLED and told me Simon Mason was downstairs to see me, I debated whether to let him in. First, I had a nuclear hangover and my mouth tasted as if I'd been licking ash trays. Second, I remembered that Michael had dropped me off at Simon's house the night before, and I didn't remember how I got home, so I was reasonably certain that Simon had seen a side of me with which he was not likely to have been impressed. Third, I was still in bed, and I looked like . . . well, I didn't look good. On the other hand, I'd only been gone from his house for a few days, and as uncomfortable as this was likely to be, I missed him. I told the doorman to buzz him up.

I jumped out of bed and ran to the bathroom. After stuffing a glob of toothpaste in my mouth and sucking a mouthful of water from the faucet, I began to multi-task. While swishing the toothpaste around, I used one hand to pull a pair of khaki shorts up beneath the red softball jersey that I'd slept in, while I worked the fingers of my other hand through the tangles in my hair. The shorts eventually came up, but my fingers stopped cold in my hair, which had taken on a texture roughly resembling a trumpet vine. I tried to loosen the thicket on my head by working at the knots with my fingers. This merely teased each wave into something akin to an over-stretched Slinky. By that time I was feeling light-headed and desperately needed to get more blood to my brain. I forgot about the hair and eased down to the floor where I lay on my back and stretched my feet up onto the toilet seat. That's when the door chime rang.

"Just a minute!" I closed my eyes and followed the sparklers that shot from my retina toward the edges of my eye sockets. The door chimed again. Enough blood had flown back into my head to engage the part of my brain necessary for ambulation, so I rolled over on my side, grabbed the edge of the sink, and pulled myself to my feet.

When I got to the door, I brushed my hands over my softball jersey, as if that would have an impact on a night's worth of wrinkles. That's when it occurred to me that I had no idea how I had gotten into the softball jersey in the first place. As I grabbed the doorknob I looked over my shoulder. Through the bedroom door I could see my cocktail dress from the night before, neatly folded and draped over the arm of the chair next to the nightstand. I couldn't imagine that I could have done that.

I pulled open the door. "Simon, what a nice surprise." I sounded like Martha Stewart welcoming a member of the ladies' club.

"I was in your neighborhood and thought I'd drop in to check on you."

"That's so nice. Come on in. The place is kind of a wreck right now."

He stepped in. "I should have called first."

I ran a hand through my hair. It dead-ended again at a mammoth tangle. I gave the tangle a tug, which had no effect except to send a shooting pain down my scalp to my ear. Standing in my wrinkled softball shirt with one hand stuck to the top of my head was not the look I was going for. I dropped my arm to my side and resolved not to touch my hair again under any circumstances. "Look, Simon, I want to apologize for last night—"

He held up his hand. "I didn't come over looking for an apology. I'm just concerned."

"But I do need to apologize. I shouldn't have bothered you at home." My stomach had been tumbling with increasing vigor since I got off the bathroom floor. Suddenly, every part of my mouth's piping that was capable of emitting saliva opened its valves. I moved my hand toward my lips.

"I'm glad you bothered me." His eyes followed my hand.

I pulled it away. "You are?"

"Yes, I am." He cocked his head. "Do you want to sit down? You don't look so great."

My stomach heaved. "Excuse me—" I sprinted to the bathroom.

After slamming the door so hard that it popped back open, I tried to flip on the fan as I dropped to my knees in front of the toilet bowl. I hoped that the rattling of the fan motor would mask the sound of my retching, but I missed the switch. There was no going back for a second chance. Simon must have heard every gag, grunt, and gurgle.

I pulled some toilet paper off the roll to wipe my face and chin, and eased to my feet. It was time for another glob of toothpaste. I stood at the sink, swishing and gargling as quietly as possible. I'm not sure why I was so concerned about Simon hearing me gargle, since he'd just heard me eject about a quart of whatever was in my stomach. I suppose, though, that every social recovery has to have a starting point.

It's difficult to reenter a room with dignity after making loud noises for five minutes with your face in a toilet bowl. Nevertheless, I straightened my softball jersey, held my head high, and walked back into the living room.

Simon was sitting on the couch, flipping through my *People* magazine. He didn't even look up. "Can I get you anything?"

His nonchalance ticked me off. "No thanks, I'll live."

He closed the magazine and looked up at me. "Would you sit down for a minute, please? I'd like to talk to you."

I knew I was about to get fired. I decided to take it with at least a hint of defiance. "I'll stand, thanks."

"Then would you mind standing over here? I don't want to have to crane my neck."

As I walked over to stand in front of him, I noticed that I had several dark blotches on the front of my shirt, none of which had been there before I ran into the bathroom—one more pleasant surprise in a nearly perfect day. I crossed my arms over them.

Simon ran his hand over the top of his head and sighed. Before he could speak, I blurted, "I quit."

He raised an eyebrow. "Why?"

"You were going to fire me, weren't you?"

"No."

"Oh." Suddenly feeling considerably less defiant, I felt for the chair behind me and sat.

He looked me in the eye. "You've got a drinking problem, don't you?"

I waved a hand in the air. "Where did that come from?" His eyes focused on the stains on my shirt. I crossed my arms again. "Okay, I know I had too much to drink last night. I hadn't had a drink for a while, and it snuck up on me. That's a long way from having a drinking problem."

"Save it, Taylor. I checked on you before I hired you. I heard about your reputation at the Secret Service."

"Then why did you hire me?"

"I had my reasons." He rubbed his hands on the legs of his jeans.

That struck me as a strange response, but I was in no position to interrogate him. I glanced at the *People* magazine in his hand.

He smiled sheepishly. "I wasn't really reading it." He tossed it onto the couch.

I smiled, too, glad for the lightening of the mood, but my stomach was rumbling again.

He lost the smile. "You've got a problem. I want to help you. Will you let me?"

"I don't have a problem. I just got a little tipsy. Why are you making such a big deal out of it?"

"If you were just a little tipsy, tell me what happened after Michael dropped you off at my house."

I glanced toward the open bedroom door and the neatly folded cocktail dress. "What do you mean? Did something happen?"

"If you don't remember, wouldn't you say that's an indication of a problem?"

I wasn't ready to allow the discussion to move past the "what happened" part. "Did anything . . . *happen?*"

He leaned back on the couch. "No, nothing happened. But according to Michael something could have—between you and some bar rat who was out trolling for someone just like you."

My shoulders sagged. "And what exactly is someone just like me?"

"I didn't mean for it to come out that way."

"I know exactly what you meant." I lowered my head. "I'm sorry I let you down."

"This has nothing to do with me."

"Please don't say that." I raised my head. "I need for it to have something to do with you."

He paused. "Okay, then it does. I want to help you."

I started to cry, then grabbed my hair in my hands and clenched my eyes and my teeth.

He looked at me wide-eyed.

"Just once," I said, "I'd like to have a conversation without bursting into tears like a twelve-year-old!"

He let out a breath and smiled again. "You had me worried there for a minute. Where do you keep your tissues?"

"In the bathroom next to the sink."

He was on his feet before it occurred to me that the bathroom was the last place I wanted him to go. Too late. He came back into the room carrying the box of tissues. He handed it to me and sat on the couch.

I pulled out a tissue and wiped my eyes. "I don't want to be this way, you know."

"What is 'this way'?"

By that time my nose was running. I had no choice but to cap off a memorable conversation by blowing it. There is no good place in a social setting to put a used tissue. I wadded it into a ball and closed my hand over it. Before I could speak, though, I began to cry even harder. I pulled more tissues out of the box.

Finally I got control of myself. "The truth is that I wish, for just one day of my life, I could be good enough. That's all I want—just to be good enough."

This is where, in my fantasies, he would have walked over, put his arms around me, and held me close. But he didn't. Instead, he leaned forward with his elbows on his knees, his hands clasped in front of him. "Good enough for what?"

I gave up on the tissues and wiped my face with my sleeve. "I don't know. Good enough to live. Just to be around decent people."

His voice softened. "Taylor, think about who you're talking to here. I'm a preacher who has committed adultery and denied Jesus in front of tens of millions of people. And you think *you're* not good enough? *Nobody* is good enough. If we had to be good enough, none of us would have a chance."

I used my fingers to wipe the spots beneath my eyes where I knew mascara must be pooling like mud puddles. "You may have made mistakes in your life, but you've done a lot of good for people. I've never done anything worthwhile for anybody. I'm a drunk and a . . . a . . ." I thought of the guy in the bar. I didn't have to say it. Simon knew what I was.

Simon got up, walked over to my chair, and knelt in front of me. He put his hand on my knee, but not in the romantic way I imagined in my fantasies. He just rested it there. It was like my father's touch. "You've done an awful lot of good for us—for Kacey and me. You are so much better than you think you are. I wish I knew how to make you see that."

There was nothing else to do. I just sat there and sobbed.

After a few moments he stood up. His voice became matter-of-fact. "Let me get you some help, Taylor. Then you'll see how good you can be."

I just nodded.

"I'll make a call. Someone will talk to you tomorrow."

I nodded again.

"Are you okay? Can I get you anything before I go?"

I shook my head.

"I'll call you in the morning." He turned to leave.

I looked up. "Simon?"

"Yes?"

"Please don't tell Kacey."

He smiled. "She thinks you walk on water. She thinks I do too. I guess we've both got her fooled. Let's leave it that way." He turned and walked out the door.

CHAPTER
THIRTY-TWO

THE NEXT DAY BRANDON called. He didn't give his last name. That was part of the deal with the version of the twelve-step recovery program that Simon's ministry offered. Everyone was first-name only. Brandon told me that at one time he'd been Simon's accountant. Then his drinking led him to bungle the annual audit so badly that Simon had no choice but to fire him. Soon thereafter, Brandon's wife walked out on him, leaving him at "the bottom," a concept central to the twelve-step theory of recovery. The idea is that until a person experiences complete humiliation, he won't have the willingness to give himself up to God—and the program makes it clear that God is the only answer to addiction.

I attended the weekly meetings even though I wasn't sure I was buying the "give yourself up to God" approach. After all, they were a church—what were they supposed to say? Frankly, my recent experience with praying for Simon had fallen short of anything that was likely to light a spiritual fire under me. The twelve-step program did provide impressive success-rate statistics, though. And while I might not buy their whole spiel, I did know one thing: I didn't want to continue in the direction my life was going.

I didn't fit the twelve-step mold as perfectly as I should have. For example, I couldn't say that I'd ever hit some sort of wallow-in-your-own-excrement rock-bottom, not in the sense that I understood the group to mean it. I'd fallen to more of an isolated rocky ledge from where I could peek over into a dark pit. I constantly had the feeling that some invisible force, like a magnet, was pulling me toward the edge, trying to suck me into the pit. To me, that pit was rock bottom, and I had never quite reached it.

At my third weekly meeting I made the mistake of describing this visualization to the group. All of them except Brandon concluded that the idea of the ledge and the pit posed a significant obstacle to my recovery, that it indicated I hadn't fully admitted the depth of my problem. Brandon pushed his heavy glasses up on his nose. "Come on, folks. She's not really on a ledge, and she's not really in a pit. She's in the basement of a church. It's a metaphor." The tone of his voice contained the unspoken addendum, *you morons!* He gave me a closed-lipped smile, which I later learned was his mechanism for hiding his crooked front teeth.

After the meeting I caught Brandon in the church parking lot. "Thank you for sticking up for me."

He hitched his pants up under the overhang of his belly. "They didn't mean anything. They just got caught up in your metaphor and couldn't get out. After all, the last thing you want in a church basement is to get caught in a girl's metaphors."

I laughed. "Good point. I'll be sure to keep them covered from now on."

He took his wallet out of his pocket, pulled out a business card, and handed it to me. It was white, and the only things on it were the name Brandon and a phone number. "That's my cell. You can call me any time you need help. I don't sleep much, so you don't have to worry about calling late."

"Did you have these printed just for these meetings?"

"Sure. I seem to be better at supporting other people than I am at supporting myself."

I put the card in my purse.

He opened his car door. "You're the first famous person to come to our meetings. I like to rub elbows, you know?" He gave me the closed-lip smile again.

"You know who I am?"

"Any person with a television and a brain knows who you are. That means the others aren't likely to identify you, so you don't have to worry." His eyes brightened. It was obvious he enjoyed being the cleverest person in the room.

"They seem like nice people to me."

"They're very nice people. I'm just gigging them a little. It can be a bit of a housewives' club."

"I noticed you were the only guy there tonight. Is that the way it usually is?"

"About half the time. You met Jason last week. He travels a lot, so he doesn't make all the meetings."

I lowered my voice. "I really don't want anyone to know I'm coming to these meetings. It could cause real problems for Simon."

"Don't worry, I know the rules. We must protect Simon at all costs."

I squinted at him.

He shrugged and stuffed his hands in his pockets. Before I could ask what he meant, he nodded toward my purse. "Be sure to use that number on my card if you need me." He got into the car.

"I will. Hey, who do you call when you need support?"

"My mother." He waved. "See you next time. I'm late for a Dread tournament. In my spare time, I'm a gamer."

Over the next couple of months I came to understand why Brandon hadn't answered my question seriously. He was always there for me, and I understood from others in the group that they also relied on him. Not a single person could recall, though, a time when he'd ever called one of them for support.

Eventually Brandon became my recovery partner. That meant that he was essentially my twelve-step mentor. Probably the smartest person I'd ever met, he leaned more than I did toward the classic addictive personality profile. He ate too much, drank too much coffee, and spent an alarming portion of his non-working hours playing video games. To top things off he was an accomplished and unapologetic computer hacker. Each of those compulsions seemed worthy of its own intervention, but he was content to prioritize his treatment and focus on licking his alcohol problem.

During my first couple of months in the program, I called him quite a few times, usually after midnight. Whenever I got the urge for bourbon, I'd ring him up and he'd talk me into having a diet soda instead. We discussed all sorts of things, but one call sticks out in my mind. I was lying in bed with my head propped on a pillow and had been talking to him for twenty minutes or so. The conversation had somehow turned to Simon. I asked Brandon why he'd never gone back to work for Simon after he got help with his drinking.

"I did go back, about six months ago."

"What were you doing for him?"

"Keeping the books, just like before."

"What happened?"

"I quit."

"When?"

"Just after Kacey was kidnapped."

I sat up and switched the phone to my other ear. "Why?"

"He was paying me too much."

"Would you please be serious?"

"Boy, your sense of humor really goes in the ditch after 2:30 in the morning."

I looked at the clock. It was 2:45. "Why did you quit?"

There was silence on the other end of the line.

"Brandon?"

"It was nothing. Little stuff, that's all. Listen, are you going to be all right tonight?"

"Yeah, I'm fine now."

"I'm going to get some sleep then. You call me back if you need me, okay?"

"Okay. Thanks for talking. You're a life saver."

After I hung up, I took a sip of my soda. Was it my imagination, or had he rushed off the phone to avoid telling me why he quit? I closed my eyes and rehashed the last part of the conversation. Before long my leg jerked and startled me awake.

I was no longer sitting up. My head was on the pillow and the covers were under my chin. I opened one eye and looked at the clock: 3:45. Without opening my other eye, I reached over and flicked off the lamp.

CHAPTER
THIRTY-THREE

THE BEST THING ABOUT Simon's discovery of my drinking problem was that I got to spend time with him and Kacey again. At first he checked on me every day, in person or by phone. He also added an additional session at the gun range for Kacey every week. Within a week or so, he gave me an open invitation to drop by for dinner whenever I wanted.

Since I'd never been a daily drinker, their constant presence was more important to my treatment than the twelve-step program. As long as I had somebody who cared about me, I didn't feel the need to drink. I was beginning to understand that loneliness had always been my real problem. The equation was simple: family equals no loneliness equals no drinking. It worked like a charm.

During that time Simon and I often sat in the family room and talked. Kacey had enrolled in summer school to make up the credits she lost during the spring semester, so most evenings she was either at the library or studying in her room. Typically, Simon would put the Rangers game on the television and pick up a book to read. When something of note happened in the game, he would look up and check the replay.

It was not unusual for me to sit with him until the game was over. I never really asked if I could, we just sort of fell into the habit. I quickly got hooked on baseball. Often I would be the one to shake him from his reading by yelling, "Get to it, get to it—yeah!" or some other admonition to one Ranger or another.

By this time I no longer had romantic fantasies about Simon pulling me into his arms. On several occasions I tried to re-conjure them in my mind, but they just weren't there anymore. The daydreams stopped cold after he told me about his son. I was happy, though, with our relationship—not just with Simon, but with Kacey too. It was comfortable. It was family.

It soon became clear that Simon's theme for the summer was martyrdom. He bought a dozen or so books on the topic and raised the issue from time to time as we sat in front of the television. One evening in mid-July we ordered pizza for dinner. When we finished eating, Kacey grabbed her backpack and headed for the library. Simon sat in his favorite chair, reading a book entitled

Heroes of the Christian Faith. I sat on the couch with Sadie curled up next to me. I thumbed through a celebrity magazine with one eye on the Rangers game.

I settled on a favorite player, Billy Johnston, the Rangers' second baseman. He was fast and scrappy, and he'd established himself as the team leader in a season in which they had rallied from a poor start to challenge for the division title. Johnston was batting with two outs and runners on second and third when Simon took off his reading glasses.

"It's amazing what some of these people went through."

I didn't take my eyes off the television. "What people?"

"The martyrs in this book. Listen to this one."

I smiled politely, but the count on Johnston had gone to two-and-two. I shifted my position in my seat to make it easier to monitor the game with my peripheral vision while he spoke.

"It's around the year two hundred," he said. "The Roman emperor decrees that no one can become a Christian or a Jew, period. He apparently didn't intend to bother people who were already Christians and Jews. He just didn't want any new ones around."

Johnston doubled off the wall, knocking in two runs, but I was careful to keep one eye on Simon.

"There's a twenty-two-year-old Roman woman named Perpetua, who has recently given birth to a baby boy. Then there's another woman who is Perpetua's slave. Her name is Felicity."

on my leg and closed her eyes. I scratched her behind the ears. "You've been reading about martyrs for weeks. I have to believe there's a reason, and I'm worried that I know what it is. You're really going to do this missionary thing, aren't you?"

"Yes, I am. I'm going public with it in a week or so."

I scratched Sadie faster—so fast that she opened one eye and peered up at me.

"And why do you care?" he said.

I took a deep breath and let it out. "Because you and Kacey are the closest thing I've had to a family for a long time. I don't want you to get hurt. I don't want it to end. There, I said it. Does that satisfy you?"

His voice softened. "I'm glad you feel that way. I want you to feel that way. You'll always be welcome here, Taylor."

That's when the question entered my mind again, the same question that Meg had raised: Why was Simon so willing to welcome me into his life? He had only known me for a brief time. I was a proven lush, and I hadn't demonstrated any strong religious beliefs. Why had he allowed me in so quickly and willingly?

"Thank you," I said. "That means a lot to me."

He smiled and nodded at the dog. She'd fallen asleep with her chin on my leg. "And Sadie welcomes you too."

The conversation died a natural death, but the question lingered. I assumed there was no single answer—and that whatever answers did exist would be complex and obscure. As it turned out, I was wrong. The answer was simple. I just didn't know it yet.

CHAPTER
THIRTY-FOUR

ONCE SIMON MADE UP his mind to promote the idea of a televised debate between Christianity and Islam, publicizing the idea was no challenge. He had been a huge international personality before the kidnapping. His additional notoriety since had ensured nearly immediate access to any talk show in America. The big issue was which show to choose for the initial announcement.

After much discussion, Elise and Simon decided on the Lawrence Sylvan show. Sylvan had been the leading political talk show host for more than ten years. No friend to evangelicals, he had roasted religious leaders many times, always probing for controversy. Elise and Simon felt that of all the major talk show hosts, Sylvan would be the most likely to seize on the debate issue and keep it—and the controversy—alive as a tool to drive his ratings.

The evening that Simon was to announce his debate challenge, Elise commented that he was the calmest she'd ever seen him before a public appearance. After the makeup people finished with him, the three of us sat in the green room of the television studio. He munched cashews and read a *Sports Illustrated*.

Elise pushed a handwritten page of notes in front of him. "I've written down some talking points that you can refer to when the camera's not on you."

Simon flipped a page of his magazine. "Thanks, but there's no need."

She frowned. "You know you have a tendency to forget things when the lights come on."

He looked up and smiled. "I'm fine, really." He bent over and tightened his shoelaces. Just as he finished, a slender blonde in a tight skirt walked into the green room.

"Reverend Mason, Lawrence is ready for you."

Simon brushed a cashew off his corduroy sport coat. "Okay, let's go."

Elise stepped in front of him. "One last hair check." She brushed at the close-cropped hair above his ears.

He swatted her hand. "Good grief, Elise, I don't have any hair!" He stepped around her and followed Miss Tight Skirt out of the room.

Elise clutched her notebook to her chest and glanced at me. I pretended to be looking at a magazine. She brushed at a wrinkle in her dress and sat down.

As Elise and I waited for Simon to go on the air, we both gave an inordinate amount of attention to the commercial running on the flat-screen television on the wall. A talking dog was selling air freshener. When the commercial ended, the intro to the Sylvan show played. The camera cut to a close-up of Lawrence Sylvan smiling out from behind his wire-rimmed glasses. He sat behind a black marble-topped table, directly across from Simon. Each had a light-blue coffee mug in front of him with the network logo facing the camera.

"We're pleased to have with us tonight, The Reverend Simon Mason, in his first television appearance since his press conference shortly after his daughter, Kacey, was released by her kidnappers a few months ago. Welcome, Reverend Mason."

Simon smiled. "Thank you. I'm glad to be here, Lawrence. Please call me Simon."

"Okay, Simon. So how is Kacey?"

"She's doing fine. She's really something. Much tougher than I am, that's for sure."

"She really is remarkable. I wish you'd brought her tonight. We would have been happy to have her."

"You've got kids, I know, Lawrence. You can understand why my sister and I do our best to keep Kacey out of the spotlight."

"Of course. Has she had any lingering problems, either physical or emotional? It was a harrowing experience."

"She's getting along very well. As I said, she's pretty tough."

"That's great to hear. I know you're not here to talk about Kacey, but if I hadn't asked about her my viewers would have rioted. She must be the most popular young lady in America right now."

"She just wants to be a college kid."

"We wish her all the best. Getting down to business, I understand that your experience with Kacey's kidnapping has made you feel that you've been called to a different kind of ministry—one that arises from the fact that Kacey's kidnappers were Muslims."

"That's right. I've decided—"

"Have you forgiven them, Simon? Kacey's kidnappers, that is?"

Simon put both hands around the coffee mug in front of him. "I'm doing my best. It isn't easy. I've gotten to the point where I no longer want to kill them." He smiled. "That's progress, I guess. It's probably better than they're doing. I'm sure they'd still be happy enough to kill me."

Sylvan laughed. "One of the things I've always liked about you is that you seem like a regular guy. I think a lot of ministers would have come on here and said, 'Of course I've forgiven them,' when in reality I don't know if they would have."

"I'm no saint, and I've never pretended to be. I know what God wants me to do. He wants me to forgive them. I'm trying my best to do that. But that doesn't mean it's easy. And just because I'm trying, it doesn't mean I'm going to be successful immediately. Over time, I'll get there."

"Do you hate them sometimes?"

"I had hatred in my heart when this happened, you better believe it. Quite honestly, I still have those feelings from time to time. Each time I see Kacey's missing finger I have to fight that darkness inside. You've got, what, two girls, Lawrence?"

"A girl and a boy."

"You can imagine what it would be like if someone did something like that to one of them."

"A nightmare."

"I'm fighting it. I'm working on it. Each day it seems to get a little bit easier to think about forgiveness."

"I can understand how difficult that must be. I'm sorry, I interrupted you a moment ago. You were about to describe the new calling you believe you've received."

"Yes. I believe God has called me to bring the story of Jesus to Muslims, not just here in the U.S., but around the world."

Sylvan leaned forward. "I don't think I have to tell you that this is likely to be a controversial calling."

"Maybe so, but I don't really understand why. Muslims are free to share their beliefs with Christians everywhere in the West. It seems that it's time for the information to move in both directions. Right now there are countries in the Middle East where handing a Bible to a Muslim can get a person thrown in jail, or worse. No one is landing in jail in the West for handing a copy of the Quran to a Christian, and they shouldn't be."

In the green room Elise clapped her hands. "This is amazing. It's the most relaxed I've ever seen him."

On the screen Sylvan tapped a pencil on the table. "I don't pretend to be an expert on the tenets of Islam, but I think Islam takes a different view of proselytizing than Christianity does. Don't you think we should respect that aspect of their faith?"

Simon narrowed his eyebrows. "I'm not aware of anything in Islam that prohibits discussion and learning. In fact, some of the great civilizations of history, Muslim civilizations, were known for their commitment to education."

"You're talking, though, about much more than education, aren't you, Simon? You're talking about converting Muslims to Christianity."

"Yes, and I want that to be perfectly clear. My long-term goal as a minister is to bring people to Jesus. But the first step in doing that is education. That's all that I'm talking about at this point. I'm calling for a series of televised debates—actually, *debate* is probably not the right word. More like discussions. I'm asking Muslim leaders to discuss with me publicly, in a respectful, professional manner, some of the basic premises of our faiths."

Sylvan leaned back in his chair. "That seems straightforward enough. But you're whistling in the wind here, aren't you? Do you think there is any chance that any Muslim spiritual leader will take you up on this?"

"Yes, I do. In fact, I would be surprised if this didn't happen." Simon folded his hands in front of him. "Sure, we all know there are radical Muslim leaders out there who aren't willing to discuss anything with anyone. History books are full of radical Christian leaders, too, so we can't be self-righteous. But I'm confident there are a large number of moderate leaders of Islam, both in this country and in the Middle East, who would welcome this sort of discussion."

"The risks may be quite a bit higher for Muslim leaders in the Middle East," Sylvan said. "Once word got out that they were planning on traveling to the U.S. for a televised discussion of the sort you're proposing, well, let's just say there could be some danger involved in that."

"They won't have to come to the U.S. I'll be happy to meet them whenever and wherever."

Sylvan took off his glasses and pointed them at Simon. "You mean you would go to the Middle East?"

"Yes. Anytime, anywhere."

"Iraq? Iran?"

"Anytime, anywhere."

Sylvan put his glasses back on and chuckled. "Well, I can see where Kacey gets her guts. It's an interesting idea, Simon. Actually, it's so simple that I'm surprised no one of your stature has proposed it before this. We will invite some Muslim leaders to our show during the next couple of weeks and see what their reaction is. Good luck to you, sir."

"Thank you, Lawrence."

The television screen flicked to a commercial. Elise turned to me, her face suddenly pale. "If he goes through with this, he could end up dead."

I did a double take. Had that thought really just occurred to her for the first time? I stood up.

"I'm afraid that's exactly what he wants."

CHAPTER
THIRTY-FIVE

A WEEK AFTER SIMON'S appearance on the Lawrence Sylvan show, I was sitting at my desk typing a long overdue report for a client when my cell phone rang. It was Simon.

"Can you come by the house? I'm making some plans, and I need your input."

I saved the page I was typing. "What type of plans?"

"I'm going to Michigan. I'd like to pick your brain on a few things."

I pulled up the Challenger Airlines flight schedule on the computer screen. "When are we going? I'll need to arrange my schedule."

"You're not going."

I spun my chair away from the desk. "What do you mean I'm not going? Am I fired?"

He sighed. "Why do you always think I'm about to fire you? I'm just going alone on this trip."

"I'm your security chief. How can I secure you if I'm not there?"

"That's what we need to talk about."

SITTING IN THE LIVING ROOM of Simon's house, sipping from a bottle of water, I watched him pace in front of the fireplace. I was struck again by the informality of the most formal room in his house. It really was more of a loose combination of library and study. Two deep leather chairs flanked the fireplace, and a giant sisal rug covered much of the hardwood floor in the center of the long room. There seemed to be little method to the placement of the few remaining tables and lamps, and the leather chairs didn't go well with the cream-colored couch that faced the fireplace. It was a man's room, apparently decorated by the man of the house. If my dad had done the decorating, the result probably would have been similar.

Simon stopped pacing. "It's time to start making things happen."

"What do you mean?"

"I'm not going to wait around for Islam to come to

me. I'm going to go to Islam. I'm starting in the U.S., in Dearborn, Michigan."

I crossed my leg. "You told me before that there are lots of Muslims in Dearborn. That's great. But what are you going to do when you get there?"

"Preach."

"On television? Radio? With a bullhorn? What are you planning?"

"Some good old street-corner preaching. I suspect the media will find me."

Something brushed against the bay window in the front of the room. We turned to look. The wind had nudged a tree limb against the glass.

I turned back to him. "You're going to be a target for every crackpot—Christian and Muslim—who thinks he's received a message from God. You know that, don't you?"

"Like I'm not already?"

"Fair point. Does Kacey know about this?"

"I talked to her about it last night."

"What does she think?"

"Believe it or not, she's completely in favor of it. She said that we can't allow ourselves to be silenced by a bunch of thugs."

"What thugs? As far as we know, the people who kidnapped her have never even heard of Dearborn."

"She wasn't talking about Dearborn." He rested his elbow on the fireplace mantel. "She was talking about people who want to foreclose all competition in religious ideas, the ones who not only won't listen to any other points of view themselves but who try to prevent others from listening too."

"She doesn't understand the danger you'll face."

"Oh, come on, Taylor. She was kidnapped, remember? Don't you think that gives her an idea? Besides, I've talked to her several times in detail about the risks. She understands that if I eventually go to the Middle East, there's going to be some danger."

"Did you talk about the possibility that you might get killed?"

"We specifically talked about that."

"What did she say?"

He pointed toward the doorway behind me. "Why don't you ask her?"

I looked over my shoulder. Kacey was standing there in an SMU Tri-Delta T-shirt, holding her backpack in one hand. "Ask me what?"

"We were talking about my plans to go to the Middle East. Taylor asked what you thought about them."

"I told Dad I wanted him to go, and that I wanted to go with him."

"Over my dead body."

Simon smiled at me. "That's one point we can agree on. Kacey is not going to the Middle East."

"We can't run from these people anymore," Kacey said. "If we want peace, we have to stand up and show some guts."

"You sound as if you want to fight them. That's not your father's point."

"It's not my point, either. I just want them to play

by the same rules as the rest of the civilized world. Every person is entitled to a free exchange of religious ideas and a free choice of which religion to pick. More than two hundred years after the American revolution I don't think that's such a radical idea, is it?"

Simon looked at me and shrugged. "Are you going to tell me that what she's saying doesn't make sense?"

Kacey threw her backpack over her shoulder and smiled. "I'd love to stay and chat about religious freedom, but I've got to go to class."

I waved and waited for her to walk out the front door, then turned back to Simon. "Okay, I heard all of that, but I'll ask you again. Are you sure she's okay with this?"

"What do you think?"

"She strikes me as a bit too matter-of-fact. She's putting on an act for you." A gust of wind rattled the window, and raindrops splattered on the glass.

He put his hands in his pockets. "I agree, some of it's an act. I'm not kidding myself. She's frightened and she's trying to be strong. Despite that, though, I'm convinced that she does get it. The kidnapping affected her more deeply than you know. She understands what the danger is, and she wants me to go."

"You know her better than I do."

"Don't jump to that conclusion. Sometimes I think the first rule of parenting is that the father doesn't know anything."

I smiled. "You're being too hard on yourself. In my experience, fathers know their daughters pretty well."

Simon walked to the window and looked out. "I wonder if she got drenched." He squinted through the glass. "Looks like it's blowing more than it's raining."

I jumped out of my chair. "The top is down on my car!"

He laughed. "Do you need an umbrella?"

I was out the door almost before he finished his sentence. The wind knocked me back a step. I lowered my head and plowed down the front walk. Grass clippings and live oak leaves peppered my head and arms. Fortunately, the raindrops were only sporadic. I hopped into the car, turned on the ignition, and pushed the button to raise the roof. As it folded into place above me, I glanced out the window. Kacey's Civic was still in the driveway, the engine running. She was in the front seat, but the window was fogged and I couldn't make out what she was doing.

After the top locked into place, I opened the door and sprinted to her car. When I got to the driver's side window, I could see that she was clutching the steering wheel, looking straight ahead. I rapped on the glass. She jerked and looked up at me. Her eyes were red and puffy. I ran around to the passenger side and got in.

She smiled, but it was hardly convincing. "I decided to wait a few minutes to see if this would blow over." She sniffled and wiped her face on the sleeve of her cotton top.

"I can see you've been crying, so you don't have to make small talk. What's wrong?"

She continued to grip the steering wheel. Outside the rain let loose, spreading out and flowing over the windshield. "Nothing."

"I'm not as dumb as I look, you know. Why don't you just tell me?"

She took her hands off the wheel and turned to face me. "I don't want Dad to die."

"Oh, honey." I put my arms around her neck and held her. Her shoulders shook. "Why don't you tell him you don't want him to do this?"

She pulled away and wiped her eyes. "What am I supposed to say? 'Dad, please think about me'? He's already thought about me. He risked his *soul* for me. That's sacrifice enough for one daughter, wouldn't you say? I'd rather die than ask him to do it again. It's my turn to sacrifice. If I love him, I have to let him do what he thinks he needs to do."

"Then I'll tell him how you feel."

Her eyebrows narrowed. "No! You have to promise not to tell him a thing about this."

"I don't know if I can promise you that. He needs to know."

"If you tell him, I'll never speak to you again." She wiped mascara from beneath her eyes with her fingers. "I may be only twenty, but I understand that some things are more important than how I feel. He believes that he needs to do this."

I squinted through the windshield. The trees in the yard were no longer swaying. "All right, I promise. But I'm still going to try to talk him out of this. I just won't mention you."

"Thank you."

The clouds had moved over quickly. The rain slackened to a mist, and Kacey switched on her wipers. "I've got to get to the library. Are you going to make a run for it?"

"I guess so. Are you all right?"

She smiled and held up her shortened finger. "I'm tougher than you think."

"There's such a thing as being too tough, you know." I wiped her cheek with my fingers.

She touched my hand. "Go ahead. I'm fine, really."

"Okay, but if you need to talk, call me."

"I will."

I took a deep breath. "Here I go!" I shoved open the door and splashed across the yard to my car.

As I turned the key in the ignition, I watched Kacey back out of the driveway. I understood the way she felt, but I also understood something that she didn't—what it was like to live without a father. With the course Simon was determined to take, I was afraid that she was about to learn. And I didn't see any way that I could stop it.

CHAPTER
THIRTY-SIX

NO ONE WAS CERTAIN how we would find out if any Muslim leader wanted to take Simon up on his debate challenge. After all, Simon didn't even know the names and locations of the leaders he was challenging. As it turned out, though, the decision to go on Lawrence Sylvan's show had been a good one.

Two nights before Simon was to go to Dearborn, Kacey and I had one of our regular practice sessions at the gun range. We finished at 9:30 because Kacey had a party to attend. Just after she pulled away from the curb, my phone rang. It was Simon.

"What's up?"

"I'm going to the Middle East. Can you come by the house?"

"What? What happened to Dearborn?"

"We'll talk about it when you get here."

"I'll be there in ten minutes." I flipped the phone shut and hopped in my car. When I arrived at the house, Simon and Elise met me at the front door.

"Where in the Middle East?" I asked as I stepped into the house.

"I'm not sure yet. The imam is from Beirut, Lebanon."

I'd never wanted to believe that the Middle East side of this idea would go anywhere, so when I heard those words I got a stomach ache. "What about Dearborn?"

"Dearborn is off. I've been spending quite a bit of time talking to Hakim, the Chicago limo driver, in the past few weeks. His family is connected in the Christian community in Lebanon—and I mean really connected. They are apparently one of a small group of families that carry major weight over there. When Hakim explained to them what I had in mind, they were excited about it. They started working back channels. There is an imam in Beirut, highly respected and a big supporter of secular government. He saw me on the Lawrence Sylvan show and was interested. He's taking a huge risk, but he wants to do this. By all accounts he's a good man."

"Why Lebanon?" Elise said. "Why can't he come to New York or meet you in Europe?"

"I told you, I'm not positive it will be Lebanon. But I'm not calling the shots on that. I promised I would go anytime, anywhere. Frankly, I don't know if the Lebanese government would even let me into the country. They've got plenty of other things on their plate right now without taking on something as controversial as this."

As we talked, we walked into the kitchen. I sat at the breakfast table. "I can get a security team together, but this will take a lot of advance planning. How much time do we have?" I pulled a pen and note pad out of my purse and scribbled some initial thoughts.

"There's not going to be a security team. I'm going alone."

Elise touched Simon's arm. "What? You can't be serious."

"There's a big difference between going to Dearborn without security and going to Beirut without security," I said.

Simon leaned back on the edge of the table. "I don't want to show up with an entourage when the point is to do missionary work. That's not the first picture I want people in the Middle East to get of me."

"Excuse me," Elise said, "but considering what you're going over there for, how do you expect to stay alive without security?"

"I didn't say that I wouldn't *have* security. I said I'm not *taking* a security team. We'll have to arrange something when we find out where I'm going. If it's Lebanon, Hakim's family can help. Besides, there are many Christians in Lebanon. They've been there a long time. Somehow they've managed to stay alive and be major players in the country. Lebanon is not Iran."

I flipped my notepad shut. "Come on, Simon. You know the distinction here. All those Christians who've been living in Lebanon for so long are not the world's best-known evangelist, and they're not running around trying to debate religious issues with imams. That puts you in a different security category, wouldn't you say?"

"I'll rely on God to keep me secure."

Elise pointed at him. "I've got a hunch God doesn't spend a lot of time working a security detail for fools who won't take commonsense precautions for themselves." She turned and walked out of the room. A few moments later the front door slammed.

Simon tilted his head to one side. "I think she was beginning to see it my way, don't you?"

I didn't want to humor him by laughing, but I couldn't help it. I was not about to let him off the hook, though. "Do you actually not see that she loves you? Are guys really that blind?"

He gave me a perplexed look. I realized that, incredibly, the answer to my second question was yes, but this was no time to try to correct a million years of evolutionary misfiring that must have accounted for that result. "Forget that for now. I agree with Elise."

"So you think I'm a fool too?"

"Well, not that part. I think you're a guy who feels that he has something to live down. I understand that feeling, so I don't think you're a fool."

"Thank you."

"Do you want my personal feeling about what you're doing?"

"I thought you just gave it to me."

"That was a specific response to the question of whether I thought you were a fool."

"Okay, then, what's your personal feeling?"

"I'm afraid for you, and I'm afraid that if you go to Lebanon or wherever over there, I'll never see you again. I'd have a hard time dealing with that." I ran a hand through my hair.

He stuck his hands in his pockets. "Thanks, Taylor. That was a nice thing to say. It means more to me than you know."

For a few moments neither of us said anything. When the silence became so awkward that I simply couldn't take it anymore, I said, "I don't suppose that anything I can say is going to change your mind?"

"Frankly, no. Nothing anyone could say would change my mind. I've got to do this. I understand everyone's concerns about me. But the reality is that there are some things more important than living."

I looked out the window. The day had been hot and clear, and the night promised to be huge and bright. Even sitting in a well-lit kitchen in the middle of the city, it was easy to spot individual stars blinking to life all over the sky. I smiled.

"What's so funny?"

"My dad said that to me once."

"Said what?"

"That there are some things more important than living." I stood and picked up my purse. "You came up with the one argument I can't dispute, because I believe it too. I hope things work out for you, Simon. I hope that God will bless you, because you're a good man."

I turned and walked out the door.

CHAPTER
THIRTY-SEVEN

THE ARRANGEMENTS FOR THE debate moved quicker than anyone expected. Hasim Saladin, a professor of religious studies at Oxford University, acted as the go-between to negotiate the rules. The imam recommended Saladin as a moderate voice of Islam, a reputation that required little time for Elise to confirm. Simon and the imam quickly agreed that Saladin would also act as the debate moderator and that the event would take place in Beirut.

They agreed to keep the location strictly confidential. Simon, Elise, and I were the only ones in the Mason camp who knew. Because there would be no live studio audience, the location of the event was easier to keep secret than it otherwise would have been. The only requirements from a production standpoint were an adequately sized room and a good camera crew.

An old friend from my Secret Service days, Roger Baines, was a pilot experienced in handling "sensitive" cargo. I'd sent him a considerable amount of business since I started my security service, and he was always eager to please. I arranged for him to fly Simon to Great Britain to pick up Professor Saladin. The plans were so secret that even Saladin, when he stepped on the jet in Manchester, would not know where he was going. From there Roger would fly them to Amman, Jordan.

On the ground we were relying heavily on Hakim's extended family. They were thrilled that Simon was coming to Lebanon, and even more thrilled about his purpose. Their connections reached into neighboring Jordan, and that came in handy in our planning. Hakim assured us they could arrange to move Simon and Saladin quietly through customs at the Amman airport. Two of Hakim's cousins would drive them from there into Lebanon and on to Beirut. We hoped that the chances of his being spotted would be greatly reduced by not flying into Beirut. We were concerned about secrecy in the imam's camp, but there was little that we could do but trust his assurances on that score. His personal risk was at least as great as Simon's.

The event was highly publicized, and media speculation was rampant about the location. Most of the prognosticators favored Dubai as the likely location, because of its elaborate efforts in recent years to Westernize and become an international tourist destination. The press surmised that Dubai would enjoy a public relations coup if it could peacefully pull off such a high-profile dialogue between faiths. The government of Dubai consistently denied that it was hosting the event. In light of the many favorable stories about its pro-Western climate, though, the denials were less strenuous than they could have been.

One thing quickly became clear: It hadn't occurred to anyone that either Simon or the imam would be crazy enough to conduct the event in a country as unstable as Lebanon. For its part, the U.S. State Department immediately informed Simon that it considered his trip, whatever the destination in the Middle East, to be a huge mistake. The U.S. government would be powerless to ensure his safety.

There were many risks of leaks, but the most significant came from the television side of the event. The parties agreed that one network would handle the live television feed and share it with any network that requested it. The chosen network was required to sign a confidentiality agreement with a hefty penalty clause that would cost it millions in the event of a traceable leak. Furthermore, the parties would not disclose the location to the network until forty-eight hours prior to the event.

The parties took a commonsense approach to the rules, keeping them as simple as possible. The discussion would address four topics: the fundamental tenets of the faith; the founder of the faith and his significance to it; the history of the faith and how that history is relevant to believers of today; and the ways in which the faith provides a better foundation for life than other faiths.

No one had any illusions that the time periods allotted would allow for much detail. It was not designed to be a theology lecture but a starting point for a continuing dialogue.

Both Hakim's extended family and the imam had connections at the highest levels of the Lebanese government, and both agreed it would be best not to notify the government at all. Lebanon had historically been one of the few countries in that part of the world where Muslims and Christians had shared power. In theory, it seemed to be an ideal location. In recent decades, though, Lebanon had been far from a peaceful haven for religious dialogue. Everyone concluded that it was impossible to determine which players in the government could be trusted. Instead, each side would make arrangements privately for its own security. In Simon's case, Hakim's family was to provide it. Many of Hakim's extended family members had served in Christian militias during Lebanon's civil war, so they had no shortage of training or armament.

The evening before Simon was to leave for Beirut, he called and asked if he could see me for a few minutes. By that time the press was stalking him, so he asked if I'd mind coming by the house. We could both imagine what the scandal sheets would say if he were seen going into my apartment.

When he called I was sitting on my bed reading a

client report. I hugged my knees to my chest. "What do you want to talk about?"

"I've got something to give you."

"I'll be there in fifteen minutes."

I pulled on a pair of jeans and a yellow Chicago T-shirt that I had bought in the Azure Hotel's gift shop when my suitcase finally hit empty during our stay there. At one time I'd have been driven to distraction by trying to guess what Simon wanted to give me. Those days of romantic fantasizing were over. I no longer viewed him as a knight waiting to rescue me from loneliness. This knight had warts, and I had seen them. Nevertheless, I was curious enough to apply a heavy foot to the accelerator on my way to his house.

Simon met me at the front door. The tail of his rumpled golf shirt hung out over faded cargo shorts. His beat-up running shoes were unlaced, as if he'd stuck his feet in them just to answer the door. "Thanks for coming," he said. "I wanted to talk to you before I leave. It's nice outside. Let's go out on the back deck."

As we passed through the kitchen, he pointed to the refrigerator. "You want an iced tea?"

"Yes, thanks."

He pulled a pitcher out of the refrigerator and filled two tumblers. "Let's see, you don't take sugar, right?"

"That's right."

He handed me the glass. I held it up and made a show of examining it. "A pitcher of tea in the refrigerator? Very civilized. Who's responsible for that? I'm guessing it's not you."

He smiled. "Meg was here today."

"I figured."

He held open the back door and we walked out onto the deck. Simon's backyard had a distinct southern look. The deck was elevated several feet above a rectangular swimming pool, and the floor and rail were as white as the rocking chairs in which we sat. Beyond the pool the long, narrow lawn stretched two hundred feet or so to a lanky stand of cedar elms that guarded the back fence.

Simon took a drink of his tea and rested the tumbler on the leg of his shorts. We sat in silence and rocked, looking out over the yard. The day had been hot and dry, typical for August in Dallas. The sun had been down for half an hour, and a surprisingly refreshing breeze curled in from around the trees, rippling the pool water and making the evening not only tolerable but pleasant. With each movement of the water, the pool light cast up translucent blue ghosts that swirled up and down and over the porch rail.

"Where's Kacey?"

"She had a thing at school. I'm meeting her near campus for a late dinner."

"It must be hard."

He looked down at his glass. "I can barely think about it, the idea of saying good-bye to her . . . It's the one thing that could make me not get on the plane tomorrow. If I can't think about it, you know how difficult it is to talk about it."

"Sorry."

He set his glass on the porch rail. "I had an interesting visitor yesterday afternoon. Brandon dropped by. I understand you've become friends."

I cocked my head. "Brandon? Hey, wait a minute, I thought the whole twelve-step thing was supposed to be confidential. Did he rat me out?"

He chuckled. "No, it wasn't about you. He called to tell me why he resigned as my accountant."

My mind flashed to my telephone conversation with Brandon and how he'd rushed off the phone when I raised this subject. "Oh? What did he say?"

"He asked me why five hundred thousand dollars was missing from my ministry's general fund. That's why he quit. He thought I was skimming money."

I turned and looked at him. "Five hundred thousand dollars just disappeared?"

"That's what he said."

"Why didn't he tell you this when he quit?"

"Brandon may be sarcastic, but he's the farthest thing from confrontational. I think it just wasn't part of his makeup to cause a scene. I don't know why he changed his mind and came to me yesterday."

"You still haven't called the man who left the note about your son, have you?"

He shook his head. "No, and he only asked for two hundred thousand anyway."

A few months earlier I wouldn't have even considered the possibility that Simon could have been involved in skimming money from his ministry. Since hearing the story behind the note, I was no longer sure what to think. I set my iced tea on the deck beside my chair and turned my rocker toward his. "Do you know what happened to the money?"

He looked me in the eye. "What kind of man do you think I am?"

I studied his face, and in an instant I knew the answer. Knew it with certainty. "You're a good man, Simon. I know you didn't take the money. Did Brandon believe you?"

"He said he did. For one thing, he knows that I've never had anything to do with the money side of the ministry."

I leaned forward with my elbows on my knees. "Then who did take it?"

"I have no idea—and I don't know for sure that anyone took anything. Remember, this was just Brandon talking. I had to fire him once for messing up an audit. No one has confirmed what he's saying."

I turned a palm up. "On the other hand, he's sober now, and he strikes me as a pretty smart guy."

"That he is."

"If you're not involved in the money side of the operation, who is?"

"A whole staff of people. We collect a huge amount of money in the course of a year."

"Is Elise one of them?"

He raised an eyebrow. "Only in the sense that they all report to her. Look, Elise wouldn't steal money from the ministry. She just wouldn't."

I rocked back in my chair. "I didn't say she would.

I just wanted to know who was in charge. So what do you want to do?"

"Obviously, I don't have time to investigate this before I leave for Beirut. I wanted you to know about it. If this were to blow up, I'd never want Kacey to think . . ." He ran a hand over his head.

"Don't worry, she never would. When you come back, we'll get to the bottom of it."

"Yes, when I come back."

He picked up his glass off the rail, took a long drink, and put it back. He crunched an ice cube as he rocked. When he stopped crunching, he tapped his fingers on the arms of his chair. "Can I show you something?"

"Sure, what?"

"Follow me."

We walked back into the house, through the family room, and into the garage. He turned on the overhead light and led me around his pickup truck to his wood-working space in the back corner. The accumulated heat of the day made the garage air oppressive. I swiped the back of my arm across my forehead.

"I know, it's like a sauna in here," he said. "This will help." He flipped the switch on a floor fan and turned it so it pointed at me.

I held out my arms to maximize the breeze's coverage.

"I've been working on something for Kacey," he said. "I put the final coat of stain on it this afternoon. This is where I've been hiding it." He stopped in front of a five-foot stack of moving boxes. He pulled the highest two boxes off the stack and motioned for me to look over the top.

I stepped away from the fan and leaned over the boxes. On the floor behind them was a mahogany baby cradle. I put my hand over my mouth.

He narrowed his eyebrows. "You don't like it?"

There was nothing else to do. I ran into the house, shut myself in the hallway bathroom, and cried.

CHAPTER
THIRTY-EIGHT

TEN MINUTES LATER I had composed myself, and we were back in our rocking chairs on the porch. My eyes were red and my mascara gone. Realizing that things could still get worse, I'd stuffed my pockets with clean tissues before I left the bathroom.

Simon rocked slowly, his eyes on the pool water. "I wanted her to have something from me—in case I don't . . . in case I have to miss some of the important things in her life."

"It's a beautiful cradle."

"I'm just glad you could identify that it *is* a cradle."

"This is no time to try to be funny."

"If I don't laugh, I'll be crying along with you."

I took a drink of my tea and set the glass back on the porch rail. "I don't know how to say this, because I know how much of yourself you must have put into the cradle, but you realize you can't give it to her, don't you? It would be like telling her you don't expect to come back."

"I thought of that too. I don't intend to give it to her."

"Then why did you make it?"

"I'm going to put it in the attic. She would never go up there unless something happened to me and she was sorting through my things. I'll attach a note to it. The only way she'll find it is if I'm gone. If I come back, I'll save it until she has a baby."

My hand went over my mouth again. With my other hand I reached in my pocket for a tissue.

A neighbor's dog barked, and Simon glanced over his shoulder at the back door. "I wonder where Sadie is." He went to the door, held it open, and whistled. I quickly wiped my eyes and stuffed the tissue back in my pocket.

Sadie ran onto the porch and shot past us down the steps. At the edge of the pool she froze and stared into the water, her tail extended and perfectly still. After a few moments she leaned back on her haunches and barked three times at the water. Then, as if that had been sufficient to discharge all of her poolside responsibilities, she turned and ran back up the stairs to Simon, her tail wagging frantically. Simon sat in his rocker and rubbed her behind the ears with both hands. Then he held his fist to his side. Sadie lay on the porch between our rockers, her chin resting on her paws, her tail flicking sporadically.

"What was that all about?" I said, grateful for the interruption.

"She sees her reflection in the water and thinks it's another dog. She's got to let it know who's boss of the Mason yard."

I patted her side. "You're funny, Sadie." She stretched her head back and sniffed my hand.

Simon slipped his feet out of his tennis shoes and put one foot up on the porch rail. He seemed to focus on something just beyond the pool. "I'm going to miss you."

I turned and looked at him. In the swirling light from the pool, his eyes glinted and he appeared younger. I could imagine him when Kacey was small—a strong, athletic father, the kind who would make a girl feel confident and secure.

"Thank you. I wouldn't have been sure."

He smiled. "I'm surprised to hear you say that. You're so much like me. We've got our flaws, but I think we're basically good-hearted. I hope you don't mind that I lumped you into a category with me."

"It depends on what flaws you're talking about."

"Minor ones in your case; more problematic ones in mine."

It was my turn to stare into the yard. "You know that I don't want you to go."

"That's nice of you to say, and it's what I wanted to talk to you about." He lowered his foot from the rail.

I quickened my rocking.

"I won't deny that I'm trying to do something—something really important—to square things with God. I mean, how does a preacher make up for denying his faith? It's all so crazy. Seventeen years ago I was just some guy working at an auto plant. I wish so much that I could go back."

"You don't deserve to feel this way."

He reached over and stopped my rocker with his hand. "Please look at me, Taylor."

I turned toward him. "This is so unfair." I pulled another tissue from my pocket.

"I'm not looking for sympathy. I don't have to do this; I'm choosing to do it. You know, Tom Carston talked about grace when he was over here that day. It's not about that. I know how grace works, and I know that I don't have to earn it. This is about owing God something. It may be irrational, but it's the way I feel. Anyway, the point is that you're right. A part of me wants to die. It may be the only way I can find peace."

"That's not martyrdom; it's suicide."

"No, I'll say it again: It's peace. Did Jesus commit suicide? He could have prevented his death, but he didn't. Did the martyrs commit suicide? Many of them could have avoided death just by keeping their mouths shut. I don't believe that it's suicide to choose to put yourself in a position where you might die as a public statement of your faith."

"What about Kacey? If you die, what happens to her? Do you think a cradle will make up for a missing father?"

His hand slipped from the arm of my rocker.

"I'm sorry. That was unfair," I said.

"It's okay. I want to talk about it. In fact, I need to talk about it. I *need* to tell someone how hard this is. I don't think I can tell Kacey. It would only make it more painful for her." He ran his hand over his head. "Do you think I haven't agonized over her? My dinner with her tonight will be the most painful thing I've done in my life—saying good-bye."

I dabbed at my eyes with my tissue. "I didn't mean what I said. I'm just upset."

He shook his head. "You don't have to apologize. I told you, I want to talk about this. The truth is that I love Kacey more than anything. And that's the problem, isn't it? Deep in my heart I've had to admit that I love her more than I love God. She's part of me. I can see her, I can touch her, I was there when she was born. How could I not love her more than someone I can't see and can't touch? That's why I have to make this sacrifice. I owe it to God. I turned my back on him once. I'll never do it again. My love for him isn't what it should be, but I will sacrifice everything for him. I'm willing to say good-bye to the one thing that matters most to me. My daughter." His voice cracked. "There is nothing more I can give."

Even if I had thought of something to say, I couldn't have spoken. For several minutes we sat in silence. He stared down at the water; I stared up at the stars. I focused on one that was particularly bright. It flashed and pulsed in a rhythm I struggled to catch. For an instant my father's face came to me, looking up at me in the moment before he died. He was happy in that moment. He'd finally found peace. Dad was wrong that night when he told me that I loved the lights. I thought of Simon and Kacey, how much I'd grown to love them, and I knew that for me it had never been the lights.

It was the stars. How I loved the stars.

I touched Simon's arm. "I understand."

He squeezed my hand and nodded.

Sadie stood, gave herself a shake, and put her head in Simon's lap. "So you want some attention, huh?" He gave her head a good rub. "I'll miss you, too, puppy." After a minute she moved back to the side of his chair, circled a few times, and lay on the porch again.

"I guess we got sidetracked from the reason I wanted to see you," Simon said. "I've thought a lot about you lately. More than you would imagine. I'll admit that sometimes I've wondered how you felt about me. That's one of the reasons I asked you to come over. I want you to know how I feel."

I leaned away from him as he spoke. He seemed to be heading in a direction that I no longer wanted to go.

He cleared his throat. "I never had a little sister."

I realized I was holding my breath. I exhaled.

"If I had had a little sister, I'd like for her to be exactly like you. I feel protective of you, and I trust you. That must be obvious after the talk we just had. It's about the best compliment I could give someone."

I leaned toward him and smiled. "I appreciate it very much."

"I want to ask you a favor, and I want to give you something. First, the favor: If anything does happen to me, I'm asking you to look out for Kacey. Be a big sister to her. Meg will give her all the mothering she could need. Kacey idolizes you, though—I've told you that before—and you could be a great influence on her. Will you do that for me?"

My eyes were moist before he even finished the question.

"You're crying again? What did I say this time?"

I waved my hand in the air. "Oh, you know me." I wiped my cheek with my sleeve. "This means more than just about anything that anyone has ever said to me."

"So you'll do it?"

"Of course I will," I said between sniffles.

"Thank you."

"You said there was a second thing?"

"Yes. I have something for you." He reached in his back pocket and pulled out a folded letter-sized envelope. "I told you I trust you. Now I'm going to give you a chance to prove I'm not a sap." He handed it to me.

I laughed, still wiping my eyes. "Is it a million dollars?"

"Clever. Actually, there are some things about me that you still don't know. For example, I knew more about you than I let on when I called you that first day from Chicago."

I raised an eyebrow. "Like what?"

"Just more. Now I'm asking you for a promise."

"What kind of promise?"

"I want you to hold onto this envelope. If I get back from Lebanon okay, you can return it to me—unopened. If something happens to me, I want you to open it. That's all I'm going to say."

"This is a bit melodramatic, isn't it?"

"Maybe. I need you to promise me, though. I know it will be tempting to open it as soon as you walk out that door tonight, and I can't stop you from doing that. But I'm giving it to you because I trust you. I'm asking you to prove that I have reason to. Will you do it?"

I turned the envelope over in my hands. Then I held it up to the porch light and squinted.

"Very funny," he said.

I pulled it back down. "Okay, I give you my word that I won't open it unless you don't come back. But you will come back, right? And when you do, you'll tell me what's in the envelope. Otherwise, I'd have a rather unbecoming rooting interest in your trip."

He chuckled. "Thank you for promising." He looked at his watch. "It's nearly ten. I've got to get down to the campus to meet Kacey." He reached down and slipped on his shoes.

We stood and picked up our glasses. Sadie trotted to the back door and looked at us over her shoulder.

Simon touched my arm. "Before you go, there is one more thing I'd like."

"What's that?"

He leaned toward me, stretched out his arms, and hugged me.

CHAPTER
THIRTY-NINE

THE MORNING AFTER SIMON left for Beirut, I was squeezing my toes into a pump in the shoe department at Nordstrom when my phone rang. It was my pilot friend, Roger.

"The package has been delivered."

"Is that some sort of secret pilot code?"

"Yeah. Sounded cool, huh?"

"As cool as you're likely to get. Were there any problems?"

"None that I could see."

"Great. Are you staying over there for a while?"

"No. I'll be back tonight. I have another job the day after tomorrow."

"Thank you. I'll make sure you get paid promptly."

"My pleasure. Maybe this is something that I'll be able to tell my grandchildren about."

"Don't you have to have children before you can have grandchildren?"

"I'm working on that."

"That's more information than I needed. Thanks again."

He laughed. "Any time."

I clicked the phone off, found Hakim's number, and punched the buttons. After a few rings Hakim answered, huffing and puffing.

"This is Taylor. Are you all right? You sound out of breath."

"I'm jogging. Here, let me get off to the side of the track." There was a shuffling sound, and several car horns blew in the background.

"Where are you, on Michigan Avenue?"

"Close. I'm at the track at Northwestern University, the downtown campus. "What you're hearing is Lake Shore Drive. Have you talked to Simon?"

"I just got a call from the pilot. Simon got to Amman okay."

"I know. I talked to my cousin Kalil. Simon is fine. In fact, Kalil and Jibran have already gotten him to Beirut, and he's checked into his hotel. It's a nice hotel, near the water."

"That's what I wanted to know. They're staying with him, aren't they?"

"Oh, yes. One of them will be with him at all times.

Jibran is staying right there in the room with him. They are both experienced men. Militia."

"That's all I wanted to know. Thanks, Hakim. Bye."

I had never been a worrier, and I gave myself a mental kick for acting like such a grandmother. I put the pumps back in their box and resolved to relax. Simon was going to be just fine without me.

CHAPTER
FORTY

THAT NIGHT I DREAMED that Kacey was standing in front of me, in the isosceles firing stance, aiming her pistol at my recovery partner, Brandon. I tried to tell her not to shoot, but my mouth was stuck shut with something like super bubble gum. I watched helplessly as she sighted the pistol and closed her finger over the trigger. Instead of a gun shot, her pistol rang, and rang, and rang again.

I sat up in bed. My phone. I leaned over and hit the speaker button. "Hello."

"Taylor, it's Hakim."

I clicked off the speaker and held the phone to my ear. I looked at the clock. Two-thirty in the morning. "What's wrong?"

"Something's happened to Simon."

My shoulders sagged. "Oh, no. What?"

"Jibran is dead. He and Simon were supposed to meet Kalil for breakfast at 9:30 in the hotel. When they didn't show up, Kalil went to their room. He knocked on the door and there was no answer. He got the hotel manager to open the door. Jibran was sitting on the floor, propped against the wall beside the door. He had a bullet through his head."

I sat back against the headboard. "What about Simon?"

"He wasn't there. There was no other blood or sign of a struggle, just Jibran lying there."

"I'm sorry, Hakim."

"So am I."

"How can we find out what happened to Simon? Has anyone contacted the authorities?"

"One might question who the authorities are in Lebanon right now. We cannot rely on the police. No one knows for sure who is loyal to what faction these days."

"What can we do?"

"My family has many connections, and not just in the Christian community. There are back channels to be worked, things to be done to obtain information. Lebanon is a country with a chaotic political climate. In some ways that may help us. Allegiances can change day to day. Often money is the thing that changes them. They will let me know as soon as they hear something."

"I want to go over there."

"That is not a good idea. An American woman traveling alone in Lebanon could be in danger."

"I get the idea that anyone traveling in Lebanon could be in danger. I'm pretty good at taking care of myself."

"I suspect that you are. If you insist on going, I wish you would allow me to have my uncle arrange an escort you can trust, someone to drive you around who knows the area, the customs. You'll want to blend in as much as possible."

"I'd appreciate that. Thank you."

"When do you intend to leave?"

"I know a pilot. As soon as I can get him on the phone and make visa arrangements."

"Your visa should not be a problem. You can get it at the Beirut airport when you arrive. You will find Lebanon a relatively easy country to get into for that region of the world. Our goal is to make sure that you come out again."

"Yes, of course."

"One more thing: I understand the type of work you are in. I have a tip for you. You may be accustomed to traveling with a weapon in your luggage. I wouldn't attempt that. My uncle can arrange for anything you need in that regard once you arrive in Lebanon."

"Thank you for the tip."

I clicked the phone off and put my head in my hands. This couldn't really be happening. Why didn't Simon listen to us? I grabbed my hair and pulled it until it hurt. I wanted to punch him, hurt him. He had no right to throw away his life. There were people who needed him.

I needed him.

And what chance did I have of helping him in Beirut?

I sat up straight and took a deep breath. One thing was certain: Whining would accomplish nothing. I might not be able to do much, but I had to do what I could. I swung my feet over the side of the bed. Before I stood, I looked up at the ceiling.

"God, if you're up there, please keep an eye on Simon. And give me some luck."

CHAPTER
FORTY-ONE

AS I WALKED TOWARD the baggage claim area at the Beirut airport, I saw a man in a New York Yankees T-shirt holding up a cardboard sign with black lettering: "Taylor Pasbury."

I waved at him as I approached. "Sakir?"

He put the sign under his arm. "Miss Pasbury? I was worried that your flight would be delayed. Look at the sky." He pointed out the plate-glass windows at dark clouds rumbling a mile or so from the airport. "They might have sent your plane back to Amman. Follow me. The baggage claim is this way."

"I don't have any other baggage. This is it." I nodded at the wheeled suitcase I was pulling. "I came in on a private jet. Any news about Simon?"

He glanced over his shoulder and lowered his voice. "We will wait and talk about that in the car."

I looked around at the passengers attending to their luggage, although I had no idea what I was looking for. A fellow in a trench coat and dark glasses?

As the automatic doors opened to let us out of the terminal, the first raindrops were splattering on the pavement. Sakir led me across the terminal drive to a silver Mercedes parked in one of the first stalls in the parking garage.

"Is this your car?"

"You expected a bombed out 4-Runner? This isn't Iraq. We've had our problems for the past few decades, and certainly during the Israeli fight with Hezbollah. Even in the days when Syria was running things, though, there were ways to make a good living in this country. Our family has been here many years. We adapt." He tossed my suitcase into the trunk and opened the passenger door for me.

"You will be staying at the Seafarer Hotel under the name Tia Gemaldi. We know many of the staff there. You will be safe, and we will be able to communicate easily. Here is a passport in case you are ever asked for identification around the hotel. Do not use this with any of the authorities, though—only with staff at the hotel and nongovernment people. If anyone in authority asks for your passport, give them your real one. You do not want to get yourself in unnecessary trouble."

I took the passport and put it in my travel bag. "Your English is very good. Better than mine, I'd say."

We ducked into the car. "I'm a graduate of Columbia University," he said as he turned the key. "Good English is a valuable asset there. You should teach it to more New Yorkers."

I laughed.

As he backed out of the parking space, he glanced at me. "We think we have news of Simon."

"What is it?"

"We believe we know who is holding him. Now we are working on finding out where."

"Who has him?"

"A small group of Shiite thugs. They have ties to Iranian security forces, but not at any official level. It appears that they are attempting to make a name for themselves."

"Have you gone to the police?"

"This is not Texas, Miss Pasbury. There is no way of knowing who can be trusted in the police or the government. Allegiances are fluid these days."

"So if you find him, what can we do?"

"We're not sure. That will depend on the circumstances. Have you ever heard Lebanese music?"

"No."

He reached for the radio and turned it on. The Beach Boys were singing "Help Me, Rhonda." He smiled.

Twenty minutes later he pulled into the circular drive of a gleaming glass high-rise with a giant fountain in the drive. "This is the Seafarer. Four Stars. I think you will find it satisfactory. Let's get you checked in."

He walked past the bellman and led me into the hotel lobby. I headed for the check-in desk. He held up a hand. "Wait, one moment, please."

We stood about thirty feet from the desk. From the corner of his eye he watched a heavyset man behind the desk who was handing a key to a customer. When the customer left, the man looked at Sakir and nodded.

"Now." Sakir led me to the desk. He did not speak to the man as I registered but stood next to my suitcase a few feet away.

I'd already been told that most of the service employees who deal with the public in Beirut speak English. That proved to be true. Check-in was no more difficult than if I'd been in Kansas City. Sakir rode with me in the elevator to the seventh floor. My room was halfway down the long hallway.

"Right in the middle, lots of people around," he said. "That's good."

I pulled out the card key.

"May I come in with you?" he said. "I have something to show you."

I paused. "Sure." I handed him the key. "You first."

He smiled. "Smart. You should do well in Beirut." He slid the key into the slot, swung the door open, and walked into the room. When he got to the foot of the bed, he dropped onto his stomach.

I took a quick step back toward the door. "What are you doing?"

"Just a minute." He rolled onto his back and scooted his head to where he could see beneath the bed. Then he reached under it and moved his hand back and forth in wide swipes. His hand stopped. "There." He swept his hand again. "And there! Thank you." When he pulled his hand from beneath the bed, he was gripping a pistol.

I lifted my suitcase in front of me and backed toward the doorway, my eyes on the pistol.

He laughed. "No, no, come back. This is for you. Sig Sauer .357 is your preference, I believe?" He flipped it so he was gripping the barrel and held it out to me.

I walked back into the room and took it. Still on his back, he reached under the bed again and dragged out three twelve-round magazines. He sat up, his back against the bed, the magazines on the carpet beside him.

"Wow, you guys are good," I said, as I got the feel of the pistol.

"I forgot something." He dropped onto his back again and felt beneath the bed one more time. When he came up, he had a silencer.

"Let me amend that. You guys are pros."

He stood and handed me the silencer. "We try. Firearms are plentiful in Lebanon, so if you need something else, just let me know. I can't overemphasize how important it is that you exercise extreme discretion with your hand gun. It could create severe problems if a woman were known to be 'packing,' as they say in the States."

I was beginning to wonder if I'd been dropped into the middle of an organized crime family. "I think they only say that in the movies. Thank you, though. Your people are very efficient."

"Efficiency is power in Lebanon. We have to be able to provide what the government cannot. That ability creates influence."

"I thought the Christians shared power in the Lebanese government."

"Sharing control of the government and having real power are not always the same thing. We exert our influence within and without the government." He moved toward the door.

"How will we get in touch again?"

"After you get unpacked and relax a bit, go downstairs and grab a bite to eat. You'll be safe in this hotel. A number of people are watching out for you. I will call your room in a few hours and brief you on what we know at that time."

"Thank you, Sakir. You and your family have gone to a lot of trouble."

"You are welcome. You must remember, we are experienced in the ways of this country. It can be a dangerous place. We know what must be done to manage that danger. That may make us appear a bit—shady, should I say? But we are Christians, and we believe that what Mr. Mason wants to do here is important. We are happy to do what we can to help." He gave me a slight bow and walked out the door.

I moved the pistol from one hand to the other. He was right about one thing: Lebanon seemed like a very dangerous place.

CHAPTER
FORTY-TWO

HAKIM'S FAMILY DID FIND Simon. He was being held in a suburb of Beirut. The group that had him was loosely organized—basically a new street gang looking to make a reputation. How they learned that Simon was in the country remained a mystery. In one way, though, we were fortunate. Simon had been grabbed by a bunch of rookies—and corrupt rookies at that. After a couple of days—and the payment of a substantial number of U.S. dollars—Hakim's uncle, Paul Malouf, purchased an informant.

Malouf was an experienced leader. About sixty years old and solid as a block of concrete, he exuded quiet confidence. He had been a general in the Christian militia during Lebanon's civil war. He assembled a team of six, including me, to rescue Simon. The others were soldiers with whom Malouf had worked on many occasions. I was allowed on the team for one reason: I knew Simon Mason. Malouf believed that could be a significant advantage when things got hot and we needed to make educated guesses about how Simon might react.

Before deciding to go it alone, the team discussed the possibility of bringing in the authorities. Simon was so high profile the government wouldn't dare botch the job. It was a testament to the deep level of distrust of the government—or more particularly of certain individuals within the government—that Malouf nixed the idea.

Our informant operated on the fringes of several radical groups in Beirut. A more experienced bunch of terrorists would never have allowed him so close. He was able to provide us with firsthand information about the guard setup and weaponry in the house where they were holding Simon. Malouf held several planning sessions over a three-day period as he continued to receive details from the informant. We met at Malouf's estate on the outskirts of Beirut's suburbs. It was apparent from the sheer size of the place that, as Sakir had informed me at the airport, the Malouf family had done well over the years.

The night of the operation we had a final planning meeting in Malouf's kitchen. By that time I was catching on to how names worked in Lebanon. I figured someone must assign them randomly. The names of the men around the table were Paul, Samir, Pierre, Hakil, and Joe. We sat at the kitchen table munching spinach pies that Malouf's wife had prepared.

The kidnappers took a hide-in-plain-sight approach. That way they didn't have to draw attention to themselves by posting an army of guards around the house. They were holding Simon in a neighborhood in which one of them lived, a fairly affluent suburb by Lebanese standards. There was no indication that the neighbors knew anything about Simon's presence or were in league with the kidnappers.

The neighborhood consisted of a narrow street of one-story block houses, each with its own small yard. Paul explained that the house drew on the typical Lebanese central hallway floor plan. Every member of our team, except me, had been in many houses throughout Beirut with similar room arrangements. The house was a rectangle, longer from front to back than side to side. On each side of the house was a strip of grass that separated it from the neighboring house. The front door opened into a living area. To access the rest of the house it was necessary to walk through a door in the middle of the back wall of the room. From there, a hallway ran to the back of the house. On the right side of the hall was a bathroom with a large bedroom behind it. On the left side of the hall was a small bedroom, with the kitchen behind it at the back.

Each room in the house had only one window, except the front living area, which had a window in the front and another on the side. The back door opened directly into the kitchen, where our informant said at least one of the kidnappers hung out at virtually all times of the day and night.

They were holding Simon in the small bedroom in the middle of the house, between the living room and the kitchen. According to the informant, one guard stayed in the room with him at all times. Both Simon and the guard slept on mats on the floor. Simon was shackled by the ankle, with a thick, two-foot chain, to a heavy wooden desk in the corner of the room near the window. The shackle was screwed into the desk leg, so Paul decided the fastest way to free him would be to saw off the leg of the desk and take it with us.

Paul's men had watched the neighborhood for the past twenty-four hours. The kidnappers posted a lookout in a parked car at each end of the street. The house had a single guard on the small front stoop. According to the informant, the guard was a burly sort who was both stupid and lazy but dangerously strong. The backyard was unfenced and watched by a smaller, more intelligent guard. Our informant said the outside guards carried only pistols, while the three to five men inside the house had a variety of automatic weapons. The front room was rarely occupied, as it faced west and was the hottest room in the house. The best television in the house was in the kitchen, so that was where most of the men spent their time.

Paul's plan called for our informant to leave the house at 2:15 a.m. He would meet us at a nearby parking lot. At that time he would let us know the latest on where everyone in the house was positioned. Samir and Hakil would then head for the opposite street corners on foot. They were to take out the street-corner sentries simultaneously at exactly three o'clock. Samir would then rendezvous with Paul in a neighbor's yard, and Hakil would make his way back to the parking lot to pick up the van in which we would make our escape.

Joe and Pierre would approach the house from the neighbor's yard on one side and take out the front guard with a silencer. Paul and Samir would approach the house from the opposite direction, move into the backyard and take care of the guard there. Paul would be the first to enter the house with Samir right behind him. Paul was to shoot anyone in the kitchen, while Samir leapfrogged him and tossed a sonic concussion grenade into the bedroom where Simon was being held. The sonic grenade would send a shock wave in a six-foot radius, stunning anyone in the room. Upon hearing the blast from the grenade, Joe and Pierre would enter the front of the house and support Paul and Samir. I was to wait in the backyard and deal with anyone other than our people who approached or left the house from the back.

Four things were essential to the plan: stealth, marksmanship, the reliability of our information, and a great deal of luck. None of us had any illusions about the odds: They were not good. But if what our informant told us was true, the kidnappers intended to kill Simon. The only thing holding them up was their indecision over the best way to maximize publicity.

As we finished our final planning meeting, Paul surprised me by praying for the success of our mission. The idea of praying before heading out to kill people would never have occurred to me. It was apparent, though, that Paul would never have considered leaving without praying. By the time he began the prayer, my level of fear was increasing exponentially. My stomach rumbled so loudly that I worried someone might comment on it. When he finished the prayer, Paul did.

He motioned to me to stay seated while the others left the room. When we were alone, he smiled. "Nervous?"

I rubbed my hand over my stomach. "I guess so."

"Me too. I take these." He pulled a small tin of antacid tablets out of his pocket and offered me one.

"Thanks." I popped it in my mouth.

"It will be fine. We live, we die—it will happen to all of us sooner or later. Better to go out doing something noble, eh?" He pushed his chair back, stood, and slapped me on the back. "You will see some action tonight, young lady. Remember to clean your weapon. Tonight would be a bad time to have a gun jam." He turned and walked out of the room.

What he said to me helped, but I still headed for the bathroom.

CHAPTER
FORTY-THREE

PAUL AND SAMIR WEREN'T paying much attention to me as we knelt behind a row of shrubs in the backyard of the house next door to where the kidnappers were holding Simon. A single light glowed in the front porch of the house. What would the residents think if they happened to awaken in the middle of the night, look out the window, and see three people in black clothing and camo face paint crouching by their azaleas? I assumed that even in Lebanon that would be cause for concern.

In the Secret Service we trained for combat situations, but I'd never actually been in a firefight. I wondered whether I'd see any of the real shooting from my post in the back of the house, and how I'd react if I did.

I thought of Dad and told myself over and over that it would be better to die than to run. I felt like throwing up.

The weather gave us two lucky breaks. The night was starless, and there was a brisk, swirling wind. We were difficult to see and hear. No more than fifty feet away, the backyard guard slouched in a cheap aluminum lawn chair. His back was to the kitchen, his leather boots propped on an empty orange crate. His head sagged so that his chin nearly touched his chest. A cigarette dangled from his lips. He hadn't taken a drag since we arrived a few minutes earlier, and his shoulders rose and dropped in a slow, steady rhythm.

The light from the kitchen reached just far enough out the back door to illuminate the guard's back but stopped at the base of his neck. With his head in the dark and his body awash in light, he had an eerie, half-human look, which made it easier for me to think that we would soon be killing him.

Something rustled in the bush next to my foot, then scurried along the shrub line. I had no idea what sorts of animals were common to Lebanon. Maybe it was a ground hog.

The illuminated hands of my watch pointed to three o'clock. We could not see into the kitchen, but the informant had told us that two men were playing cards at the kitchen table when he left. According to the informant, we had one more reason to be thankful for our luck: Besides the two in the kitchen, there was only one other man in the house: The one in the bedroom with Simon.

Paul nudged Samir, who eased his head above the bushes. He aimed his pistol at the guard. The wind increased the difficulty of the shot, but we were close enough to the target that it should have been manageable. I had no idea how well Samir could shoot. While I spent my spare time at Paul's estate practicing with my new Sig Sauer, I hadn't seen Samir do any shooting. It was a shot we couldn't afford to miss. Just in case, I quietly took a knee, found a gap in the shrubs, and leveled my Sig at the guard's head.

Samir didn't seem comfortable in the wind. He shifted his weight from foot to foot, raised the pistol and lowered it. We were surrounded by windows, and I worried that his head had been exposed for too long above the bush. His fidgeting stopped and he became still. A bug landed on my ear. I forced myself to ignore it. Samir's silencer zipped. The guard yelled and grabbed his thigh. I followed his head through my sight as he bent to look at his leg, which was already bleeding through his pants. I squeezed the trigger. His head snapped sideways. He slumped from the lawn chair to the ground. Samir and Paul spun toward me, eyes wide. Paul smiled.

Someone in the kitchen shouted, "Ali!" It was more of a question than an alarm. Paul and Samir ran around the bushes, heads low, guns pointed at the ground. When they reached the wall of the house, they flattened their backs against it. The wind rose again. I strained but could not hear what was going on in the kitchen.

Paul lifted his pistol in front of his chest and rocked slightly from his heels to his toes. He took a breath, then spun around the corner and through the back door into the kitchen. Samir followed close behind. I heard several pops.

They were not the sound of silencers.

I waited for the boom from the sonic grenade. Nothing happened. I peered through the gap in the shrubs, but there was nothing to see. A light came on in the neighbor's house behind me. I was doing no one any good squatting behind a stupid bush, so I ran around the shrubs toward the back of the house. As I got there, Samir stumbled out the back door, the shoulder of his shirt stained with blood.

He lifted his hand, which was closed around the grenade. "Take it! They're all down." I grabbed the grenade and clipped it to my belt. "Go!" he said.

I backed against the house and peeked around the corner into the kitchen. Two men sprawled on the floor near the table. Paul lay on his side near the door, blood puddling under his head and his leg. He moved his leg and groaned.

I spun through the door, stepped over him, and moved to the rear of the kitchen. Stopping with my back to the wall, I held my gun in both hands and peeked around the corner into the hall. The light was off, but I could see that the hallway was empty. I turned the corner and looked for the bedroom door on the right that I remembered from the floor plan Paul had drawn.

Just before I got to it, I heard a click from inside the bedroom.

I dropped to my stomach. The wall above me exploded with a spray of automatic weapon fire. I covered my head with my gun hand and unclipped the grenade from my belt with the other. Chunks of drywall rained on my back. I was practically kissing the floor as I lowered my hands in front of my face and pulled the pin on the grenade. The firing from inside the room stopped.

Stretching my left hand out in front of me, I rolled the grenade around the corner, then curled into a ball on my side and covered my ears. The explosion lifted me an inch off the floor.

Popping up to my knees, I held my pistol in both hands and lunged sideways. I skidded in front of the open doorway. The first thing I saw was Simon. He was kneeling, on the far side of the room, his back to the doorway. Several feet to his right, sitting dazed on the floor, was my target. His beard was thick and dark, and he cradled an AK-47 to his chest. I squeezed off two shots. One entered the wall next to his head. The other entered his heart.

I stood up just as Joe and Pierre ran into the hallway from the living room. "Paul and Samir are down. Back there!" I pointed toward the kitchen. They ran past me.

I looked back at Simon. He was still kneeling, his head leaning against the side of the desk. I walked into the room. As I approached, he still didn't move.

Then I understood, and I began to cry.

When I reached him, I knelt beside him and put my arm around his shoulder. I touched my cheek against his. It was cool and dry. I leaned forward and looked at his face. His eyes were closed. His throat was slit from side to side. Blood soaked the front of his shirt, and dull red blotches were already forming on his face and neck. We had been hours too late.

I stood up and hid my face in my arm. My shoulders shook, and I wanted to run, to fly out of the house. Something, though, made me turn back.

I looked down at Simon's hands. His fingers were clasped and resting in his lap, the way that a child would hold his hands to kneel and pray. I smiled, then raised my hand and ran it over his bald head, just as I'd seen him do so many times.

We had tried our best, Paul and the team, but Simon had done better. He got what he wanted.

He'd found peace.

CHAPTER
FORTY-FOUR

IF IT HADN'T BEEN ten o'clock in the morning, I'd have been far more tempted to have a bourbon. Sitting alone in the private jet that Elise had chartered to bring Simon's body home, I watched out the window as Beirut disappeared behind me. I was in no hurry ever to return.

The authorities in Beirut took three days to sort out the situation and conduct an autopsy. By the time they were finished, much of the international media—including many outlets in the Middle East—were loud and persistent in their condemnation of the unwillingness of fundamental Islamic groups to accept an open competition of religious ideas. Simon was right. His death had mattered.

While waiting in Beirut for the release of Simon's body, I'd been tormented each time I passed the hotel bar. Two things kept me straight. First, I owed it to Simon not to take that first drink. And second, I leaned on the principles of the twelve-step program. One of those principles was reliance on a spiritual power greater than I am.

I began to pray in Beirut, not just for me, but for Kacey. I wasn't very good at it, but I figured no one was awarding style points. I just stumbled along in a beginner's dialogue with God, assuming this was one area of life in which it was okay to learn as I went. I can't honestly say I've been overwhelmed by the spirit, but I'm keeping an open mind. I owe that to Simon too.

Paul was hurt worse than Samir, but both would be okay. I invited them to Dallas and promised the entire team that I'd send them custom-made cowboy hats. They seemed to be more interested in Dallas Cowboys jerseys, so I promised those too. Their willingness to risk so much for a man they didn't even know was something that would have been more difficult for me to understand had I never known Simon and my father. Dad was not the only person who believed that some things were more important than living.

When I called Kacey to give her the news of her father's death, her voice broke but she didn't cry. I think she expected it as much as I did. She would have to grieve in her own way, but I worried that she would hold her emotions too close. If she'd been my own sister, I couldn't have been any more eager to get home to her.

She *was* my family now. Simon had wanted it that way, and so did I.

During the past few days I'd pulled out Simon's envelope several times, but I hadn't opened it. Beirut hadn't seemed the right place. Now, as I folded a leg beneath me and settled in for the long flight, I reached into my purse, found the envelope, and held it in front of me with both hands. I pictured the evening when Simon gave it to me. Already the details were receding, leaving more of a sense than a verbatim transcript of what he'd said. I pictured his face, focused hard on it. It was the one thing I wanted to burn so deep into my memory that it would never blur.

I slid my fingernail beneath the flap of the envelope and pulled out two folded sheets of computer paper that contained Simon's crisp handwriting in black ink. I flicked on the light above me and began to read:

Dear Taylor,
If you're reading this, I'm not around anymore
(assuming you kept your word . . .).

I nodded. "I did, Simon." I said aloud.

I told you once that I knew more about you
than you thought. That's because I've followed
your life from a distance for a number of years.
Doing the math in my head, you must have been
about ten years old when I met your mother. I'll
let the shock of that settle in for a moment. Yes,

I met your mother just before I learned that Marie had had an affair. We worked together at the auto plant in St. Louis.

Your mother was a brilliant woman. In the beginning I didn't understand why she was working on an assembly line. As I came to know her better, I realized that she was troubled in ways I could not hope to sort out.

You probably can see where this is going. The boy referred to in the note that you found— my son—is your mother's son also. Our affair was brief, but long enough that she mentioned you a number of times. It was not until I read in the newspaper about a teenage girl who shot her father's killers at a campsite in West Texas that I recognized your name and learned where you were and what you were doing. I told you the truth when I said that a friend referred me to you after I received the threats. I just didn't tell you the rest of the story.

Your mother left the auto plant soon after I broke off the affair. I don't know where she is now. We've not been in touch since she told me about my son shortly after he was born. She didn't ask for anything. She said she was calling from New Mexico and just thought I should know.

I do know that your and Kacey's brother's name is Chase Franklin. He lives in Katy, Texas. I hope you and Kacey will decide to meet him. I hope you'll find your mother too.

If I had more courage, I'd have gone public

about Chase and accepted the consequences. But if I had more courage, I'd have done many things differently. When you meet him, please tell him that I love him. I don't expect him to believe that, but I wouldn't want him to go through his life without at least hearing it from me, even if secondhand.

Now, a word for you. You're strong, Taylor, much stronger than you know. If you had been my own daughter, I couldn't have been more proud of you. There is a goodness in you that is as beautiful as you are, and you've maintained that even though you've had more than your share of bad breaks. I have one thought for you, to help you in your life, I hope. This is more important than anything else I could tell you. Invite God into your life, as I did. Then rely on him. Don't be put off by flaws in men like me. Our flaws are not God's flaws. If you follow this advice, you will never be alone again.

I am glad to have known you. When you remember me, I hope you will forget the bad and think of the good. If it's possible to miss someone in heaven, I will miss you until I see you there.

Love,
Simon

I read it again, and then again. The news about my mother was almost beyond belief. Despite that shock, though, my focus kept drifting to the last sentence of the letter. If there was a heaven, could Simon really see me from there? And miss me? If he could, then maybe Dad could too.

I looked out the window. Beneath the plane the sun glinted off the whitecaps in the Mediterranean. Everything sparkled, just like a star. I closed my eyes and pictured Dad and Simon, both of them looking down at me from up among the stars. Watching me. Missing me. From the one place where Dad had always wanted to be—the one place where there was peace.

I leaned my head against the window. And for the first time in a long time, I smiled.

CHAPTER
FORTY-FIVE

THE AIR WAS UNSEASONABLY warm for mid-November in Dallas, and the wind flipped and snapped our hair as I slid my Camaro onto the ramp toward I-45 south. The top was down and the stereo was up. Kacey tapped her fingers on her leg as Duane Allman and Dickey Betts slung guitar runs back and forth in "One Way Out." It was good to see her forget for a while. Watching her out of the corner of my eye, I felt young,

I hadn't felt that way for a long, long time.

I pressed my foot on the accelerator.

I'd contacted a private investigator about my mother a couple of weeks after I returned from Beirut. He was a friend and was happy to see what he could dig up about her. I was confident he would find her soon. It's more difficult to disappear than people think.

I was still debating whether to give him another assignment—to look into who wrote the note that was in Simon's Bible. I talked to Brandon about the missing money, and he was preparing a comprehensive review of the ministry's books. For now, I intended to handle that investigation myself. That's the way Simon wanted it.

I'd only seen Elise once since the funeral. She left town for a few weeks and returned with a tan. When she dropped by to pick up Simon's files, she didn't have much to say to me. She told Kacey that she'd taken a vacation to clear her mind. Since then she'd thrown herself into winding up the business affairs of the ministry. I thought that someday maybe we should talk, clear the air. I wasn't ready for that yet, though, and it was a safe bet she wasn't either.

With Meg's encouragement I moved into Simon's house for a while. Kacey was living at home for the fall semester. She was doing okay—better than could be expected. Though she missed Simon terribly, she was proud of the way her father died, proud of what he did. I was proud too.

Kacey and I continued to shoot together regularly. Michael Harrison had taken an interest in her welfare and had met us several times at the gun range. He was becoming a good friend to us both. Kacey had already developed into a better-than-average shot. After Simon's death, she became even more insistent about learning self-defense, so I signed her up for a Krav Maga class.

With her athletic ability, she was sure to be a quick study.

Traffic was light, and as I merged onto the highway, I looked over at Kacey. She was bobbing her head to the music. She turned to me and smiled—that smile that starts in her eyes and illuminates her entire face. I saw so much of Simon in that smile.

My eyes began to mist, and I turned away. This was not the time for that. This was a happy time.

We were going to meet our brother in Katy, Texas. He was waiting for us there.